TALES from the ARENA
PLAYING FOR KEEPS

Elizabeth Schechter

Circlet
Press

Also by Elizabeth Schechter:
Chains of Light
Fools Rush In
Heart's Master
Her Captive
House of Sable Locks
Princes of Air
The Rebel Mage Series

Playing for Keeps © 2018 by Elizabeth Schechter
Previously published as Tales from the Arena: Playing for Keeps

Cover credits:
Male figure © Design Pics | fotosearch.com
Background art © Algolonline | fotosearch.com

ISBN 978-1-61390-199-1 paperback
Also available in digital formats.

Circlet Press, Inc.
39 Hurlbut Street
Cambridge, MA 02138

www.circlet.com

Chapter One

Rakesh looked out the window of the meditation chamber and judged how long it would be until twilight. Just long enough, he decided, and settled himself onto the floor in proper mediation position, resting his hands on his knees and closing his eyes. Silently, he started to recite the Code.

I will be as supple as the graceful Li-ahn.

Rakesh had never actually seen a *li-ahn* tree. He'd been told that once there had been forests of them in the northern mountains, and the wood had been prized for its beauty, its incredible flexibility and its astonishing strength. During the early days of the war, the trees had been harvested almost to extinction for use in weaponry. He'd heard gossip, though, that the Council was talking of reforesting the *li-ahn* groves; Virin had said.... Rakesh grimaced at his lack of focus, banished Virin from his thoughts, and returned to the Code.

I will be as calm as the great Melnamore.

Virin spoke often of taking him on holiday to a place on the northern coast of Lake Melnamore. He called the place a small slice of paradise.... Rakesh opened his eyes, shook his head, and rubbed his face, then rubbed his fingers over the red collar he wore around his throat, feeling the ten studs that marked his years of service. Usually, touching the collar helped calm him, but this time, it had no effect; it had been two months since he'd last seen Virin Zaan-ti-ar, and if Rakesh had harbored any doubts about his feelings for the man, this would have dispelled them completely. His thoughts were too scattered for meditation, and even the rituals of the Code weren't enough to calm and center him. How was he going to serve tonight if he couldn't pull himself together? He took a deep breath and closed his eyes to try again.

I will be as supple as the graceful Li-ahn.
I will be as calm as the great Melnamore.
I will be as strong as the oldest mountains.
I will serve with grace,
I will serve with compassion,
I will serve with love.
I offer my blood as a balm,
I offer my body as a gift,
I offer my life to the greater good.

This time, the silent recitation yielded the quiet that Rakesh sought, and he slipped into the half-trance that was so much a part of the Discipline, so much a part of his life. He slowed his breathing and his heart-rate and examined his body and mind for signs of illness or weakness, anything that would be a detriment in the Arena. Satisfied that the healers had not missed anything, he allowed himself to float on waves of warm solitude, until a soft chiming broke into his meditation and called him back to himself. He took a long, cleansing breath, followed by two shorter ones, stretched slowly, then opened his eyes. In the doorway, looking nervous and with his hands still on the signal bell, was one of the Novices-candidates—an attractive young man dressed in loose, white trousers and a white wrapped shirt. Rakesh nodded, and the youngster bowed from the waist. Ah. Aakari-born. Either a refugee, or else he was the child of refugees, as was Rakesh.

"What is it..." Rakesh paused, just for a heartbeat, until he could remember the Novice-candidate's name. "...Linter?"

"Begging your indulgence, sir, but there's a Black Sword asking for you," Linter answered, his accent marking him as having been born outside of Tyesean borders. "He wishes to know if you're serving tonight."

Rakesh blinked and turned towards the window; it was fully dark outside. "I was in trance longer than I thought. Who is it who asks, Linter?"

"I..." The flush on Linter's olive-dark skin was alluring, and Rakesh smiled. Hopefully, this one would take the collar; his reactions in training were perfect, and his empathy rating was very high. "I am sorry, sir. I didn't hear his name."

"His rank, then?" Rakesh asked, trying to keep his hopes under control.

"Zaan-ti-ar, sir."

Rakesh gave in to his emotions and grinned. "I was hoping. Thank you, Linter. Please return to the Lounge and let the honored Zaan-ti-ar know that I will join him shortly? Offer him Friasin water and tonic while he waits, and have the bar put it on my account."

Linter bowed again and backed out of the room, leaving Rakesh shaking his head in amusement. The boy was lovely, and would be a wonderful Novice once he took the Collar.

"That one is going to have them fighting over him," Rakesh murmured as he got to his feet. He stood in place for a moment, then took a short, sharp breath and started to run through a series of exercises that would leave his muscles warm and flexible. All the better to serve.

Once he was done, he went to the bathing room, stripped and quickly washed, then went back to the living quarters, where one wall contained rows upon rows of the tiny sleeping spaces that the Collared laughingly called the cells. The facing wall was lined with counters, shelves and lockers, and Rakesh went to the ones that were his, taking out the flat box that contained his Arena garb. Opening it, he took out the series of synth-leather control bands, all of them in a brilliant crimson that matched his collar, and laid them out in sequence on the counter. First the belt, with the attached loincloth that hung to his knees, then the bands that encircled each of his ankles, his knees and his thighs. Similar bands went on his wrists, above and below his elbows, around his upper arms, and around his waist. He examined himself in the mirror briefly, checking each band in turn, the crimson standing out bright against his olive skin, then took a moment to comb his dark hair out until it hung straight and shining down his back, reaching past his waist. Virin always commented on how much he liked Rakesh's hair, how much he liked it loose. Rakesh looked at himself in the mirror again, nodded, then grinned and hurried out of the room.

As soon as he passed from the Dormitory and entered the corridor that led to the Arena, he felt his collar pulse—he was being summoned. The signal didn't extend into the living quarters, which was why someone had come to fetch him. "I hear," he said aloud. "And I am coming."

Recognized. The Patrons will be informed. The pulsing stopped as the Arena control computer answered.

"Patrons? I was only informed of one. Identify the Patrons who requested me?"

Two Patrons have requested Rakesh Taramar. Virin Zaan-ti-ar. Martiri Kian-ti-os.

Rakesh stopped, surprised. "The Kian-ti-os? Oh, that could be awkward... Which claim was entered first?"

The Zaan-ti-ar filed his request seven minutes prior to that of the Kian-ti-os.

Rakesh let out a shaky breath. "Good. Ah, inform the Kian-ti-os that I have a prior commitment. Offer him an appointment in no less than three...no, five days. As soon as I have something open." Rakesh smiled as he passed through the security doors and entered the private lift that would take him to the third floor and the Lounge. If Virin was as eager for this meeting as Rakesh was, then Rakesh was probably not going to be cleared to be back on the floor in the usual three days.

The Kian-ti-os accepts. He offers his regrets and his good wishes for your evening's pleasure. The appointment has been added to your calendar for eight days from now, and he has accepted.

"Well, that was nice of him. Tender my thanks, and offer him a drink in my name." As the lift slowed, Rakesh took a long breath, let it out slowly, and drew the mantle of Discipline around himself. When the doors slid open, he was ready, and entered a room whose occupants would send most men fleeing in terror.

Chapter Two

The Lounge was full of a swarming sea of black uniforms, the dark clothing occasionally punctuated by a man or woman dressed as Rakesh himself was, saving only that their bands and collars were white. This was the Lounge, the informal gathering place for some of the most dangerous men and women in Tyese—the Ishkarin. Rakesh knew the stories about them—who didn't? Created in secret, bred to be the perfect soldiers in order to win a stalemated war, the Ishkarin were perfect hunters, perfect killers. Perfect sadists. They had broken the stalemate with a wave of violence and terror that had left the Aakari Empire reeling, and when the war ended, they had demanded as their reward a place in Tyesean society. They'd volunteered to became peace-keepers, to channel their inborn tendencies into something positive. The Council had agreed, and in order to offer the Ishkarin another outlet, the Arena had been created. Here, the Ishkarin could release their aggressions without threatening the people they were supposed to protect.

As Rakesh came out of the lift, the conversation hushed, and people turned to stare. The whispers started as he moved into the room, but Rakesh was used to that by now. Most of the Collared who volunteered to serve in the Arena and who made it through the rigorous testing and training served the required five years, then turned away from the Arena and accepted their rewards of high-caste status and a generous pension. Some chose to stay on, taking the red collars and becoming Taramar, but only for a year, perhaps two.

Rakesh had worn his collar for ten years, five of them as a Taramar. At twenty-eight, he was the oldest among the Collared, and he was the only Red-Collar currently in service. Because of that, he was widely regarded as one of the most skilled, and therefore was the most sought after among the Collared. People wondered aloud at the depths of his servitude, his capacity for pain, never knowing that that the reason for his long service was a single man. A man who had just turned away from his viewing station near the large, interior windows to smile as Rakesh approached.

Virin Zaan-ti-ar was older than Rakesh by perhaps a dozen years. He was well-built and trim like all of his brethren, his once bronze-colored hair gone mostly silver. He was a mid-ranking Sword, one who might someday see the commissioned rank of Kian, if he were lucky enough and diligent enough in his duties. Rakesh certainly hoped so. Rakesh stopped less than an arms-length away from Virin, and sunk to his knees.

"I serve, Zaan-ti-ar," he said quietly, and heard the buzz of admiration from those around them. "What is your pleasure?"

"Rakesh," Virin purred softly in his deep voice, and Rakesh felt as if his spine were melting. "Have you eaten, Taramar?"

"Yes, Zaan-ti-ar, thank you," Rakesh raised his eyes slightly, no higher than Virin's legs, taking in strong thighs encased in black synth-leather. *Oh, please hurry and finish the niceties, Rin!* "May I offer you a meal? Or a drink?"

"You already brought me a drink," Virin reminded him. "And I've eaten."

Rakesh bowed slightly, crossing his wrists behind him. Above his head, he heard Virin catch his breath. "Then how may I serve, Zaan-ti-ar?"

"Rise," Virin commanded. Rakesh stood up slowly, keeping his eyes downcast and watching through his lashes as Virin reached towards him; there was a moment of pressure as Virin pressed his personal sigil to the front of Rakesh's control collar. The collar warmed and pulsed softly, and Rakesh knew that his collar was now marked with Virin's identicon, marking Rakesh as off-limits to anyone else for the rest of the evening.

"Control," Virin murmured.

What is your will, Patron?

"Activate the wrist bands and the belt."

Immediately, Rakesh's wrists were encircled in steel, his wrist-bands fused together and sealed to the belt around his waist by the now-active magnetic beads embedded in the synth-leather. For a moment, his control slipped, and he moaned softly; prompting a smile from Virin and a chuckle from the Swords surrounding them.

"Oh, are you the lucky one, Virin?" An older man with Kian-ti-os rank-pins on his collar came closer, openly admiring Rakesh. "Looks like you got to him ahead of me."

"You bid on him, Kian-ti-os?" Virin asked, his eyes darting from Rakesh to the higher-ranking officer.

"Yes. Too late, by only a few minutes, according to Control." Martiri raised his glass to Rakesh. "Thank you, Taramar, for the drink. And for the appointment. I look forward to seeing if I can make you scream."

Rakesh bowed, then slowly went back to his knees at Virin's side as Virin and Martiri spoke, their voices pitched low. Rakesh breathed deep, keeping his eyes lowered and setting himself the task of not listening, focusing on the timber of Virin's voice, and not the words. There was an odd intensity to their conversation—something of some importance was being discussed. Not classified, though, or they'd not be speaking of it in the Lounge. If it was something that Virin thought that Rakesh needed to know, Virin would tell him after their time on the Floor. And if it was not something that Virin thought that Rakesh needed to know...gossip was a form of currency amongst the Collared.

Rakesh was suddenly alert when Virin tapped him on the shoulder. "I'll keep your words in mind, Kian-ti-os. Thank you."

"Of course, Virin," Martiri said. He paused, then asked, "Would I be able to convince you to share him?"

Rakesh felt his muscles tense slightly, and fought to keep himself under control. After two months without a single word from Virin, he didn't want to be shared—he wanted his Zaan-ti-ar alone. He relaxed when he felt Virin's hand running over his head, stroking his hair the way a woman might stroke her pampered pet.

"I've been two months in the field, Kian-ti-os. Tonight, I prefer to take my pleasures alone."

"A fair answer. Have a good night, Virin. Make him scream."

Virin grabbed a handful of Rakesh's hair, tugging it hard and pulling his head back; Rakesh sighed softly, his eyes closing as he pressed his shoulder against Virin's leg.

"I intend to, Kian-ti-os."

———————◆———————

AS WAS PROPER, RAKESH followed three paces behind Virin as they made their way through the crowd towards the lift that would take them to the Floor of the Arena. All along the way, Swords stopped them, admiring Rakesh, congratulating Virin. There was some good-natured teasing from one female ir-Kian that Rakesh remembered had been a member of Virin's cadet class, and who commented on just how often Virin seemed to be choosing to spend his time and coin on the Taramar. Then they were through, and inside the lift. As the doors closed, Virin sighed and turned towards Rakesh.

"You look wonderful, Kesh," he murmured. "I missed you. I almost strangled my commanding officer over you; he wanted me to stay in the field another month."

Rakesh stepped closer to Virin, feeling his heart pounding in his chest, unable to quiet it, no matter how he tried to invoke Discipline. "I've missed you, too," he said. "I was worried. You always send word if you're going to be gone longer than a week."

"You never got any of my messages?" Virin asked, sounding shocked. Wordlessly, Rakesh shook his head. Virin grimaced and looked up."Control, hold the lift."

Holding. The lift shuddered as it came to a stop.

Virin looked back at Rakesh, and the heat in his eyes made Rakesh's mouth go dry. Virin stalked towards him, slowly driving him backwards until his back pressed against the side of the lift, his bound hands splayed on the cold metal. Virin grinned, his teeth bared, and touched the control pad on his wrist-comp; Rakesh gasped as all of the magnets in his control bands activated, bonding to the wall of the lift. He strained and squirmed while Virin stood and watched, his eyes half-lidded and a lazy smile on his face.

"Very nice. Very, very nice. I dreamed about you, Kesh. And I wrote down every single dream. I sent a message once a week, the entire time I was gone," Virin said, his voice low. He moved closer, running his hands over Rakesh's chest, then up and down his upper arms. "Long messages, telling you exactly what I was going to do to you once I had you under my thumb again. How I was going to make you scream and cry. How I was going to fill you in every way possible, until your sweat and your tears smelled of me. How I was going to completely destroy you...."

Rakesh shuddered, feeling Virin's fingers digging into his arms, the pressure of the other man's chest against his as Virin pressed against him. It was so easy to forget how much stronger the Swords were than other men, how dangerous they were...until they were at your throat. He moaned as Virin's thigh pressed against his painfully-hard cock, gasping out, "Rin...."

Virin laughed, stepping back and folding his arms over his chest. "Oh, you have missed me, haven't you? I don't recall ever having gotten you to break in the lift before." He tapped his wrist-comp again; Rakesh stumbled and went to his knees as the lift wall released him. "Come and show me how you've missed me."

It was the invitation Rakesh had been waiting for; he steadied himself as well as he could with his wrists still sealed behind him, then crawled towards Virin, pressing his cheek against Virin's inner thigh, nuzzling at his crotch and feeling Virin's erection trapped behind the synth-leather. He pressed harder, and Virin's hand settled on the back of Rakesh's head; he combed his fingers through Rakesh's hair and murmured, "Up now, Kesh."

Rakesh sat back on his heels and looked up, "I'm not sure I can. My legs are shaking. I haven't felt this...undone since I was a Novice."

"I'm flattered," Virin said. He smiled and leaned down, effortlessly picking Rakesh up and steadying him on his feet; Rakesh leaned against Virin for a moment, taking long breaths and trying to reestablish Discipline. When he'd finally managed to calm himself, he nodded and heard Virin say "Control, resume." The lift shook slightly as it began to move.

"You're still not quite there, you know," Virin said, sounding amused. Rakesh smiled slightly.

"I know," he answered, very much aware of the erection prominently displayed through the thin silk of his loincloth. "It's been two months, Rin."

"I know you haven't been celibate, Taramar."

"It's not the same," Rakesh murmured, hearing the lift slowing. He shifted, taking his place behind Virin's shoulder.

"No. No, it isn't," Virin agreed as the door slid open.

Chapter Three

Entering the Floor for the first time, the noise was horrifying, especially if you didn't realize that both the lift and the lounge that overlooked this area were highly soundproofed. Novices who came on to the Floor for the very first time were always startled senseless when they first came out of the lift and heard the screams and cries of agony. But Rakesh was used to it, and had long since learned to hear the passion and pleasure beneath the pain. To others, the sounds of the Floor might be those of a torture chamber, but to Rakesh, these sounds were the sounds of home. Today, it cut through his disorientation like a knife, and helped pull him back to his center; he took three quick breaths and steadied himself even more, following Virin out of the lift and onto the Floor.

The Arena had once been just that—a sporting arena—and the Floor had been the field. It might have been any large gathering space, if not for the screams, and the vast array of torture devices that ranged from the most primitive to some technology that had been developed specifically for the Arena. There were groups of men and women in black uniforms at every station, watching, laughing, offering advice to whomever was currently working over their Collared. Some of the bystanders were attended by a White Collar of their own, and were obviously waiting their turns.

"I've some very special plans for you, Taramar," Virin called over his shoulder.

Rakesh felt a rush of excitement and started to move a little faster. He was trying to close the distance caused by Virin's longer stride when someone grabbed him from behind, and a heavy, synth-leather glove clamped down over his mouth. Startled, Rakesh tried to break free, but the black-clad arms tightened around him, and he was dragged into the shadow of one of the tall barriers that separated one station from the next.

Being pulled out of sight was enough to completely shred any traces of Discipline and send Rakesh into a mindless panic; with his wrists bound, he couldn't fight back, and his captor was taller than he—his feet barely touched the floor. This could not be happening—*no one* touched a Collared who was marked to another Patron! Rakesh kicked, and his heel connected hard against his captor's thigh. The man cursed, and Rakesh realized that he'd been cursing softly the entire time. Man's voice. Young sounding. Strange to Rakesh.

"Damn you, stop fighting me!" the stranger snapped. "I'm trying to warn you! Stop fighting me and listen!"

Rakesh shook his head, trying to shout around the hand still over his mouth. His collar started to pulse—Virin had noticed he was gone.

"Listen!" his captor repeated. "You're in danger. You're in grave danger. Do not leave the Arena! Do you understand me? Do not leave! You're safe here. Nowhere else. They want you...."

"Rakesh!" Virin's voice cut through the normal sounds of the Floor. "Control! Locate!"

Immediately, a bright light surrounded Rakesh and his captor as a spotlight pinpointed their location. The man cursed and pushed Rakesh away; Rakesh went flying, tumbling uncontrollably and crashing into the barrier. He lay there, gasping and shaking, hearing the commotion around him as people came running. Strong hands grabbed his shoulders, and he tensed until he recognized Virin's scent. He blinked, tossing his head to try and get his hair out of his eyes, and saw Virin looking down at him.

"Kesh?" he said softly. "Are you all right? Control, release!"

"Yes," Rakesh answered as his arms fell free. "I'm fine. He didn't hurt me. Didn't even try. I... Help me up?" He pushed his hair out of his face and took Virin's hand, letting himself be pulled to his feet.

Virin's hands lingered for a moment on Rakesh's arms. Then he straightened, and Rakesh saw Virin as he was when he was in the field—a trained killer, searching for a target. A thrill went through him, and he stepped closer to Virin.

"Who was it?" Virin demanded.

Rakesh shook his head. "I... I never saw him. He grabbed me from behind. Never saw his face. I didn't know his voice."

Virin turned, pointing at several Ishkarin. "You three, fan out, find anyone new on the Floor, or anyone who seems to be in a hurry to leave. Where is Security? I want to see the surveillance video...."

"Zaan-ti-ar, stand down," another voice broke in, and Martiri Kian-ti-os pushed through the crowd. Virin stiffened, and looked as if he were about to attack when Martiri held both hands up in front of him. "I will see to this, Virin. You see to your Taramar. He's had a bad time of it. Take care of him." He looked past Virin to Rakesh. "Taramar? Are you all right?"

Rakesh took a long breath and started to work on steadying his nerves. "Yes, Kian-ti-os. Just...shaken. I'll be fine."

Martiri nodded. "Good. Virin, take him off. I'll find who did this."

"When you do, Kian-ti-os, I want him," Virin growled.

"Of course." Martiri turned away and started barking orders. Virin hesitated for a long moment, long enough that Rakesh moved to stand at his shoulder, gently touching his arm.

"If you want to join them on the hunt, I'll be fine," he murmured. "I'll go back to the Dormitory, see the medics, spend the night in meditation."

Virin snarled and turned, grabbing Rakesh around the wrist. "You're staying with me," he snapped, tugging Rakesh with him through the crowd. Then, without warning, Virin stopped. He looked over his shoulder, then turned, and for the first time, Rakesh saw Virin hesitate.

"Kesh, I need to hurt something right now. I'm angry enough that I need to tear something apart." His voice sounded almost apologetic, and he stepped closer to Rakesh and lowered his voice, "I...would rather not hurt you. Not that way. Not in anger. And I wouldn't blame you if you didn't want me now. I should have protected you from that, and I didn't."

Rakesh stared at Virin for a moment, unable to believe what he was hearing. "Rin..." he breathed. Then he stepped forward, pulled the taller man's head down and kissed him firmly on the lips. Virin coughed in surprise, then looked startled as Rakesh knelt in front of him, his eyes never leaving the Sword's.

"I serve, Zaan-ti-ar," Rakesh said softly. "I want to be with you tonight." He lowered his eyes, closing them as he crossed his wrists behind his back and whispered, "I want you to hurt me."

There was a long moment of nothing, and Rakesh wondered if he'd misjudged himself—was this really what Virin needed? Then the bands around his wrists fused together once more, and he felt a heavy hand clenching in the hair at the back of his neck. He gasped as Virin hauled him to his feet, and when the Sword looked down at him, his eyes were hard and cold; for a moment, Rakesh felt more like prey than he ever had before in his life.

It was intoxicating, and he moaned softly and swayed towards Virin, who just smiled. He turned, never releasing Rakesh, dragging him along by the hair. Stumbling after Virin, Rakesh thought for a moment that they were heading towards the whipping frames—Virin's usual favorite for working out aggression. But Virin steered Rakesh past the racks and whipping frames, towards the more advanced equipment. When he realized where they were going, Rakesh moaned, and heard Virin laugh.

"You asked for this, Taramar," Virin growled. He waved off the attendant by the neuro-disruptor. "I'll see to him myself."

Rakesh slowed, digging in his heels as Virin started forwards; the Sword turned, stepped in close and pitched his voice low, "Kesh?" It was the closest he'd come to his normal speaking voice since they'd come out of the lift.

"I'm fine," Rakesh said. "Just... I need a moment."

Virin smiled, all arrogance and teasing cold cruelty that made Rakesh want to whimper and beg for things he wasn't even sure he wanted. "All right. Take your time. Just remember, the anticipation only makes it worse."

It took Rakesh three tries before he could run through the Code without stumbling, and a fourth time before he even caught a glimmer of the calm that he'd had once possessed. Finally, he nodded and felt Virin's hand close like a vice over the back of his neck, forcing him towards the machine.

There was a reason the neuro-disruptor was empty, even on a busy night like this one; it was a delicate machine, and required specialized training and a more subtle touch than many of the Ishkarin possessed. In all his years in a Collar, Rakesh had never been subjected to the disruptor, had only ever seen the machine in use twice, and both times, it was being operated by the Ran-ti-ar, the absolute leader of the Ishkarin. Dizzy with a heady combination of fear and lust, Rakesh allowed himself to be released, only to be imprisoned in the machine's capsule, his control bands bonding to the metal walls and the insulating mask lowering itself over his head and neck, cutting off both sight and sound. There was a moment where it felt as if everything itched, as the transmitters in the capsule synced with his nervous system. Then...nothing, for what seemed like an eternity; Rakesh licked his lips and took a long breath, blowing it out slowly and starting to recite the Code once more. As he finished the third line, he heard Virin's voice in his ears, and realized there were speakers in the mask.

Level one and building.

It started as a gentle warmth, spreading out through his limbs and making him wonder what he'd been afraid of. Warmth turned to heat, an all-over heat that made Rakesh grimace and want to try to move, even though he knew full well that the heat source wasn't external. It reminded him of falling asleep in the sun as a boy, and the resulting painful sunburns. The heat grew, becoming more painful, and he gasped and tugged on the control bands, only vaguely hearing Virin's voice:

Level two and building.

Painful heat became white-hot pain, making Rakesh moan, trying to fight the bonds, trying to pull away and get away from the burning. This was like nothing he'd ever felt before, no pain he'd ever experienced. Other pain had been localized, he'd been able to focus on it, envelope it, pass through it. This pain enveloped him, consumed him, made him feel as if his skin were about to burst into flames. As he heard Virin's voice marking the change to level three, Rakesh started to scream, only to hear mocking laughter.

You asked for it. Level four and building.

Conflagration. Virin had warned him, told him that he needed to tear something apart, and Rakesh knew that was just what was being done. He was being taken apart so completely that he might never be whole again; Rakesh shrieked until his voice and his mind both failed him, passing into a twilight state where pain meant nothing, save only to stimulate his growing lust, his achingly hard cock and his desperate need for Virin's touch. He heard Virin's voice, first through the speakers, then clearly as the mask was removed. He was aware of applause, of excited chattering all around him. Then he was being picked up, put onto a stretcher, and taken...somewhere.

Chapter Four

Rakesh's next awareness was of someone massaging him, strong hands kneading at the muscles in his shoulders and back, making him moan and whimper in pleasure. He breathed, smelled Virin's musky scent, and relaxed.

"With me yet?" he heard Virin ask. He tried to answer and heard laughter. "Not yet, I see. Soon." Rakesh felt himself being rolled over onto his back, and groaned as the movement made every muscle in his body ache. Virin continued to massage him, moving his limbs and making the muscles pull and hurt. The massage changed, became simple touches, gentle and erotic, until Rakesh felt as if he were floating on pleasure. Some dreamless time later, Rakesh smiled and tried to move, only to find that he couldn't. He blinked, and noticed the blindfold for the first time. Then he noticed what Virin was doing to him.

"Rin?" he asked. "What...?"

"Ah, there you are. I was wondering when you were going to come back," Virin said.

"How... What...?" Rakesh paused, then gasped in pleasure as Virin twisted the fingers he had buried in Rakesh's ass. "Oh...!"

"How long were you out?" Virin asked. "About twenty minutes. I haven't kept exact time, though. I've been busy. What did I do? Ankle band to thigh band, wrist band to ankle band. Belt and arm bands to the table, so you're not going anywhere. Oh, and part of your loincloth for the blindfold, since I forgot to pick one up. A very nice package, and all for me." He laughed, adding another finger and making Rakesh writhe and moan. "I've wanted this for weeks, Kesh. Creator, I've missed you."

Rakesh tried to draw a full breath, tugging hard on his bonds and spreading his legs as wide as he could, hissing through the pain that every movement caused. "Rin...please...."

"I know," Virin soothed gently. "I know what you want. I've known what you've been wanting since the lift. Do you have any idea how hard it was for me not to take you there?" He slid his fingers free, trailing them up the inside of Rakesh's thigh. Rakesh whined softly, wanting to move. He could hear Virin moving, something wet-sounding, then a warm hand came to rest on his knee. "You are magnificent, Kesh."

"Rin..." Anything that Rakesh was going to say was lost in his moan as the head of Virin's cock pressed against his ass. He took a long breath and relaxed, moaning as Virin slowly filled him. He heard Virin groan, and tried to roll his hips in response. The small movement he managed still drew a gasp from Virin; he pulled out almost completely and slapped Rakesh's cock hard enough to make him yelp.

"You're not supposed to be moving, Kesh," Virin scolded. "Not unless you want this over before we've begun. I'm about to go off like a missile."

Rakesh whimpered at the thought of being left unfulfilled. "No...please, Rin...."

"Patience, Kesh," Virin whispered. He started to push in again, his hands gripping Rakesh's legs hard enough that Rakesh knew that he'd have bruises. He didn't care, wanting only to be filled, to be fucked, hard and fast, and until he screamed his throat raw. He struggled to stay still, to control himself until Virin's body was pressed hard against him and Virin was panting with effort.

"Now," Virin purred, his hands grabbing onto Rakesh's forearms. Braced, he started to move, thrusting hard against Rakesh, who howled and struggled, trying to move with Virin. He managed to shift just enough, roll his hips enough, and his howls turned to moans and gasps of pleasure, punctuated with Virin's heavy breathing and the wet slapping of their bodies as they slammed together. Virin groaned, panting out, "Control...release...release left hand."

As Rakesh's hand fell free, Virin growled, "You know what to do."

Rakesh did, ignoring the pain in his muscles as he wrapped his hand around his own cock and started pumping. It was easy to imagine that it was Rin's hand on his cock, and he moaned as Virin started pumping faster, harder, his breathing becoming more ragged. Rakesh worked his cock harder, moaning as Virin's hand covered his own, squeezing tightly.

"Mine," Virin snarled, the sound hitting Rakesh right at the base of his cock; he made a sound something between a scream and a groan and came, splattering his stomach and both his and Virin's hands. He heard Virin's groaning grow louder, more high-pitched, and his movements became sharper, harder. Then Virin collapsed over Rakesh, and Rakesh could feel his breathing, fast and hot against his neck. He turned his head and rubbed his cheek against Virin's short hair. "...love you, Rin."

"I love you, too. Crazy Collared," Virin murmured, moving off of Rakesh. "Where's my comp? Do you see... Oh...blast it all. Control, release all bands."

Rakesh groaned as his right arm and his legs fell free, and his legs fell off the edge of whatever he was laying on. He lay still for a moment, then stretched, reaching up and pulling the blindfold from his eyes. He looked around and smiled.

"On the table, Rin?"

"It was the right height. Now budge over," Virin climbed onto the table next to Rakesh and pulled him into his arms. "I mean it, Kesh. You are magnificent. When are you going to give up the Collar and be mine alone?"

Rakesh smiled, resting his head on Virin's chest, "When are you going to get promoted so you can marry me?" The question didn't elicit the usual response, the one that Rakesh expected after almost three years of the same conversation; he looked up to see Virin staring at the ceiling, his face expressionless. "Rin?"

"We could live together. Not get married. Just...live together," Virin answered softly.

"What? Rin, what's wrong?"

Virin shook his head, then looked at Rakesh. "I don't think I'm ever going to make Kian, Kesh. I was passed over again." He put his arm around Rakesh and continued, "Apparently, there's some talk about my bloodline. About how I'm not...pure enough, not enough of an Ishkarin to be a commissioned officer."

Rakesh propped himself up on his elbow, "What does that mean? Rin, you're one of the best officers in the field. Every Sword who comes to the Arena says so."

"Perhaps. But enough to be in command? Whoever it is in my line of command who makes the decisions apparently doesn't think so. I suspected something, before. Other people getting rewarded for things that I'd worked on. I thought... I don't know what I thought. But this time...they told me direct. It's my bloodline—"

"Your father was Kian-ti-os! He'd be Ran-ti-ar now if...."

"If he hadn't been assassinated. I know, Kesh. No one knows that better than I. They mean my mother, I think. Since she's not a Sword. 'No fault of your own, Zaan-ti-ar. You understand. You're a fine officer. But the purity of the higher echelon must be maintained,'" he said, his voice mocking, as if he were reciting.

"They told you that?"

Virin sighed and nodded, rubbing one hand up and down Rakesh's arm. "They told me that. Oh, they were very apologetic. But still...I'm never going to be promoted. So...I'm afraid I'm going to have to renege on my proposal, Kesh. But you could still retire and live with me. I checked before I came here tonight. The rules say I can't marry until I reach the rank of Kian, but there's no rule against living together."

"I know that. My oldest sister lived with a Sword for years. A Za-an-ti. They were supposed to marry when he had the rank, but he died in the field." Rakesh settled back down next to Virin, closing his eyes and resting his cheek on Virin's shoulder. "I had dinner with Iras," he said, and felt Virin tense.

"You did *what*?"

"Dinner. With Iras. Two weeks ago. I was completely shocked when I got the invitation. She's a legend in the Arena."

"I know. One of the first women to wear a collar, the first woman ever to take the Red. You probably have a serious case of heroine-worship regarding her." Virin sighed. "So...what did Mother want?"

"Her exact words were 'So you're the Taramar who stole my son's heart.' What have you been telling her about me, Rin?"

Virin snorted. "Not as much as you'd think, and probably less than you've told *your* mother. Mother is a meddler."

"She was very gracious. She remembers my parents from their time in the Arena, and she asked after them," Rakesh said. "And...she mentioned something that I don't think either of us thought of. Rin, have you given any thought to how our relationship will change if I give up my Collar?"

"Why should it change?" Virin demanded. "And what do you mean *if*?"

Rakesh tipped his head back, waiting for the pain to subside before saying, "Rin, think about it. I give up my collar. I become a private citizen...."

"A high-caste, extremely wealthy private citizen," Virin murmured. "Maybe that's the answer. You could keep me as a pet."

"Be serious, Rin. If I'm a private citizen, what happens to you when it gets to be too much for us? What happens when I beg you to hurt me... and you do?"

"I don't follow. Why...?" Virin stopped. "Oh."

"A Sword doesn't prey off the battlefield or outside the Arena. Rin, she was warning me. Warning us. She doesn't want to see what almost happened to them happen to us."

Virin's eyes widened, and he looked at Rakesh, "Wait...my mother said *what*?"

"She said it almost happened to your father, before you were born. He was disciplined, but the Ran-ti-ar kept it from going further. She doesn't want to see you in the camps, Rin. Neither do I. And...I know I'm not going to be able to keep from wanting what we have now. I love what you do to me. But even if you get promoted, even if we can marry...."

"If you're not in a Collar, then we can't ever..." Abruptly, Virin sat up, and Rakesh winced as the movement jarred his body and set everything to aching. "How did we miss this, Kesh?"

"I don't know." Rakesh rolled onto his side and watched as Virin paced the length of the room, then started to push himself up into a sitting position. His muscles didn't want to cooperate, and he almost pitched off the table; Virin caught him before he fell and helped him to sit, then sat down next to him, his arm around Rakesh's shoulders.

"So...I won't get promoted, and you won't give up your collar," Virin said. "Which leaves us...?"

"Right here," Rakesh answered, resting his head on Virin's shoulder. "Same as we are now. We'll neither of us lose anything. We'll still be able to be together."

"Every third night. If I'm lucky enough to get here first," Virin grumbled.

"I did some research of my own, after I spoke with Iras. She gave me the idea. Said there was a rule when she served here. Apparently, it never changed," Rakesh said. He smiled "Rin, did you know that I could set my preferences?"

Virin sounded surprised when he answered, "You can?"

"One of the benefits of wearing the Red. I can give certain Patrons priority. Or, in your case...a certain Patron. I don't know why I didn't know about it. But if you want me to, I'll set it so that any night you want me, I'm yours."

Virin chuckled, and Rakesh felt him kiss the top of his head. "Thank you, Kesh."

"So, are you going to tell me where you were?" Rakesh asked.

"In a moment. I want to make you comfortable," Virin answered. He stood up and picked Rakesh up in his arms, carrying him over to the wide bed and laying him down. Then he stretched out next to Rakesh and pulled him into his arms. "You should try not to move, Kesh. It will take a day or two before the effects of the disruptor wear off." He paused, then laughed and kissed Rakesh's shoulder. "Hm...."

"What?"

In answer, Virin pushed Rakesh onto his stomach and pulled his arms behind him, saying, "Control, activate all bands." Rakesh yelped as, in an instant, he was immobilized, his legs bound from thigh to ankle, and his arms sealed behind him, elbow meeting elbow as the bands bonded together. He struggled for a moment, making Virin laugh again as he pulled Rakesh back into his arms so that they were laying chest to chest. "For your own good, Taramar. You shouldn't move. Now, you've been waiting all night to ask me where I've been, haven't you? You really are the most amazing creature. And where haven't I been, these past two months? I think I've been everywhere."

"Is there something wrong?" Rakesh wanted to know. "Is it Aakar again?"

"Oh, no," Virin assured him quickly. "Things are quiet there. I was in Felanore for...a week, I think? No, probably more. I keep hearing rumors. something about a missing heir to the Imperial throne, but that rumor is older than I am, and there's never been any proof to it. Then I was north, in the Gap. I was in the Highlands, and your parents send their love."

Rakesh blinked in surprise. "You saw my family?"

"I was in the area," Virin said. He started to trace abstract patterns on Rakesh's back.

"Rin, why?" Rakesh asked, trying to focus on the conversation, and ignore his reactions to the bondage and to Virin's idle caresses; he was getting hard again

"There's a reason I was out in the Highlands, and checking in on your parents," Virin said, his voice suddenly stern, his hands falling still. "I wanted to warn them. And now I'm warning you. Kesh... I don't want you leaving the Arena. Not alone, not with a group. Not unless you are with me."

"What? Why?" Rakesh asked, alarmed by how serious Virin had gone. "What is it?"

"Something is happening, Kesh," Virin said. "That's why I went to visit your parents. They were both Collared, even if they only wore the White. Retired Collared, both Tyesean and Aakari, have been disappearing. From Arena City, from every city and town in Tyese where former Collared have settled, there have been disappearances. There have even been disappearances in Felanore, from the embassy staff. No one knows what is happening or why, and there have been no traces of the missing found. And worse, no missing persons reports have been made to any authorities, and for that many high-caste citizens to just...disappear.... It's unheard of. The rumor mills are going wild with it—they say that the Council are kidnapping former Collared to sell as slaves overseas."

"That's ridiculous," Rakesh snorted.

"It is," Virin agreed. "But until we know what is happening, I don't want you to leave the Arena unless you are with me."

Rakesh frowned slightly. "Rin...that's what he said. The Sword who grabbed me. He told me it wasn't safe for me outside. That I was in danger."

Virin sat up, tipping Rakesh onto his back. "He was warning you?" he demanded. "What did he say? Exactly?"

Rakesh closed his eyes, thinking back. "He said..." he paused for a moment, then repeated what he remembered being whispered in his ear, "'You're in danger. You're in grave danger. Do not leave the Arena! Do you understand me? Do not leave! You're safe here. Nowhere else. They want you....' and that's when the spotlight hit us. He pushed me away and ran."

"'They want you,'" Virin repeated. "Blast it all, Kesh. I never thought to ask you, and...why didn't Martiri ask you to report?" He frowned and shifted so that he was sitting facing Rakesh, his eyes distant. "I'll need to speak to him; this is the first real lead that we've had. Martiri will probably come to speak to you tomorrow, if they don't find whoever it was who grabbed you by looking at the surveillance videos." He smiled, resting his hand on Rakesh's stomach. "When we find whoever it was, I don't know if I'm going to thank him or kill him. I should go and report this."

Rakesh caught his breath as Virin stood up, "You... You're leaving?"

Virin nodded, pulling on his pants as he answered, "Kesh, you've given me something to go on. I've been hunting whoever is doing this for months. I was starting to think I was never going to make a breakthrough. I need to get back on the hunt."

"But...Rin.... " Rakesh squirmed, knowing it would do him no good. It wouldn't be the first time that Virin's duties had called him away, but this time, somehow, was worse than ever before. He closed his eyes and took a long breath, licking his lips and trying to center himself. "Just...let me know what happens?"

He felt the bed shift, and opened his eyes to see Virin sitting next to him, fully dressed in his black uniform, smiling at him with enough heat in his eyes that Rakesh moaned. The moaning grew louder as Virin ran his gloved hand down Rakesh's chest.

"Oh, Kesh, you really didn't think I'd leave you here like this, did you?" he murmured. "We just need one more thing." He held up the silken strip that had once been part of Rakesh's loin-cloth, doubling it and twisting it between his hands before leaning over Rakesh and forcing it into his mouth. Then he ran his gloved hands down Rakesh's chest, his fingers finding pressure points that quickly left Rakesh, already sensitized by the neuro-disruptor, writhing in alternating waves of pain and pleasure and crying into the gag. Virin laughed as he worked, sliding one hand up Rakesh's chest and tightening it around his throat. The other hand he wrapped around Rakesh's cock, laughing as the Collared bucked his hips.

"Impatient pet," he murmured, squeezing both hands firmly and starting to pump his fist as Rakesh gasped for air. "Come for me, Kesh. Come for me," he crooned. "Now!"

Rakesh screamed as he shot, his body stiff as a board as he came hard enough to splatter his own chest. It seemed to go on for several minutes, as Virin continued to cut off his air and pump his cock, until at last Rakesh fell limp, curling onto his side as Virin let him go. Dimly, Rakesh was aware of Virin standing up, leaning over the bed and kissing his forehead.

"I've sent for the attendants, and they'll take you up to the medics. I'll be back in a few days, my love. If you're not ready to take Patrons, I'll take you out for dinner. Stay inside, and stay safe."

Unable to move, unwilling to move even if he'd been able, Rakesh smiled around the gag, hearing Virin moving away, and drifting off to sleep as he heard the door close.

Chapter Five

Rakesh settled into a comfortable chair in the Collared common room and opened the book he'd chosen, but after a few minutes of staring at the page without seeing, he set it aside. It had been five days since he'd last seen Virin, and there had been no word. He'd sent messages to Virin's barracks, but had only been told that the Zaan-ti-ar was out in the field, and could not be reached. He ran his fingers down the sleeve of the blue silk shirt he was wearing; it had been a gift from Virin, and he'd hoped that tonight he would be able to wear it when they had their dinner date, since the medics had not yet cleared him to serve on the Floor. But it was well past the usual dinner hour, and Rakesh was starting to doubt that he would see Virin tonight at all. His stomach grumbled, and he abandoned the book altogether, getting up and starting towards the door. He moved stiffly, a slowly fading reminder of his evening with Virin and the punishment of the neuro-disruptor. Dinner, he thought to himself, and then perhaps the gentle workout that was all the medics would allow him. Hopefully he'd be cleared to return to service tomorrow, or the day after. His frustration at being left idle was starting to become unbearable—he'd spent the past few days working with the novices, but that wasn't enough, and he was starting to get snappish. He needed to be on the Floor. As he walked out into the corridor, he heard someone call his name. Turning, he saw Linter coming towards him.

"Excuse me, Rakesh? There are two Swords down in the receiving room. They wanted to speak to you."

Rakesh went cold, resting his hand on the wall to keep from losing his balance completely. His collar felt suddenly too tight, and he had to swallow twice before he could answer, "Two Swords? I'll... I'll be right there."

Linter looked at him, obviously concerned, turning away only when Rakesh waved him off. Rakesh leaned against the wall and closed his eyes. Two Swords... Was this his greatest nightmare? Had they come to tell him that Virin was...? His mind shied away from even the thought, and he swallowed once more, took a very long, very shaky breath, and drew himself up, starting down the hall towards the lift that would take him down to the receiving room.

As he walked in, two Swords turned towards him. One, with the rank pins of an ir-Zaan on his collar, stepped forward, "Rakesh Taramar?"

"Yes," Rakesh answered, forcing the words out. "How may I serve, ir-Zaan?"

"Taramar, we need you to come with us," the ir-Zaan said. "There's been an accident. Virin Zaan-ti-ar was injured..."

"Is he...?" Rakesh choked out.

"He'll be fine, Taramar," the other Sword—a Zaan— said gently. "It is serious, though. He's in the medical center, and he's asking for you. Won't go into regen without seeing you. Will you come?"

Rakesh dragged his fingers through his hair, nodding absently. "Yes. Yes, of course. Just...let me.... " He stopped, looking around, trying to gather his thoughts. It was impossible to think of Virin being hurt. But he was alive. Thank the Creator, he was alive.

"I'll let the trainers know where you're going and why, Taramar," the ir-Zaan offered. "Go on. There's a car waiting. I'll go speak to them, and meet you outside."

"Thank you," Rakesh said gratefully, and followed the Zaan out of the receiving room and into the courtyard. There was a sleek, black aircar waiting; the Zaan opened the rear door for Rakesh, then climbed into the compartment with him. Rakesh settled back into the seat and looked at the Sword sitting across from him. "Thank you again, for coming for me," he said. "What happened?"

"All I know is that it was an aircar accident," the Zaan replied, glancing out the window. Rakesh looked, and saw the ir-Zaan coming towards the 'car. The other Sword quickly entered the 'car, slamming the door behind him. The Zaan nodded at him and knocked on the partition separating them from the driver. "Let's go!"

The 'car lifted, passing out of the gates and turning right. Rakesh blinked in surprise and turned to the ir-Zaan next to him. "The medical center is the other way," he said, suddenly wary.

"There was heavy traffic as we came in. We don't want to delay you, so we're taking a different route," the Zaan answered quickly. He glanced at Rakesh and smiled. "It's all right, Taramar. We'll be there soon."

Rakesh nodded, his mind racing. The 'car turned a few more times, and after the third turn, Rakesh knew that the Zaan was lying. They weren't going to the medical center; they were heading towards the other side of Arena City. So where were they going? He reached up and rubbed the studs on his collar, looking out the window at the buildings going past.

How soon, before someone noticed he was gone? Before they started to look for him? Was he going to be one of the ones who disappeared without a trace? The idea was terrifying—of course there was no report made, no trace of the former Collared who'd disappeared. If it was the Swords who were taking them, they could very well make any reports disappear as well. And if they said there was no signs of the missing, who would doubt them?

"I know we're not going to the medical center. So, where are we going, really?" Rakesh asked.

The ir-Zaan laughed once. "He's quick."

"Too quick," the Zaan grumbled. "Get him ready."

Rakesh turned to see the ir-Zaan taking a syringe out of his belt-pouch. "Nothing to worry about," the ir-Zaan said. "A mild sedative. You'll take a nap, and we'll have a nice quiet drive in the country."

Rakesh swallowed, staring at the amber-filled needle. "And Virin?"

"Oh, he's probably dead, or he will be soon," the Zaan answered, as calmly as if he was talking about the weather. "We sent him into a trap. The mixed-blood meddler should have stayed out of our business."

Rakesh closed his eyes, took a long breath...and went for the Zaan's throat. His attack took both men by surprise, and the aircar pitched and rolled as the two Swords wrestled Rakesh to the floor, the ir-Zaan jabbing him in the upper arm with the syringe. As Rakesh's consciousness faded,he felt a moment of satisfaction that he'd managed to do some damage to the Zaan—there was blood pouring down the man's face from a broken nose. Then the Zaan moved into Rakesh's line of sight, and he saw the knife in the Sword's hand.

"Should have played nice, Taramar," the Zaan murmured. He ripped open Rakesh's shirt, and the last thing Rakesh felt before he passed out was the knife digging into his shoulder.

Chapter Six

R akesh woke up cold and confused, in darkness, on the floor, with rough rope digging into his wrists,and ankles. His throat felt naked where his collar should have been, and his shoulder was on fire with pain, making it hard for him to think. Moving slowly, he managed to get into a sitting position with his back against a wall, but from there, he could go no further. In the distance, he heard heavy footsteps, and flinched as a door opened and the room was flooded with light.

"Well, it's good of you to join us, Taramar," a familiar voice said. Rakesh blinked, looking up to see Martiri Kian-ti-os standing in the doorway. There was movement behind him—he wasn't alone.

"Our appointment was for next week," Rakesh said weakly, unable to think of anything else. Martiri laughed.

"Well, I've moved the date up a bit. Are you ready to serve the pure Ishkarin? Are you ready to serve the Ishamar?"

"Ishamar? Red-Swords?" Rakesh asked, confused. "I don't understand. What are you talking about? Why am I here?" He looked around, seeing the room for the first time—dirty, with cracks in the walls and rubble on the floor. "Where are we?"

Martiri smiled, stepping into the room and letting the others file into the room; they ranged around the room and stood against the walls, watching Rakesh. He could feel the hunger in them, and started to shiver. There were, Rakesh saw, five men and three women, and he recognized all of them. The two Swords who lured him from the Arena were there, and the others were high-ranking officers whom he had served in the Arena. All of them were wearing red uniforms instead of their usual black.

"You've got very good instincts, Taramar. You understand, I think. You're here to service us. To service the pure bloods. The ones who should never have been limited to the rules of the lesser beings."

"You're the ones taking the Collared," Rakesh whispered. "But, you're supposed to *protect* us. That's what the Swords do." But Martiri was already shaking his head.

"No, Taramar," he said. "That bargain was made by someone who should have known better. The Swords were created to rule the world, not coddle the weak. We aren't protectors. We're predators." He moved over to crouch in front of Rakesh. "And you, my dear, were created to be the perfect victim." He rose and smiled. "We are going to enjoy you. For a little while, at least."

"WHAT DO YOU MEAN HE's not here?" Virin demanded. It had been a very long week; it seemed as if everything that could have gone wrong had gone catastrophic, with the capstone being a transport failure that had killed three members of his team, and left Virin himself unconscious and in regen. Once he was awake, he'd pushed to come home, and now he was tired and aching, and all he'd wanted was a quiet evening with Rakesh. But he'd arrived at the Arena to find out that Rakesh was gone, and no one knew where. "I told him to stay put. He wouldn't just leave and not tell anyone."

The novice shivered and paled, but refused to be cowed, "I'm sorry, Zaan-ti-ar. But Rakesh Taramar isn't here."

Virin growled and was about to snap another question when the door to the receiving room opened and an older woman wearing a gold collar entered, leading a young man by the hand. Virin stared at her in surprise, "Chief Trainer? I'm honored...."

"Zaan-ti-ar, are you here about Rakesh?" she interrupted.

"Yes. Where is he?"

"Tell him, Linter," she said, turning to the man who had entered with her. He nodded and clasped his hands behind his back.

"There were two of them, sir. Two nights ago. They... They said they'd been sent to get Rakesh. He... He was so worried... He was waiting for you to come. When they came instead, he looked so scared... I thought he might need help. So I followed him. I stayed and listened behind the door," he swallowed and looked down at the floor. "They told him that you were hurt. That you were in the medical center, and calling for him. He left with them. They told him they'd tell the trainers, but no one did. I got Security, but by the time they got outside, the 'car was gone."

"They. Who is 'they?'"

The boy flinched, looking at the Chief Trainer, then whispering, "Swords, sir. They were Swords. A Zaan and an ir-Zaan."

"Naturally, we reported Rakesh missing. But nothing has been done, and it's been two days now," the Chief Trainer said. Virin could see the worry in her eyes. "Virin...."

He nodded, "I'll find him, Marga. I promise. I'll need his identichip signal."

She held up a memory disc. "I thought you might. The signal is here, as well as the surveillance videos for that night. The Swords didn't come through the Arena, so we don't have them registered. No identities, I'm afraid."

Virin nodded, then cocked his head and asked, "Marga, what was found on the surveillance videos of the night that Rakesh was attacked in the Arena?"

She looked startled, "What? Attacked? When was this?"

"A week ago. Marga, you didn't know?" Virin asked, incredulous. "How could you not know?"

"Indeed. How could I not know?" she repeated, her eyes gone cold. "Come with me, Virin." Virin found himself following in her wake, feeling very much like a cadet as she led him through a maze of passages and into a lift. When the door opened, Virin was certain that they were underground, but he didn't have a chance to ask how far before Marga swept off again. She opened a door and walked inside, and Virin followed her into a room filled with computers and monitors and all manner of equipment. An older man looked up as they entered, rising when he saw Marga.

"Chief Trainer?" He sounded surprised to see her there.

"Virin, this is Security Chief Delan," Marga said. "He'll help you however you need. Delan, anything that the Zaan-ti-ar needs...."

"Of course, Chief Trainer." Delan bowed slightly, then straightened and looked at Virin. "What's this about, then?"

"Who was on duty a week ago tonight?" Virin asked.

"Ah..." Delan frowned, reaching over and picking up a tablet. He tapped the screen, and his frown deepened. "A week ago? My second. Warrel."

Virin nodded. "And where is Warrel?"

Delan set the tablet down. "Zaan-ti-ar, what is this about?"

"Rakesh Taramar was attacked on the Floor a week ago. Whoever it was who grabbed him gave him a warning. Told him 'they wanted him.' Now...."

"Now Rakesh is missing. I know. I ran the surveillance videos for Marga," Delan said. Then he looked startled and grabbed the tablet again. "Oh... Warrel was on that night, too."

"Oh, no," Marga breathed.

"I repeat. Where is Warrel?" Virin asked.

Delan met his eyes and shook his head. "Zaan-ti-ar, Warrel is dead. He didn't report for his shift this morning. We called his sister, and she found him dead in his bed."

Virin swore, then pointed at the computer banks, "Were the surveillance videos run for that night? They should have been. Martiri Kian-ti-os was supposed to be leading the investigation."

"I'll check," Delan sat down at a terminal and started typing. After a moment, he shook his head. "No. Nothing was pulled. In fact...looks like someone tried to erase them. Did a shitty job of it. Missed the redundancies."

"Who tried?" Marga demanded. "Can you tell?"

Delan frowned and leaned forward over his keyboard, intent on his screen. Then he sighed. "Warrel. It was Warrel. Creator, Marga, Martiri was Warrel's commanding officer, before Warrel invalided out of the Ishkarin...." He turned and looked at them. "Zaan-ti-ar, what do you need from me?"

"I need to see the videos. Then... Blast it. If Martiri is involved, I have no idea who I can go to in the Ishkarin ranks. We'll have to go to the Council and the Ran-ti-ar, and I don't have that kind of rank..."

"I'll go to the Ran-ti-ar, Virin. Molari and I are old friends. I can call on him and no one will be the wiser," Marga said softly. "Just...find him."

Virin met her eyes and nodded, turning back to the screens as she left. "Delan, show me one week ago. I had Control locate Rakesh. That should have been caught."

"Working," Delan muttered, his fingers flying over the keyboard. The largest monitor lit up, and showed the Arena Floor. "I started this about a minute before the locate command was given."

Virin nodded, watching as he moved onto the screen, walking quickly and purposefully towards one of the stations. Then Rakesh came on screen, and Virin watched as a young Sword moved in behind him, grabbed the Taramar, and dragged him into the shadows. "Can you zoom in? Show me his face?"

"Better," Delan grinned. He tapped the keyboard, and Virin whistled in surprise as the image of the Sword filled half the screen, with all his identifying information listed next to his picture.

"Once you lot register at the entryway, we scan your 'chips. Then the images in the surveillance videos are tagged with the signal, so we can identify any troublemakers. This is your attacker. Serris ir-Zaan."

Virin nodded and clapped Delan on the shoulder, "Nice work. How's your tracking ability?"

"Outside the Arena?" Delan asked. When Virin nodded, he shrugged. "Limited. But you have an aircar, don't you?"

"Yes. Why?"

Delan stood and went over to a shelf, picking up a box and dusting off the top. He opened it and pulled out something that looked to Virin like a mess of wires and circuitry. "Because once I get this installed, we can track him from your 'car. Oh, and let me burn Serris' identichip signal, so we can find him, too. And I need to find my gun."

"Your gun?" Virin repeated. He shook his head, "No. Delan, you're not coming with me."

Delan drew himself up and looked Virin in the eyes. "You are not going alone, Zaan-ti-ar," he said firmly. "I only ever made Zaan, myself. And that was a long time ago. But I can still shoot, and I can still fight, and I am not going to let that boy down. So, you're the commanding officer. Command, already."

Virin sighed and shook his head, "Get what you need. I'll get the 'car ready."

———◉———

IT TOOK DELAN BARELY ten minutes to wire his device into the on-board computer in Virin's aircar. Virin drove out of the Arena courtyard, listening to Delan's tablet ping and beep.

"The signal is coming from the western part of the city. Looks like...the warehouse district. Near the lakeshore."

Virin nodded once and took the 'car airborne, flying over the rooftops rather than staying in the slower streets below. Delan, thankfully said nothing about the breech of protocol. Instead, he made an odd sound in his throat.

"What?" Virin asked.

"Something strange about the signal. Not sure...oh."

"What?" Virin glanced over at Delan, seeing the older man frowning. "What oh?"

"Oh as in, I don't think that Rakesh is there."

"Delan, if you don't start making sense, I'm going to push you out of the 'car," Virin growled. "If the signal is coming from there, how can...? Oh. They took his 'chip, didn't they?"

"I think so," Delan agreed. "Look, the 'chip is powered by the body. Something bio-electronic that I don't fully understand. Person dies, the signal keeps up for about a day."

"Locator function."

"Exactly. But if you take the 'chip out, it goes onto battery power. Which has a different failure curve. Locator signal, that dies all at once. Burns itself out, you know?"

"I know that, Delan...."

"But when the 'chip is out, if it just...runs out of battery, so there's a long tail with a weak signal. That's what I'm getting. We might as well turn around, Virin. He's not there."

Virin growled softly under his breath. "You're sure?" he asked.

"Yeah. I'm sure. Want me to put in the other one?"

"I want to see where the 'chip is. Give the 'car-comp the coordinates, then start looking for the ir-Zaan."

Delan grunted assent, and a moment later, Virin felt the 'car's automatic control take over. He took his hands off the controls and turned in his seat to look at Delan, who was frowning over his tablet.

"You're very technical for a retired Ishkarin," he said.

"Man needs a hobby," Delan answered. "Nothing untoward ever happens at the Arena, it's a nice place. A good place, especially for an old warhorse like me." He looked up at Virin and grinned. "Older than I look, son. Antigeria works really well with me. So let me see...you're...third-gen Sword?"

"Yes."

"Thought so. You're Iras' boy, aren't you? And Gavir's"

Virin rolled his eyes, "Everyone knows my mother. Yes."

Delan smiled. "Thought so. You have his eyes. Should have known, but I haven't seen you since before you went off to the school."

"You knew my parents?"

"Yeah, I remember your father. Good boy. Grew into a fine officer. One of the best I ever served with. I should have known who you were. And you might say that you're my fault. I bought Gavir his first night with Iras." Delan nodded over his tablet.

"If you served with Father, you... Delan, you can't be first-gen, can you? You must be..." Virin asked.

Delan nodded, "Past eighty, son. One of the last ones still kicking. Just...whatever they did to the rest of the lot, it didn't take so well with me. I got most of it, but not the killing need. So...I never got that far. Now, I do what I can. But I never wanted to do anything but go down fighting."

"Hopefully, we won't see fighting," Virin murmured, taking over the controls as the 'car beeped it was approaching the coordinates. He landed the 'car and looked around—they were in the still ruined area of the warehouse district. It would be a fine place to hide a prisoner...or an ambush.

"If you believe that, you're a damned fool, and I don't think there are any fools in this 'car," Delan said. "I'll cover from here. I've almost got the other. He's on the move, and I can't quite nail him down." He fished in his pouch and pulled out a smaller tablet, scowled at it, poked the screen a few times, then handed it to Virin. "Here. It's set to Rakesh's 'chip. Don't be too long."

Virin took the tablet and drew his gun, letting himself out of the 'car. He sniffed the air, then scanned the area around him, searching for movement. They appeared to be alone, so he glanced down at the tablet and started to follow the signal. It led to a pile of rubble, and Virin crouched down and looked closer. He sniffed again, and growled when he scented old blood. He jammed the tablet into his pouch and pulled out a finger light, playing the thin beam of light over the ground until he saw a glimmer of metal.

The chip was small, no larger than a woman's smallest fingernail, and Virin could see that the dirt around where it lay had darker splotches that might have been blood. He looked around again, then started back to the 'car, only to see Delan pop out.

"Virin!" he called. Before he could say anything else, Virin heard a footstep behind him. He turned, his gun drawn, to see the face of Serris ir-Zaan. The young man was pale, his uniform torn and dirty, and his open hands were held up before his chest.

"Zaan-ti-ar, please!" he blurted out. "I want to help!"

From behind him, Virin heard Delan's voice, "How long you been running, son?"

Serris looked past Virin, his eyes wide and frightened. "...two... Two days. I think...I've lost track. I ran...after they took Rakesh Tara-mar. I couldn't get to him, and I couldn't.... Zaan-ti-ar, I couldn't find you. I knew you'd look for him, though. So I kept watch here. I knew... I knew this is where they threw the 'chip. I... I drove them that night."

"Delan?" Virin called out.

"I think he's telling the truth, Zaan-ti-ar."

Virin nodded and lowered his gun, watching the young man sagged, his hands falling to his sides. "Come and tell us what you know, Serris," he said.

Serris nodded, "Thank you, sir." He followed Virin back to the 'car, sagging gratefully into one of the rear seats, then looking up hopefully. "You don't have anything to eat, do you?"

Virin fought back a laugh, but Delan snickered. "Delan, under your seat, there's a box. Should be some field rations in there. Now, Serris, talk."

Serris nodded, taking the package from Delan and tearing the wrapping open. He started talking, his words interrupted at intervals as he wolfed down the rations. "They recruited me a few months ago, just after I came down from the mountains. They told me that I was special, that they thought I was pure, and that I could be a part of the Ishamar, if I was pure enough." He stopped to lick the inside of the wrapper, then wiped his face. "I hadn't been the best cadet, and I never really expected to go far in the Ishkarin. My parents never did. But to have a Kian-ti-os coming to me, courting me personally, taking an interest in my career. I... I was flattered. Then...." He looked down and crumpled the wrappings in his hand. "Then they showed me what they meant by pure-blooded. They brought me to their headquarters—a ruin! A fucking ruin, out in Amali City. They told me that they had the place shielded, that our 'chips couldn't be scanned there, so no one would know. And they showed me what they meant. It... It was a woman. They told me she'd been Collared, once. A Tarken, a White Collar. That meant she was ours for the taking. And..." he stopped, looking up. "Do I have to tell you? It... It was pretty horrible. I... I threw up, and they all laughed at me. Then they told me their next target...."

"Rakesh," Virin said.

"Yeah. I... You know what it is when they bring the new Swords down to the Arena for the first time?"

Delan laughed, "Tempering the new Swords, the Collared call it. Yes."

"When my cadet class came in, Rakesh was the one who met us, gave us our first introduction to the Arena and assigned us to our Collared. He... He was..." Serris' voice trailed off, and Virin could see him blushing.

"Oh, I know," Virin said. "He does have that effect on people."

"I liked him. I kept on hoping that I might have...I don't know, the seniority? Whatever it took to have him agree to serve me. He seemed so..." Serris shrugged. "When they told me that they were going to take him, were going to...torture him to death, I couldn't go through with it. So, I went to the Arena that night. I thought about requesting him myself, but he went with you, Zaan-ti-ar. I followed you down to the Floor, and I tried to warn him."

"And you botched it," Delan said. Serris nodded.

"I didn't think. I just wanted..." he shook his head. "And I didn't know the Kian-ti-os was going to be in the Arena that night! I didn't see him until it was too late."

"Serris, do you know where they took him?" Virin asked.

"That same ruin, in Amali City. I can take you there," Serris answered. "I want to help, Zaan-ti-ar."

"We're going to need help," Delan murmured. Virin turned to see him looking down at his tablet. "Aircars with official signals. Homing in on us, from the looks of it."

"Blast!" Virin slammed his door closed and activated the defenses. "Delan, can you get through to Marga? Tell her we need a strike force. Give her my signal and have them home in on it. And tell her we need it ten minutes ago. Serris, there should be another gun underneath the seat there. Get yourself ready, and give Delan the coordinates for that ruin. Just in case."

"Yes, sir," Serris said. "What's the plan?"

Virin grabbed the controls and took the 'car into the air, seeing the other aircars approaching as the 'car moved above the roof-tops. "Survive."

Chapter Seven

R akesh had known pain. Or so he thought. Innocently, he'd thought that nothing could be worse than what had been done to him in the Arena.

Now, he understood just how naïve he had been. Just how sheltered.

Just how wrong.

Now, he truly knew pain.

He was no longer bound—there was no need, after they'd beaten him, a beating that culminated with them crushing his feet and breaking both of his legs. They had laughed about it, commented on each others technique as Rakesh had struggled and screamed. They'd held him down and made jokes as one pretty, female Sword had delicately ripped each of Rakesh's fingernails out, then broken each finger. Martiri himself had held Rakesh in position and urged on the Zaan whose nose Rakesh had broken in the aircar, and who had repaid Rakesh in kind. And Martiri had favored using hot irons, leaving behind gray stripes of seared flesh that ached and burned long after he'd stopped.

Somehow, Rakesh had managed to maneuver himself into a corner, partially hidden behind some rubble. That was as far as he could manage, and he prayed that it would at least slow them down when they came back for him. He knew they would be back; they'd promised as much. He was, Martiri told him, the best they'd ever had. He'd lasted the longest. He hadn't passed out, or thrown up, or cried, or even begged for mercy. They promised him more pain, then they left him alone in the dark. A cold draft trailed over the back of his neck, and he winced; Martiri had made a grand show of taking Rakesh's hair as a trophy before they'd left him the last time.

Rakesh curled up, fighting to breath around the pain in his chest, trying not to shiver. Trying not to think, or to remember Virin's words: anticipation *did* make it worse. Logic told him that soon would come the sexual assault, and he prayed that he would die before they came back. Futile prayers—he could hear heavy footsteps and laughter, coming closer. The door swung open and light filled the room.

"Where...? Oh, there he is. How did you get there, Taramar?" Rakesh heard Martiri ask, his voice light and laughing. Rakesh didn't open his eyes, trying to ignore them, but that lasted only until his arms were grabbed and he was dragged into the middle of the room and dropped there. He lay there, gasping in pain, as they gathered around him. A foot in the ribs prodded him onto his back, and Rakesh opened his eyes to see Martiri, three other men, and one of the women. All of them were carrying short-bladed knives.

"Time to play, Taramar," Martiri crooned.

Rakesh shook his head, "No... No more...."

"Oh, he's started to beg," the woman murmured. "How sweet. Will he break soon, do you think?"

"Only one way to find out," another man said. He crouched down and traced the line of Rakesh's ribs with his blade. As the pain lanced through him, Rakesh moaned, trying to push the man away. The Sword laughed and cut Rakesh again, drawing a line down the center of his chest. "No, he's still got some fight in him," he said as he stood. "Who's next?"

"We should suspend him for this," the woman suggested. "That way, we'll all get a chance, and we won't have to crawl on the floor."

Martiri grunted his assent. "Good idea," he said. "Rope. Where did we leave it?"

"I saw it." Rakesh heard one of the men leaving; he closed his eyes in resignation and waited for the pain to start again. Then, distantly, he heard something that sounded like gunfire. At first, he was convinced that he was hallucinating, that it was a delusion brought on by fear and pain. But then he heard it again, and he heard shouting. Someone screaming Martiri's name.

"What...?" Martiri stepped over Rakesh and went to the door, in time to catch the ir-Zaan as he ran down the corridor.

"The Ran-ti-ar!" the ir-Zaan gasped. "A strike force, and it's being led by the Ran-ti-ar himself. And that Zaan-ti-ar...Martiri, I saw him. He didn't die!"

Zaan-ti-ar? Virin? Rakesh stirred and groaned, turning his head towards the door and whispering, "...Rin?"

"Martiri, how did they find us?" the woman demanded. "You said the 'chips couldn't be read—"

"They can't!" Martiri snapped. "They did it some other way. We need to get out of here." He prodded Rakesh with his foot. "Get him up. We can use him as a hostage."

"What? Martiri, he can't walk!"

"Carry him!" Martiri snapped.

The woman sniffed, "You carry him. You told us that they'd never find us. Now...if they catch us, we're for the camps. If we're lucky." She turned and bolted from the room. To Rakesh's surprise, the men followed her, leaving only Martiri and the ir-Zaan.

"Sir, what do we do?" the ir-Zaan asked.

"Get him up," Martiri repeated. The ir-Zaan nodded, crouching down and grabbing Rakesh's arm. As he dragged Rakesh up into a sitting position, Rakesh felt a shooting pain in his side; he gasped in pain, coughed, and was amazed to see a splatter of blood on the young Sword's sleeve.

"Kian-ti-os! He's coughing blood!" the ir-Zaan shrilled, letting Rakesh fall. "He's dying. We should leave him." The ir-Zaan didn't wait for another order, edging his way to the door and running off after the others. Outside, the sounds of fighting were closer, and Rakesh was certain he could hear Virin's voice, shouting his name. At least he would see Virin again before he died. He smiled slightly and mouthed, "Here. I'm here."

"Oh, he'll find you, Rakesh," Martiri said softly. He knelt down next to Rakesh, and held up the short-bladed knife. "He can weep over your corpse."

There was nothing Rakesh could do, no way to stop him, and as he felt the knife entering his chest, he heard, as if at a great distance, Virin screaming his name.

———❦———

RAKESH OPENED HIS EYES to see a gray ceiling, subtly inlaid with a cream-colored staring pattern that he recognized. It was something that Ishkarin used in their own meditations, and this was one that he'd seen the few times he'd been in Virin's quarters in the barracks. He turned his head, amazed at the lack of pain, and looked around to see that he was in a dimly-lit bedroom, lying in the middle of a wide bed. He flexed his bandaged fingers, feeling small aches that told of unfinished healing, and slowly sat up. As he did, the lights brightened.

"Don't push it," Virin said softly. Rakesh turned to see him standing in the doorway, dressed informally in a wrapped shirt and loose trousers. He smiled and continued, "You're not even a day out of regen. This morning, actually."

"Rin?" Rakesh looked around again. "Where are we?"

Virin came the rest of the way into the room as he answered, "My new living quarters. Hungry? You should be."

Rakesh smiled, "I think so. Yes."

"Good. Relax. I'll get something for you to eat, and then I'll bring you up to date. Just...don't move. You're still not completely healed." He left the room, and Rakesh looked around. The bedroom was nice, the furnishings attractive without being overbearing. Everything looked new, and the fact that there was more than one room said that this place was much larger than Virin's old quarters.

"How long have you had these quarters?" Rakesh called.

"Moved in three days ago," Virin called back. "It's been a busy week, Kesh. Just wait. I don't want to shout."

Rakesh looked around again, smiling at the books on the shelves, and noticing something he'd never before seen in Virin's quarters—a trophy case. Many of the Swords kept them, displaying carefully preserved pieces of defeated enemies. Fingers, hands and ears, usually. Virin had always called the practice barbaric, and Rakesh wondered if the case was a legacy of the previous occupant. Then Virin came in, carrying a tray that he set down on the bed next to Rakesh.

"Eat. The medics said that you'll want to eat more than usual for a while. And that you'll sleep more, too. It's normal, after extensive regen. You were under for a week, which beats any stay of mine by three days. And, since I know I'm usually ready to eat the regen capsule when they decant me, you must be ready to eat the blankets." Virin sat down and pointed at covered bowls. "Grain porridge, stewed *sava* fruit, that herbal tea you like, and your mother's Aakarin stew.

Rakesh picked up the bowl of stew and lifted the lid, breathing in the scent, then looked at Virin. "My *mother* made this? Did she send it from the Highlands?"

"Ah...no. Your mother is here in the City. She's staying with my mother," Virin grinned as Rakesh groaned. "I knew that they were old friends. I just didn't know how close they were. My mother was one of your mother's trainers in the Arena. And your father's, too. Shouldn't have surprised me, really. I don't think they're planning weddings yet. At least, they weren't yesterday."

Rakesh sighed and started to eat. "How bad was it?" he asked around mouthfuls.

Virin sobered. "They almost lost you, Kesh. Twice. Once in the transport, and again just before they stabilized you for regen. Your lungs collapsed. One from being punctured by broken ribs, and the other from Martiri's knife. You want the list?"

"It can't get any worse than dead," Rakesh said. "How bad?"

Virin looked thoughtful. "I suppose when you look at it that way. Your feet may never heal properly. Some of the bones were crushed to dust, and regen can only do so much. You're not to walk at all without help for another week, and you're to stay off your feet as much as possible after that. Your hands should be fine, though, but it will be a while before the nails come back completely. That is the reason for the bandages. You'll have scars, from some of the burns. And you have a very fetching little bump, right here." He reached out and tapped the bridge of Rakesh's nose. "Now, what was this I heard about you breaking someone's nose?"

"In the aircar, when I realized that they were lying to me, and weren't taking me to you," Rakesh said, scraping his spoon around the inside of the bowl of stew, then licking the spoon. "They told me you were dead, Rin."

"I almost was," Virin answered. "Well done, Kesh. We're going to have to see about getting you some extra training, once you've healed. So, what else? Ah... that young man who tried to warn you? He turned to our side, led us right to you. He's hoping you'll see him; he wants to apologize, both for being involved with that lot, and for scaring you in the Arena."

Rakesh nodded, looking at the other bowls. Without looking up, he murmured, "And Martiri?"

"He's over there," Virin said, sounding very satisfied. Rakesh looked up, and saw that Virin was looking at the trophy case.

"Rin?"

"I never thought I would take a trophy. I thought it was a bar-baric custom. And then...I reached the door in time to see him shoving a knife into your chest. I thought he'd killed you, and I went...insane. When they pulled me off of him and told me you were alive, he didn't have enough blood left in him to fill a tea-cup." He nodded towards the case. "His heart is right there. Frankly, I was amazed he had one. And I've learned a few things in the past couple of days. Delan and I had a long talk while we waited for you to come out of regen. Apparently, this whole pure-blood thing has been growing for a long time. From what Delan says, Martiri's father was sent to the internment camps because of it. He turned rogue and turned on my father."

"That makes no sense. None of this makes senses." Rakesh swallowed hard and licked his lips. "And now?"

"Now? Now, if you want, you are my guest. At least until the medics clear you to return to the Arena...."

"No!" Rakesh blurted out. He covered his mouth with one hand, fighting down a wave of nausea and panic. Virin just nodded.

"I thought that might be your reaction. So did the Council. If you want to leave the Arena, Kesh, no one will blame you. And...if you want...." He took something from his pocket and passed it to Rakesh. Rakesh looked down at the insignia, his mind stubbornly refusing to recognize the rank pins. Then he blinked and looked up.

"Kian-ti? You've been promoted to Kian-ti?"

Virin nodded slowly and smiled. "In recognition for my service to both the Ishkarin and the people of Tyese and Aakar. Kesh, you could have knocked me over with a feather. The Ran-ti-ar told me there was a promotion coming, and I figured, one rank. I never imagined he'd award me every rank that Martiri kept me from making."

"That's why..." Rakesh looked up and around the room. "So, these are—?

"Officer's quarters. And all attendant rights and privileges. So...if that offer is still on the table, Taramar, I'd be interested."

"Offer? Rin, are you sure you still want to marry me?" Rakesh asked. In answer, Virin leaned forward and kissed him gently, cupping the back of his head with one hand and stroking the bare nape of his neck with his fingers.

"Does that answer your question, Kesh?" Virin asked. "Yes, I still want to marry you. I love you. Now, that being said," he said as he straightened. "There is another offer on the table."

"Another...what?" Rakesh asked.

Virin took something out of his other pocket and laid it across Rakesh's lap. Rakesh picked it up and looked at it, then looked at Virin.

"What is this?" he asked, holding up the collar that was similar in almost every way to the red one that he had worn before. Similar, and yet very different. This collar was black.

"The Council thought that you might want to leave the Arena. And, like I said, no one blames you. But they don't want to lose you, Kesh. Your experience in the Arena, your knowledge.... They want you to apprentice to Marga, and take over from her as chief Trainer someday. They want you to wear the gold. So, they're offering this. A new rank, created specifically for you. Now, don't shake your head!"

"But...the Collared serve the Swords. That's the way it works," Rakesh said weakly. "I can't... I can't let someone hurt me again like that, Rin."

"Take a closer look at that Collar, Kesh."

Rakesh frowned and studied the collar again. This time, he saw it—the plate at the front, usually a mutable screen, was already marked with Virin's insignia. He rubbed his thumb over the plate and discovered that it was made from etched metal.

"You would be bound to me, and to me alone," Virin said softly. "From this point on, Collared will have the choice. They can leave the Arena after five years, or they can take the Red. That won't change. But now, now if they have someone among the Swords that they love, that they want to continue to serve, they'll be able to take the Black. If you take this Collar, Kesh, the only person who will ever be allowed to touch you is me." He rested his hand on Rakesh's knee. "Kesh, you can take your time to decide—"

"Help me?" Rakesh interrupted. He held the collar out to Virin. "Help me put this on?"

Virin's head dropped, and for a moment, Rakesh couldn't tell why. Then the Sword looked up, and Rakesh could see that he was laughing. "You didn't even give me a chance to try and convince you!"

"I don't need convincing. I need you. And I need your help."

Virin took the collar from Rakesh and leaned forward, fitting it around Rakesh's throat and locking it on. He trailed his fingers down Rakesh's chest and stopped with his hand over Rakesh's heart. "I can't touch you yet. Not that way. Not until you heal. I will still marry you, you know."

Rakesh smiled, trying not to yawn. "I know."

"I will never hurt you. Unless you ask me to hurt you."

"I know that, too."

"I love you, Rakesh Tarkarin."

"I love you, too, Virin Kian-ti."

Virin smiled and patted Rakesh's chest, then picked up the tray. "I can see you're fighting sleep, so...take a nap," he said as he rose.

"You're tired, too," Rakesh said, sliding back down under the blankets. "Come nap with me."

"Thought you'd never ask. I'll be right back." Virin hurried out of the room, and was back a moment later, stripping his shirt off over his head and climbing into the bed next to Rakesh. Gently, he pulled Rakesh into his arms, kissing his bare shoulder.

"Go to sleep, Kesh. I'm here. You're safe," he murmured.

Safe, warm, whole, Rakesh slept.

ENDGAMES
Chapter One

R akesh looked out into the crowded room and smiled. At seventy-three men and woman, this was the largest training group he could remember, and the most promising. Time to greet them, and see them made comfortable. He leaned on his canes and walked slowly out to the podium. He could feel them staring at him, could almost taste their sudden rush of fear. Had serving in the Arena done *this* to him? Every training group over the past five years had asked that question. Rakesh faced the group and smiled.

"Good morning," he said, the hidden microphones in the podium catching his voice and projecting it around the room. "Welcome to the Arena. I am Rakesh Tarkarin, Second here in the Arena, and I'll be your training master.

"Now, let's clear the air before I begin the orientation. You're wondering now if my service in the Arena did this to me." He held up one cane, and heard nervous laughter. He grinned. "Don't worry. Everyone in your position asks that question, and I'm used to it. After five years, I'd think that my story would be old news, but I see a good number of Aakari among you, so perhaps not. The quick answer is no. This didn't happen in the Arena, and I value my calling and my time spent in the Arena more than anything except my marriage. If I did not, I would not still wear a collar." He reached up and touched his collar, black to signify his status, bearing fifteen gold studs to mark both his years in service and his rank as Second. "As of today, you are only committed to serve a single year. You will wear gray, to show that you are novices. No one will touch you during that time. Even if you ask. The Gray are strictly off-limits. In your time here, you will work in every area of the Arena, from the Lounge to the Floor to the medical facilities. You will learn about life in the Arena, learn about life as a Tarken, see for yourself what is and is not true. At the end of the year, you will make the decision to take the Collar yourself. Or not. That isn't a decision that I or anyone else can make for you. If you decide to leave, you will leave with the wages you earned over your year here, which adds up to quite a pretty sum. If you stay, that money is banked for you, and given to you when you leave, along with any interest earned. You can also draw on that account for luxury items during your time in the Collar. Everything else, from clothing to food to medical care to entertainment, is provided.

"You've passed the preliminary testing or you would not be here. You all are here because you have a high empathy rating, strong personalities, higher-than-average intelligence and an aptitude for pain." There was a soft susurration of laughter at that, and Rakesh smiled. "That last might be the most important part. From this point on, you will learn to harness your empathy, learn to challenge the Swords and how to submit to them. You will learn how to help them through their own pain, and you will learn how to take whatever pain they choose to give to you with joy and with pleasure.

"Now, before you start your orientation tour, what questions do you have?"

Silence, then a pretty dark-skinned girl at the front raised her hand. "Sir?"

"Yes?" Rakesh smiled at her. "What's your name?"

"I'm Lela, Sir. From Felanore." She clasped her hands in her lap. "I...have heard that when one takes the collar, that one can never leave. That we become slaves, and that the Tyesean Council can sell us beyond the seas."

Rakesh sighed. That old rumor *still* hadn't died out? "No, Lela. No one has been sold. You are not a slave. If you take the Collar, you will serve five years. If you choose, you will serve only five years. At the end of five years, you can leave. You will receive a pension, and be granted high-caste status. No one is forced to remain past their contract period."

"But—"

"I can introduce you to every living former Tarken, Lela," Rakesh added gently. "If you wish. It would take most of the day, so we'll have to make sure you have a day off from training." He looked around the room. "I've heard this rumor before. I've also heard the one that says that the Collared are the first, failed creation of Mathias, creator of the Swords. I can assure you that neither are true."

"What about the one about the Red Swords?" someone called out. Rakesh went very still.

"The Red Swords," he repeated. "That... That one is true." He backed away from the podium for a moment, struggling to keep his composure. Five years, and the mention of the Ishamar still sent him into a near panic.

"Sir?" It was Lela, who had gotten to her feet and was halfway to the podium. Rakesh waved her off and moved back into place.

"I'm sorry," he said. "Yes, the Red Swords exist. You wondered if these canes, if my injuries came because of the Arena? They did not. I was targeted by the Red Swords. I was lucky, and survived. But because of what was done to me, I am no longer able to serve in the Arena. Instead, I train you lot." He looked around and forced a smile. "And some of the things that you will be trained in are self-defense, evasion and escape. In my time, the Collared were never taught such things. It was thought there was no need. Perhaps things might have been different if we had."

"If this is so dangerous, why are we here?" someone else shouted. "Why are you asking us to put ourselves at risk?"

"No one asked you. No one forced you," Rakesh replied. "You volunteered. If you wish, you can leave now, and no one will hold it against you. Or you can walk through these doors behind me and let me teach you why. And when my fellow trainers and I are done with you, you will be counselors without equal. You will be recognized among society as part of the elite. You may choose to remain in the Arena, to take the Red. If you are as lucky as I am, then perhaps you'll find love, and take the Black." He smiled, then saw a figure in black at the rear of the room. His smile broadened, and he forced his attention back to his trainees. "Are there any other questions? No? Then, please, through these doors." He gestured to the double doors behind him.

"You will not be coming with us?" Lela asked.

"Not for the tour, no," Rakesh answered. "I already know where everything is." When the laughter died down, he smiled. "I'll meet you at the end, and we'll get your room assignments taken care of and see you all settled. Now, off with you!" He remained standing as the trainees filed past him and through the doors, then walked over to one of their abandoned chairs and sat down. Even wearing the special boots, it was hard to stand for very long. The medics were talking about another round of surgery, implants to replace the crushed bones that refused to heal....

"Sir?"

Rakesh looked up to see Lela, hovering nearby. "What is it, Lela?" he asked gently. "You're going to be late for the tour."

"There are so many, it will be a moment before they start," she answered. "May I ask you a question, sir?"

"Go ahead."

"You are Aakari?"

Rakesh shook his head. "I was born in Tyese. My parents were from Aakar, though. They were refugees who came to Tyese just after the war, and they both served in the Arena."

Lela looked startled. "Your father?"

"Yes," Rakesh answered. "Why is that surprising?"

"Because in Aakar, men don't sleep with men," a familiar voice answered from behind Rakesh. Lela went pale, and slowly backed away from the footsteps Rakesh heard coming closer.

"Lela, it's all right," Rakesh said, wondering why the girl looked terrified. "Lela of Felanore, this is my husband, Virin Kian-ti-ar. He won't bite."

"I don't know you that well," Virin added.

"You're not helping, Rin."

Lela froze, her eyes wide. "You are married to a man?" she gasped. "That is allowed here?"

"Allowed?" Rakesh repeated. He looked up at Virin. "It's not in Aakar? Father never told me that."

"Raizi left holes in your education, I see," Virin said, shaking his head. "Yes. It's considered obscene in Aakar, and the last I heard, was a criminal offense."

Rakesh let out a long breath. "Well... I wondered why we got so few male trainees from Aakar. I'll speak to the trainers, let them know to be mindful of that."

"You never asked?"

"I didn't. That was lax of me. Go on, Lela. You'll be late." Rakesh smiled as the girl bowed and darted out through the doors. Once she was gone, he slumped in the chair and groaned.

"Largest training group to date," he said, closing his eyes. "Seventy-three this time, and if the test scores are any indication, at least sixty will take the collar. And we have twenty-seven Aakari this time, and twelve of them are men. We're running out of places to put them, Rin. Even with the renovations and the additional dorm space that was added last year."

"Can you double up on bunk space?" Virin asked, dragging a chair over so he could sit facing Rakesh.

"Not without trouble. When you spend so much of your life in close proximity to others, be it other Collared or Swords, you value what private space you can get. Asking the Collared to share...that's just asking for conflict."

Virin nodded, humming softly. "Well, can you farm some of them out to the satellite Arenas?"

"Perhaps some of the more experienced Tarken and a few Taramar, but again, there's no place to put them! The Maryst Arena is full, and so is the one at the main Garrison. The one in New Amali isn't finished yet. The corps of mobile Collared for Ishkarin on maneuvers is fully staffed, and has a waiting list that will take years to get through. There's talk about starting a new Arena in Felanore, attached to the Embassy—"

"How did you hear about that?" Virin interrupted.

"Marga told me. This morning, as a matter of fact." He yawned, and Virin laughed and reached across to pat Rakesh on the thigh.

"Tired?" he asked. There was a note to his voice that made Rakesh look at him and smile.

"Never that tired. But you know I don't sleep well when you're gone. How was it in Aakar?"

"It's a mess," Virin said simply. "The garrison there has been mismanaged since it was founded, and heads are going to roll. Six ranking Swords have already been sent to the camps for abuse of power, and more will probably follow. Two weeks wasn't nearly long enough to put things right."

Rakesh shook his head. "That's terrible."

"It's worse than terrible. I really have no idea what has been going on there. Records range from bad to cryptic to nonexistent. Serris is still there, trying to make sense if it all. And I'm to go back as soon as possible," Virin said. Then he looked away for a moment.

Rakesh sat up straighter in his chair. "All right, Rin. Out with it."

Virin looked at him and smiled. "You know me too well. They've asked me to take command of the Aakari garrison." Virin reached into his pouch and held his hand out to Rakesh. "If I take it, it comes with this."

Rakesh held his hand out, and Virin dropped small gold pins into his palm. They were rank pins. Terrifyingly familiar rank pins. The last time Rakesh had seen these particular pins up close, he was being tortured. He stared for a moment, then looked at Virin.

"Kian-ti-os? They... They're promoting you to *Kian-ti-os*?"

"With the transfer, if I take it. If not...Molari says I might have to wait a year or two. But..." Virin let out a huff, running one hand over his short-cropped silvering hair. "He's been without a second for five years now, and he's feeling his age. He wants me to succeed him."

"Creator," Rakesh murmured. "I... Tell him yes. And I'll tell Marga yes."

"Tell her yes about what?" Virin asked.

"That I'll take on the gold for the Aakari Arena," Rakesh answered. "That was why she talked to me this morning. She offered it to me—"

"No."

Rakesh stopped, stunned by Virin's interruption. "What? What do you mean?"

"I mean no!" Virin snapped. "You are not going to Aakar."

"But...Virin, I don't want to stay behind," Rakesh protested. "You taking the garrison, that means you'll be living in Felanore. It won't be for two weeks, you'll be gone years!"

"It's only a few hours by aircar. I'll be here whenever I have leave—"

"And we left that kind of relationship behind when I took the Black." Rakesh grabbed his canes and pushed himself to his feet. "I'm not letting you walk away from me, Rin. Not without a fight."

"That's exactly what I'm worried about!" Virin bolted to his own feet. "A fight! I just told you what they think of men like us in Aakar! Think about the diplomatic damage we'd cause, being public as a married pair of men! We'd be breaking every law they have, or living a lie. Worse, they think of the Arena as a glorified brothel! You're not going to be an honored Tarkarin there, Kesh. You're going to be an expensive whore. I'm not going to be able to protect you from that. And with the way you are—" He stopped, but Rakesh already knew what he was going to say.

"Because of these?" Rakesh asked slowly, holding up one cane. "You want me to stay behind, because of these? Because I'm crippled now?"

"Kesh—"

"You told me that it didn't matter that I was never going to walk properly again."

"It doesn't matter! Not to me!" Virin protested. "Kesh, I just want to protect you! I never want that to happen again." He looked away, shaking his head. "I... I couldn't live through that again, Kesh. I almost lost you the last time."

"And I'll be in the Embassy. With the whole weight of the Aakari Garrison between me and the rest of the world. And with you by my side. Not hours away, in another country. Not alone." Rakesh growled softly and started to limp towards the doors.

"Where are you going?"

"To change. I'm tired, and I'm starting to hurt. And not the good kind of hurt. Linter offered to do the room assignments for me, since he's still off-duty and bored." Rakesh stopped at the doors. "Control!"

Acknowledged.

"Inform Linter Tarken that I'm sending the new trainee room assignments to his box, then do so. The file is on my terminal. Ask him to attend them after their tour. And tell the Chief Trainer that I'm leaving."

Confirmed. There was a pause, then the computer spoke again. *Chief Trainer bids you good evening, and requests that you call her to further discuss Aakar.*

"I will." Rakesh reached for the door, only for Virin to touch the control pad first. The doors slid open, revealing a long, empty hallway beyond. Rakesh didn't say anything, starting towards the lift at the far end of the hall.

"Kesh, I just don't want to see you hurt again."

"Rin, you won't see me at all if you take this," Rakesh pointed out. "You'll get leave...what? Every fourth week? And only if there is someone to take your duties? And you've just told me that things are in terrible condition there. So you won't be able to take leave at all until you get everything straightened out and running the way it ought to be. So how long, Kian-ti-os? How long before I see you again?" Rakesh turned and looked at his husband. "Do you remember what I told you, about what it was like for me, that first tour you took after the wedding?"

Virin sighed. "Yes. I remember."

Rakesh leaned against the wall, remembering the long nights. The panic attacks. Waking screaming whenever he finally passed out from exhaustion. "It hasn't gotten better," Rakesh said quietly. The lift door opened, and he limped inside. Virin followed. Rakesh continued as the doors closed. "Third level. Rin, the only reason I haven't been staying here while you were in Felanore was that there wasn't room for me! I've been tempted to take leave and go back to the farm, just for the distraction. Kezia had another baby a few weeks ago. A girl."

"A new niece for Uncle Kesh to spoil, " Virin murmured. He moved to stand behind Rakesh and put his arms around him. "I didn't know it was still that bad, Kesh. You never told me. Love, it isn't that I don't want you with me. I do. I just want you safe—"

The lift jerked to a stop and the light blinked out for a moment. Then emergency lights clicked to life, bathing the inside of the lift in sickly yellow light. "Damn it!" Rakesh snarled. "Again?"

"What just happened?" Virin asked, an odd tightness in his voice.

"Power failure," Rakesh answered. "It's been happening on and off for almost a week. Rin?"

"How... How long?" Virin let Rakesh go and backed up slowly, looking around. "Kesh, how long?"

Rakesh turned, dropping one of his canes in his haste. He'd never seen Virin like this before, never heard that particular growl in his voice. "Rin, what's wrong?"

"How long?" The growl was stronger now, and there was a wildness in Virin's eyes when he looked at Rakesh. "Don't come closer. Don't."

"Why? Rin, what's wrong?" Rakesh stumbled closer, then staggered backwards as Virin howled and attacked, diving across the small space and catching Rakesh around the waist, carrying him to the floor so quickly that his head bounced off the floor. Rakesh gasped, shook his head to clear it, then yelped and tried to push Virin off, bringing his legs up and shoving hard, feeling the pain shooting up from his feet as Virin fell back. The Sword just howled again and attacked once more. Rakesh fought back as hard as he could, hating that he was having to turn his hard-earned skills of defense on his own husband, knowing that Virin would expect no less of him. He caught Virin across the jaw with an elbow strike, then delivered a solid jab to the throat. Nothing he did stopped the Sword, who pinned Rakesh down, howling with wordless insanity.

"Rin!" Rakesh shouted, trying to calm Virin. Then his voice froze in his throat as he watched Virin pick up one of the abandoned canes. He raised it high, and all that Rakesh could do was cover his head with his arms....

———————◦———————

THE RELAXATION MANDALAS in the medical wing were very familiar, so Rakesh knew exactly where he was when he opened his eyes. And he knew from the slightly foggy feeling in his head that he'd been in regen. But he had no idea for how long, or what had happened to Virin. He sat up slowly, looking around for an attendant. And was startled to find Delan, the head of Arena Security, dozing in a chair across from the bed.

"Delan?"

Delan jerked awake, blinking. He scrubbed at his face and winced. "Nodded off, didn't I?"

"Yes."

"I'm getting too old for this," he grumbled. "How do you feel, Rakesh?"

"Fine," Rakesh answered, then asked, "Any reason I shouldn't?"

"Well, your husband damn near caved your skull in to start. After he broke both your arms. Took five men to bring him down once we got that lift open. You've been in regen for a full day, Kesh."

Rakesh stared, then whispered, "Why? Why...? He attacked me. I...." Panic closed around him like a fist, and his voice faltered and failed.

"It wasn't his fault, Rakesh," Delan said slowly. "Not entirely. He went feral. It's something that happens..." Delan's voice trailed off. "Oh, Creator. He never told you about that? No one has ever told you about that? About going feral?"

Rakesh shook his head, his hands clenched in the sheet covering his legs. He could feel them shaking, and his head was pounding. "I... I don't know what that is."

"It's a fail-safe," Delan explained. "Something Mathias put into us in case any of the Ishkarin were ever captured. If we're trapped, we essentially go insane, turn into the killing monsters that Mathias' opponents always painted us as being. It was to keep the Aakari from learning what was done to us, how we were enhanced. Tragar had some damned good geneticists of his own, back in the day. Mostly, he used them to create monsters for his menagerie. But they might have been able to duplicate what Mathias did...or undo it."

"Undo it?" The words startled Rakesh most of the way out of his growing panic. "Undo...that's even possible?"

"Anything that can be done can be undone, son," Delan said with a shrug. "And only Mathias knew for certain. I've heard that there are researchers trying to figure that out, but I don't think they will. Not in my lifetime, anyway. Or yours."

"So...wait. Wait a moment." Rakesh leaned forward, frowning. "Every time I hear about the camps, I hear about solitary confinement. But—"

"It is the single worst punishment a Sword can face," Delan said, his voice flat. "Lock him in a cell and throw away the keys. We all experience it, in training. So we know what it's like, and we know we want to avoid it. The longest I've ever seen a Sword last was about fifteen minutes, and that was Gavir. But he was...a special case."

"I know. Virin told me. What happens?"

"The ones that are sent into solitary... They don't last long, I'm told. They go insane. Tear themselves up trying to get out. If they live long enough, they go catatonic. Then..." Delan shook his head. "I don't want to give you nightmares, Rakesh."

"To go with the ones I already have, you mean?" Rakesh looked around. "Where's Rin?"

"Home. He asked me to stay with you, take you home if you wanted to go there—"

"What?" Rakesh interrupted, suddenly icy-cold. "He... He doesn't want me to come home?"

"Not what I said. I said if you wanted to go there." Delan leaned forward and sighed. "He's afraid you're going to divorce him, Kesh. That he's lost you over this. He's feeling guilty as all fuck, he's ashamed of himself, ashamed of what he is, and he's... I've never seen him this far into the dark before and I've known him for more years than you have."

Rakesh listened in silence, staring down at the smooth weave of the sheet. When Delan stopped talking, the only sound other than their breathing was the hum of the ventilation unit overhead. Slowly, Rakesh dragged his thoughts into order, only to discover that there was never really any question.

"Delan? Take me home, please?"

Chapter Two

Rakesh hesitated outside the door to the apartment that he and Virin shared. Would Virin be there? Or would he walk into an empty apartment, to find his husband already gone for Felanore? He licked his lips, then took a step forward; the door recognized his identichip signal and opened for him. He walked slowly inside and let the door close behind him. The front room was empty, the apartment quiet, and for a moment, he thought Virin was gone—

"You came back."

Rakesh turned, saw Virin standing in the doorway that led to their bedroom. He was out of uniform, looking tired and unkempt. And far more nervous than Rakesh could ever remember seeing.

"I came back. Rin—"

"I'm sorry," Virin interrupted. "If... If you want, I can be out of here tomorrow. I'll sign anything you want—"

"Rin, shut up," Rakesh said gently. Virin stopped and stared at him as Rakesh raised his left hand, baring the pledge bracelet that encircled his wrist. The matching one was, he noticed, still around Virin's.

"You are an idiot. You are a fucking idiot. And I love you," Rakesh said. "That hasn't changed. You scared me, but you've been scaring the piss out of me on and off for over ten years now. I have never expected that to change. I am surprised you never told me about that whole feral thing. That's really something I should have known. And I expect you to tell me anything else like that before I run face first into it. Deal?"

It took Virin a moment to realize what Rakesh meant. "You're not leaving?"

"And neither are you. Idiot." Rakesh watched as the tension flowed out of Virin, leaving him sagging against the doorframe. "You look like shit, Rin."

Virin grinned. "And you're awfully sweary, Kesh. How are you feeling?"

"Pretty good, all things considered. You?"

Virin shrugged. "I haven't slept since the drugs wore off. I've been... Well, I've been packing. I thought you'd want me gone. I wouldn't have blamed you." He straightened and looked at Rakesh. "Why don't you want me gone?"

Rakesh walked over to him, leaned one of his canes against the wall, and reached up to curl one hand around the back of Virin's neck. "Because I'm not blaming you for something that you were made to be," he said, looking into Virin's eyes. "I love you, Kian-ti-os. I'm not rejecting you for being a Sword. That's part of you, part of the man I love. That I loved enough to marry. And now that I know about this part, I can help you avoid being placed in that situation."

Virin closed his eyes, and Rakesh felt the shudder than ran through him. He pulled Virin closer, wrapping his free arm around his husband, feeling strong arms sliding around his own waist. "I love you," he repeated. "And I forgive you."

"Thank you," Virin murmured against his neck. "I love you, Kesh." His arms tightened slightly, then loosened as Virin straightened. "So...do I unpack? Or do I help you pack?"

Rakesh blinked, startled. "Why...? I told you you're not leaving!"

"No, but I did think we'd be taking our things with us to Aakar—"

"Rin!"

"I was wrong," Virin said simply. "I know that. I've taught you the best I can. And, look here..." He tipped his head back, and Rakesh saw the livid bruise that crossed Virin's throat. "If I'd been a normal man, you've have laid me flat with that strike. Possibly killed me. You did well, Kesh. I'm proud of you."

Rakesh felt his face growing warm, and smiled slightly. "I had a good teacher," he murmured. "How much packing have you done?"

"Not a lot. My clothes. A few personal things. Why?"

Rakesh smiled and stepped closer, his chest against Virin's. "So...none of the toys?"

"You are just out of regen!" Virin said with a laugh.

"So?"

"So, I don't want to put you back in!"

Rakesh laughed, a laugh that was cut short when Virin grabbed him and kissed him, hard enough to steal his breath. He dropped his second cane and wrapped both arms around Virin's neck, letting Virin push him back against the wall. He groaned as Virin released his mouth and started working with teeth and tongue over his jaw and down his throat.

"I know what to do to you," Virin whispered against Rakesh's skin. "I know. Come into the bedroom."

"Thought you'd never ask." Rakesh took the arm that Virin offered, letting Virin support him as they walked into the bedroom. These quarters were larger than the ones that they'd had before Virin had been promoted to Kian-ti-ar two years ago, so there was room in their bedroom for things that they couldn't fit in their old space. The whipping cross on the wall across from their bed, for example. Or the rack of whips, restraints and various other things that they both enjoyed. Rakesh looked around as they walked into the room, and groaned at the sight of clothing piled all over the bed, some of it balled up haphazardly and half stuffed into packing boxes. "Rin!"

"I know. I'll clean it up tomorrow. Now...sit down. I want to show you something."

Rakesh nodded and sat down on the edge of the bed, watching as Virin dug through one box and pulled out a long tube. He held it up and grinned. "I brought this back from Felanore. Tarason Kian-ti-ar had a truly impressive collection of these in his quarters, and I...appropriated them after he was sent north. I'd heard stories about this kind of thing in Aakar, read about them in my father's notes, but never I've never actually seen them before. I didn't think any of them still existed, really. They were supposed to all have been destroyed."

"Tarason?"

"The former commander of the garrison. I'll tell you more about him later. For now...." He passed the tube to Rakesh. "Open it."

Rakesh examined the tube, found that it twisted open. Inside was a scroll that, when unfurled, revealed calligraphy that Rakesh could not read, accompanying a beautifully-detailed drawing of a blindfolded woman. Her skin was covered by what looked like intricate lattice work.

"This is lovely," Rakesh murmured. "What is that supposed to be, a tattoo?"

"No. That's ropework, Kesh."

Rakesh looked up, then back down at the artwork. "Rope? Wait... Yes. I see the knots now. That's... extraordinary. And you found this in Aakar? I thought that they didn't..." Rakesh frowned, then looked over at Virin. "What are these?"

"Apparently, it's an ancient art form, part of the religion that was suppressed when Tragar decided to deify himself. That's all I know—there's nothing about this in any of my father's books. But he'd heard stories, though, about these kinds of scrolls, and he wrote about them in his notes on Aakar. From what I could see, Transon just thought these were pornography. He had them hanging in his quarters. But they're not meant to be."

"I can see why he thought so. So what are they?"

"Well, if my theory is correct, these are partially prayer books and partially meditation guides," Virin answered as he sat down next to Rakesh. "Honestly, I don't know. Father might have known more.

Mother says that he was studying the old Aakari religions when he died. She was interested, because some of what he learned was very similar to things Mother told him she was taught in the Arena."

Rakesh looked at his husband, "So many of the trainees we get from Aakar are so...shocked at what is expected of them in the Arena. But this... This is something that I think would have gotten them ready for it. If can adapt something that is part of their own culture, it might help. Do you think she'd loan me those books?"

"She already did," Virin answered. He reached over and took the scroll, slowly rolling it back up. "Here's the funny part. Mother told me that after their first time together in the Arena, Father gave her a book to read while she was recovering. The book was on the Aakari religion, and it turned out that she already had it. She borrowed it from one the the first Aakari refugees to take the collar." He looked sidelong at Rakesh. "Your father."

"What?" Rakesh shook his head. "Father never speaks about what his life was like in Aakar. Nothing. He's never even told us about his family in Aakar, even when I asked. Nor did Mother. I don't know if they have any living relatives there. I don't even really speak the language!"

"I thought you did."

"Not much." Rakesh shrugged. "Father and Mother were firm about us speaking Tyesean, but we learned Aakari because they would speak it to each other when they didn't want us to understand."

"We're both going to need to be fluent before we get to Aakar. We'll have to undergo immersion hypnotics before we leave. Ever done that?" Virin asked.

"No. The refugees who don't speak Tyesean get it when they join the Arena, but perhaps I should have learned more Aakari."

"In your oh-so-plentiful spare time?" Virin teased. "

"I could have gotten a tutor in the Arena. There are more than enough fluent speakers to teach me what I don't know." Rakesh frowned, thinking. "I should mention that to Marga, too."

"Later. You can think about your work later. Now, I'm thinking about you. And I want you thinking about nothing at all."

Rakesh laughed. "And how do you plan to manage that?"

Virin smiled and held up the scroll. "Meditation, my dear. Let's get you out of those clothes."

Rakesh took off his shirt and watched as what had turned into a daily ritual between him and Virin started. Virin went to his knees in front of Rakesh and slowly took Rakesh's right foot into his lap. He tugged on the straps of the knee-high boots that Rakesh wore, slowly loosening them until he could finally, gently, tug the heavy boot off. He had to be gentle, or the pain would be excruciating. The compression stocking came off next, slowly peeled down Rakesh's leg and over his crippled feet. Once it was off, Virin started to massage Rakesh's foot, using a strong-smelling liniment that the medics said would do no harm. A phrase that Rakesh privately thought meant that they didn't think it would do any good either. But Virin insisted, claiming that the salve was used in the training camps in order to speed the healing of minor wounds and breakages. Once he was done with the right foot, the entire process was repeated with the left. Then, and only then, was Rakesh allowed to take off the rest of his clothes, since having a naked Rakesh with his cock at eye-level was, according to Virin, entirely too distracting.

"Now," Virin said as he wiped the salve off his hands. "On your knees."

Rakesh nodded and slipped off the bed, positioning himself on his knees and watching as Virin got up and walked over to the rack. He picked up a coil of cream-colored rope that Rakesh didn't remember seeing before.

"I got this special," Virin explained, shaking it out. "Brought it home from Aakar. This is made from fedelis tree fiber. Feels like silk."

"Isn't the fedelis tree poisonous?" Rakesh asked.

"The nectar is. The fibers were used to make clothing for the royal family, or so I'm told. And, I'm also told that fidelis rope is what they call for in those scrolls."

"You didn't have them translated?"

"I didn't want them to disappear."

Rakesh nodded and watched as Virin fussed with the rope a little more, until he nodded and made a satisfied noise. "Good. All right. Arms at your sides. Don't move."

Rakesh did his best to follow the directions, but he was fascinated by what Virin was doing, and kept breaking position to try and see. The rope was doubled, and a knot tied off to form a small loop at the doubling point. That first knot went behind Rakesh's neck, so that the loop hung down between his shoulder blades. A second knot was tied over his heart, a third a few inches lower, and a fourth—

"Hey!"

"Sorry," Virin said, not sounding sorry at all. "Didn't mean to hit you. Your cock is in the way."

"I think that's the first time I've ever heard *that* said about my cock."

Virin laughed, kissed Rakesh, and set the fourth knot to rest at the root of his cock, then tied another knot and snugged it right behind his balls, drawing the long tails of the rope between Rakesh's legs and up. Rakesh squirmed as the soft rope slithered up the crack of his ass.

"That tickles," he said, looking over his shoulder. "What are you doing now?"

"I'm only half done. Stay still."

Rakesh couldn't see, but he could feel as Virin tied more knots, then ran the tails through the dangling loop and pulled until everything snugged down tightly.

"Comfortable?"

"Yes. Now what?"

"Well, if I've done this right..." Virin reached around and ran the tails through the paired rope on Rakesh's chest, just over the first knot, pulling them tight and bringing them back behind. Then he brought them forward again, weaving them in between the knots, forming the rope diamonds that they had seen on the woman in the scroll. Each diamond pulled the ropes tighter, pulled that one knot more firmly into Rakesh's balls. Finally, Virin tied the rope ends off under the curve of Rakesh's ass. "Very nice," he murmured. "Very pretty. I think I've gotten it. Most of it."

"Most of it?" Rakesh asked. "And...may I touch?"

"Go ahead." Virin reached out and tapped the closet door; it faded into a reflective surface. "Admire yourself. This suits you, Kesh. I'll be right back." He walked out of the room, and Rakesh looked at himself in the mirror. The pale ropes nearly shone against his dark skin, and the effect was striking. Rakesh was suddenly reminded strongly of his days as a Tarken, the white collar and control bands that he'd taken off so many years ago. He hadn't thought of those days in a long time.

"Deep thoughts?" Virin asked as he came back in, carrying one of the straight-backed chairs from their dining room.

"Thinking that these remind me of my days in a white collar," Rakesh answered. "What are you doing?"

"Making sure I don't hurt you." Virin set the chair down and gestured to it. "Sit down."

Rakesh pulled himself up and went to sit down, stumbling and almost falling as the movement pulled the knot under his balls even tighter, the pressure abruptly painful. Virin caught him, and helped him to sit.

"She had the same pattern down her legs, didn't she?" Rakesh mused. "How do you do that?"

"That, I'm not sure," Virin admitted. "I'm not going to worry about it now, either." He picked up shorter lengths of the fedelis rope and bound Rakesh's ankles and knees together. Then he moved behind the chair and took Rakesh's arms, drawing them back behind the chair and binding his wrists. He moved off, and before Rakesh saw him in the mirror, doing something at the rack. When he came back, it was with a length of black silk between his hands.

"Lights out, love," Virin murmured, lowering the blindfold over Rakesh's eyes. The cloth tightened, cutting off Rakesh's sight, and he moaned softly.

"Very nice," Virin repeated, running his fingers up Rakesh's arm, down his chest. He tugged on one of the ropes, then twisted one of Rakesh's erect nipples. "Very nice indeed. Now that I have you so nicely wrapped, what do you suppose I should do with you?"

Rakesh didn't answer. It was part of the game. If Virin had really wanted him to speak, he'd have called him by name. Instead Rakesh tugged against the ropes, feeling the silky-smooth fedelis digging into his skin, the hard knot pressing up into his balls. The tightness of the bonds was intoxicating. It made him want to struggle more, and he shifted, pulling hard and slipping down on the chair, stretching his legs out and leaning back.

"Yes, that's nice. Wait... Wait, Kesh." Virin took Rakesh by the waist and lifted him, taking him out of the chair and back onto his knees. Rakesh heard the soft hissing of rope sliding against rope, then felt the slither of it over his skin as Virin laced his arms into the body harness, creating sleeves out of rope that completely immobilized Rakesh's upper body. Then Virin helped Rakesh lay down on his stomach; Rakesh's ankles were pulled up and bound off to his wrists, then more rope was wound around his legs, binding calves and thighs together. Rakesh heard Virin rise, then felt a nudge on his side. "Now fight it. I know you want to."

Rakesh tugged against the ropes, then pulled harder, finding no slack. Not that he expected any. Not from Virin. The only way he could move was from side to side, the motion driving his erection into the floor and scraping his nipples against the pile of the carpet. He tried harder, gasping as the knots seemed to grow tighter, his bonds more stringent, that one strategically placed knot even more stimulating. One particularly hard twist tipped him over, onto his side, and he lay there for a moment, trying to catch his breath. It was only then that he realized what a mistake he'd made—on his side, he couldn't move at all. He tried to roll back onto his front, and couldn't.

"Stuck?" Virin asked, his voice rich and heavy. Rakesh knew that voice, the darkness that heralded wonderful pain and pleasure both. He whimpered, and heard Virin laugh.

"I'm enjoying watching you struggle," Virin said. Footsteps, and a strong hand ran down Rakesh's thigh. "I wonder how easy it would be to make you scream, tied like this?" Rakesh moaned, arching his back, his body rocking back and forth slightly. He heard a soft rattle, then yelped as sharp pains shot through his chest, one nipple after the other. There was a sharp tug on the chain, then Virin ran his hand up Rakesh's chest and over his throat. "I'd gag you, but I'm enjoying listening to you. Next time."

His hand moved away, and Rakesh licked his lips before rocking his shoulders forward once more, trying to get back on his stomach. One strong twist, and he tipped, teetered, hovered for a heartbeat, then fell forward. As he landed, the clamps on his nipples drove into his chest, and the knot dug painfully into his balls; he screamed as he came, whipping his body from side to side as he thrashed in place, riding wave after wave of pleasure until he fell into their still, dark depths.

———◈———

VIRIN SMILED AS RAKESH fell still, his breathing slowing and his head resting on the floor. "That was impressive, Kesh. I wasn't expecting you to come just from being tied up." he said. "Is it my turn now?"

No answer. Virin frowned, kneeling down next to Rakesh and touching his shoulder. "Kesh?"

Again, no answer, and Virin grabbed his knife, cutting Rakesh's legs free and rolling Rakesh back onto his side, unfastening the clips on his nipples and letting them fall to the floor. To Virin's shock, there was no reaction to the opening of the clips—usually, Rakesh would howl in pain when they came off. This time, he didn't even move, and Virin cursed softly. He stripped the blindfold next, letting it fall to the floor as he lifted Rakesh up and moved him onto the bed. As he set Rakesh down, the bound man groaned and his eyelids fluttered. Then he blinked, looked around and frowned.

"Rin?" he said, sounding shaky. "Why are you untying me?"

"You scared me," Virin said. He sat down next to Rakesh, resting one hand on Rakesh's stomach. "You passed out, I think."

"I did?" Rakesh asked. He tried to move and gasped, his head falling back against the pillows. He shook his head, and it seemed to Virin that he was trying to keep the rest of his body as still as possible. "I—damn that knot!—I don't think so. I... I remember. I heard you. I just... It was more like a deep trance, I think."

"Was it?" Virin turned and looked at the scroll tube. "These are supposed to be meditation techniques. I am going to have to try and find someone to translate the text, find out what we really have here."

"Can we think about that later?" Rakesh asked. He squirmed, hissing softly. "Did... Did you tighten these?"

"No."

"They feel tighter. It feels so good. Please, Rin..." Rakesh dug his heels into the bed and rolled towards Virin. "Touch me, please?" He arched his back again, and Virin was surprised to see that his cock was starting to get hard once more.

"You're not usually this needy, love," Virin said slowly. "Or this quick to recover."

"I... I don't know. I don't *care*! Please?" Rakesh moaned, closing his eyes and drawing his knees up to his chest. "Rin...please, I want you...."

"Well, there isn't much I can do to you with that rope in the way." Virin rose and started taking off his clothes, tossing them haphazardly to the side before climbing onto the bed with Rakesh. He pushed Rakesh's legs out of the way and pulled his husband into his arms, claiming his mouth in a deep kiss. He ran one hand down Rakesh's side, enjoying the contrast between soft skin and softer rope. As he brought his hand back up, he reached between them and tugged hard on the knot that sat low on Rakesh's belly, drawing a near-scream from Rakesh. Intrigued, Virin did it again, pushing Rakesh onto his back and watching the reactions as he tugged and plucked at the ropes. Rakesh threw his head back, moaning and gasping, struggling against the bonds, pumping his hips frantically. His cock was hard again, the tip already glistening, and Virin smiled slightly as he leaned down and licked the bead of moisture away. Rakesh howled in a voice that Virin had never heard before, and he only just barely missed getting hit in the face as Rakesh came for the second time, splattering his own chest and the bed with the force of his climax.

"That.... All right." Virin leaned forward, looking at Rakesh. Once again, his husband looked as if he'd passed out, his face slack, his eyes closed. But there was movement under his lids—Rakesh was dreaming. This time, Virin sat back and watched, waiting.

After ten minutes, he went to the corner and turned on the sat-comm, carrying the receiver over the bed so that he was within arm's reach of Rakesh. He made two calls, and neither conversation did anything to make him feel better.

Twenty minutes after Virin returned the sat-comm to its place on the corner table, Rakesh groaned and opened his eyes. He blinked, then looked around. "Rin?" he said slowly. "What happened?"

"You tell me. Where were you, love?"

"I'm...not sure. I... I dreamed. I think," Rakesh shook his head and tried to move. "Rin, can I be untied now? This is starting to be uncomfortable."

"I should think so, considering you've been tied up like this for nearly an hour and you came three times."

"Three?" Rakesh gasped. "I... How is that possible? I've never... In under an *hour*?"

"Within the space of about half an hour, actually. And I think it was three. That last one, if it was an orgasm, was dry. The first was before I moved you to the bed. The second was after I got into bed with you, and the third was while you were in trance."

Rakesh licked his lips and blinked. "That explains why I'm sore. I need something to drink."

"Of course." Virin raised his knife and slowly started to cut Rakesh's ankles free, noticing the red marks under the ropes that looked far too livid for simple rope-burn. Rakesh hissed as Virin pulled the ropes away, closing his eyes as if he were in pain.

"Kesh?"

"It feels like you're pulling off skin," Rakesh said. Then he yelped as Virin picked him up. "What are you doing?"

"Taking you into the bath. I think we might have to soak this off." Virin headed into the bathroom, setting Rakesh down in the bathtub and starting the water. "There's a reason they used this kind of rope in these rituals. There is some kind of hallucinogen in the fibers. And I think you might be especially sensitive to it, whatever it is." He turned around to see Rakesh staring at him.

"You knew there was a hallucinogen in the rope and you used it anyway?"

"No!" Virin snapped. "You know I would never put you in danger like that, Kesh! No, I didn't know about it until I sat-commed your father—"

"You *what*?" Rakesh sat up straight, the water sloshing around his legs as he visibly struggled to keep his balance with his arms still bound.

"He's the only person we could think of who might know what was happening to you!" Virin said, hearing the fear in his own voice. Rakesh must have heard it, too, because he fell silent. "Kesh, I had no idea what I'd done to you. I'm not ashamed to say that I panicked. I sat-commed Mother first. She didn't know, and she suggested I talk to Raizi. He... Kesh, I'm pretty sure he's on his way here."

Rakesh groaned, tipping his head back against the side of the tub. Then he gasped and cursed. "Damn that knot!"

"That probably didn't help," Virin admitted. "The skin there is kind of thin. Let me see if I can get them off now." He picked up his knife and slipped into the bath, kneeling over Rakesh's legs. "If this hurts, I am sorry. I didn't know—"

"Apologize later, Rin."

"Yes, love." Virin slowly slipped the knife underneath one of the submerged ropes and cut it, watching as the cut ends floated away from Rakesh's skin. "That's good. Soaking breaks the hold. Good. I'll have you loose in a minute." He focused on cutting the ropes, freeing Rakesh from the web, releasing his arms and legs and unwinding the cords from around his torso.

"Next time, I'll get plain rope," he muttered.

"Good," Rakesh answered, his voice low and tired. "I do want to do this again, Rin."

"Am I losing you?" Virin asked, looking up. Rakesh blinked and looked at him, his eyes half-lidded. He smiled sleepily.

"I think so," he answered. "I'm exhausted, Rin."

"That isn't surprising. Stay with me, though. Tell me about what you saw." Virin slowly tugged the ropes from between Rakesh's legs; Rakesh gasped and flinched away as the cords caught on his balls.

"Sorry," he said with a laugh. He tipped his head back and closed his eyes. "Too sensitive."

"You probably feel like I went at you with sandpaper. I'm the one who should be sorry, Kesh. And I am. I should have waited for a translation." Virin tossed wet ropes out off the tub and picked up Rakesh's arm, looking at the marks on his wrist. "I wasn't planning on hurting you tonight."

"I know," Rakesh answered without opening his eyes.

"Going to tell me what you dreamed?"

Rakesh shook his head. "Not yet. Let me sleep."

Virin smiled. "Let's get you into bed, first." He dropped the last of the rope fragments on the floor and got out of the bathtub, helping Rakesh out and steadying him while they both dried off. Rakesh leaned heavily on him as they moved to the bed, and he was asleep before Virin pulled the blankets up to cover him. Virin looked down at him for a long moment, then leaned down and kissed his cheek.

"I'm sorry, love," he said softly.

Chapter Three

Rakesh woke up to the sound of voices coming through the closed bedroom door. He knew both of them. Virin had been right, he thought as he sat up and groped around the side of the bed for his robe and his canes. The robe was there, but his canes weren't. Then he remembered—he'd dropped them in the front room. He waved the bedside light on and examined his wrists and arms before pulling on the robe. The marks were still red, a little swollen, and still a little tender. Almost like burns.... And he shied away from a strong memory of burning irons and the smell of his own burned flesh. Trying hard not to think about it, he stood up, steadied himself, and hobbled to the door.

The two men sitting at the table in the front room looked up as he came out. Rakesh smiled.

"*Aba*. It's good to see you," he said to his father.

Raizi got out of his chair and came towards him, hugging Rakesh hard, then offering him an arm. "And you, my son. Where are your sticks?"

"Out here. I can make it to the table on my own, *Aba*."

Raizi didn't move. Didn't say anything. And Rakesh knew that he'd already lost the argument. He sighed and took his father's arm. "Yes, *Aba*."

Once Rakesh was seated at the table with a mug of tea, he looked at his father. "You didn't need to come, *Aba*. This is a busy time of year for you on the farm."

Raizi snorted. "Listen to this one, will you?" he said to Virin. "I don't need to come. Of course I need to come. My son needs me." He reached out and took Rakesh's hand, pushing back his sleeve to reveal the marks on his arm. He clicked his tongue and shook his head.

"You don't have the right training to dance in the Dark Spider's webs, Kesh-*na*. You were lucky. Very lucky that She did not drain you dry. The strength of your blood, I imagine. Later, you will tell me where you found spidersilk rope. I did not know there was anyone who still knew how to make it. So, did you dream true?"

"How did you know he dreamed?" Virin asked. "I didn't tell you. I don't even know what he dreamed yet."

Raizi looked at Virin, then at Rakesh. Then he sighed. "Have I told you, or has my Kesh-*na* told you, of his birth?"

Virin blinked and looked at Rakesh, who shook his head. "No, *Aba*. I'm not even sure what you mean. What about it?"

Raizi's hand on Rakesh's tightened, and he hesitated a moment before he spoke, "Six daughters, my Akesha gave to me. Six daughters alive, and three sons lost to the Dark Gods before they had a chance to draw breath. It was, I thought, my punishment. A fitting punishment for the sins of my father, that I should have no sons. But still, I hoped. And I prayed, even in this wild country, where your only religion is war and your gods are the gods of caste. And on the Midwinter night of the dark moons, when the Dark Ones are strongest, I went into the fields and I prayed once more. I opened a vein, for the first time since I left my home, and I let my blood flow." He paused, absently touching a scar on his arm that had been there for as long as Rakesh could remember. Raizi let his hand fall, and continued. "As my blood flowed, I felt her, and I prayed. Please, I begged the Spider, please to give me a son of my own." He smiled at Rakesh. "Ten months later, she gave me you. Alone of all my children, you are like me."

"*Aba*, I didn't know!" Rakesh gasped. "I... I always thought I was...well...."

"You thought you were perhaps a mistake? Late born, so long after your sisters?" Raizi asked. "No, Kesh-*na*. You were very much wanted. And...you are very much like I was, when I was young." He stopped, looked down at the table. "Virin tells me that you are to go to Felanore."

"Yes. Marga wants me to become Chief Trainer of the new Arena there."

"I wish that you would not go," Raizi said softly. "I think it would be very bad if you went. Very bad. There are some..." He stopped and shook his head. "There are things I have not told you. Things I have not told anyone living. I swore not to speak of it. But believe me when I say you should stay out of Felanore, my son."

Rakesh looked at Virin, at the stunned expression on his husband's face. Then he looked back at his father. "*Aba...* I think I have to go. You asked me what I dreamed. If I dreamed true. I... I think I did."

Raizi sat up straight, his eyes wide. "Tell me!"

Rakesh nodded, looking down at his mug and the dregs of the tea. "I... I was wearing the Gold. I was in a room, a place I'd never been. It looked... I don't know. It had been a nice place once, I think. A very fine place. But it was a ruin. It was dark, and cold, and it was full of cobwebs. I was alone. And there were two doors in front of me. Behind each of them was something important. And I had to choose one. I could only choose one. The other one would be lost to me if I didn't take it. And...I woke up before I opened either door." He frowned, then looked up at Virin. "I think you were behind one of those doors, Rin."

Virin stared at him, his eyes wide. Then he looked at Raizi. "Cobwebs. He said there were cobwebs. You're talking about webs, too. And a Dark Spider. I've read all of my father's books about Aakari religions. I'm not the scholar he was, but I do have a good memory. There's no mention in any of the books of a Spider, and or about these...web meditation things. All I know is apparently just enough to get us in trouble. Raizi, what are you talking about?"

"That I cannot say," Raizi answered. "Believe me, Virin, son of my heart. If I could tell you, I would. I swore an oath, over my own mother's body, that I would not reveal the secrets of the Spider."

"But...*Aba,* isn't this something that we're going to need to know?" Rakesh asked. "Something I need to know? You said... You said that I don't have the training. You thought that this would have hurt me, or else you wouldn't be here. Where do I get this kind of training? And how? The scrolls—"

"Scrolls?" Raizi interrupted. He ignored Rakesh's question, staring at Virin, and the look on his face was enough to make Rakesh shiver in fear. "You have *scrolls* that showed you this?"

"I thought I told you on the sat-comm," Virin answered. "Yes. That's where this all started. I found the scrolls in the Ishkarin garrison in Felanore. I'll get them."

"*Aba?*" Rakesh asked when Virin left the table. "What's wrong?"

"These things... These scrolls... This..." Raizi shook his head. "I thought them all gone and burned. I thought that when the Mad One rose, that all of the knowledge of the Spider was lost. I thought...that perhaps I was the last, and me sworn never to reveal—" he stopped as Virin returned, carrying an armload of scroll-tubes. He laid them down on the table and sat back down, reaching across and taking Rakesh's hand.

"Raizi, what is it that we've found?" he asked, his voice low. "Do I need to report this to Molari? Is it dangerous?"

Raizi picked up one of the scroll-tubes, took out the scroll and unrolled it. He studied it for a moment, then rolled it back up, set it down, and covered his face with his hands.

"Virin, my son," he said, his voice muffled. "Do you by chance have anything to drink in this house stronger than tea?"

"*Aba!*" Rakesh gasped.

"Hush, Kesh-*na,*" Raizi chided. "Once, this once, She will forgive me. This... This is a shock to an old man."

"Why do I get the feeling that the she you mean isn't *Ama* Akesha?" Virin asked. He got up and walked into the tiny kitchen, came back a moment later with a bottle and three small cups. He filled all three cups and pushed one towards Raizi. "I know you don't drink, Raizi. So I know why Rakesh is looking at you like that. But I think I understand. You look as though you've seen the dead."

"I think, perhaps, I have," Raizi answered. He picked up the cup, sipped the amber-colored liquid, then swallowed the contents of the cup and set it down. "I think...that perhaps the Spider moves once more, trying to move out into the world. I promise you both, with my own eyes I saw the last of these scrolls burned. I was but a boy, already sworn to follow my mother into the webs, when the Mad One declared himself a god and overthrew all other gods. He imprisoned us in the Spider's temple, my mother and me. We were starved, beaten, to convince us to turn away from the webs. I was there when at last he came to the temple, when he ordered my mother to worship him alone as her Lord and God. I was there when she refused, when she cursed him and he cut her down, and when he threw the scrolls into the sacred fires."

"There were no others?" Rakesh asked. "No other priests? No one to help her?"

"No," Raizi answered. He reached out and rested his hand on the scrolls. "The worship of the Spider was different. It was a sacred line, traced through the blood, and there was only ever the Priestess. Or the Priest. Only one who stood between the Spider and the waking world. Of all my family, all my sisters, I was the only one who the Spider claimed, who would follow my mother into the webs. In my time, I would become Priest, when the Dark Spider took my mother and drained her. And one of my children would follow me." He looked at Rakesh. "It appears that one is you, my Kesh-*na*. You asked where would you get the training? It is all here, in these scrolls. Everything I know, and more. I never completed the mysteries. I was too young to dance in the webs when my mother died. Now...you will take the place that once was to have been mine. And now you are called to go to Aakar. I cannot help but wonder if this is somehow a part of the web, to draw Her bloodline back to Aakar. I cannot think why, though. You have no children, nor are you likely to have children—"

Virin scowled. "This... This is ridiculous, Raizi! Spider gods and sacred bloodlines? These religions were all destroyed—"

"And you are such an expert in religions? You, who swear by the name of the geneticist who made your kind?" Raizi snapped. "Temples may be destroyed, Virin, but so long as there is belief, there are the gods. I am old, but I am not the only one who remembers the days before the Mad One."

"Why don't you ever call him by name?" Rakesh asked softly. Raizi turned, and Rakesh hurried to finish, before his father could stop him. "You always call him the Mad One. You never call him Tragar. Why?"

Raizi shook his head. "It is...complicated. To deny him the afterlife. If no one speaks your name, then you become..." he frowned, staring at the table, drumming his fingers. "Not a person? The word...does not translate. You cannot go on, you cannot be reborn, if no one will speak your name to remember you."

He fell silent. Unable to think, shocked to the core by the idea of being claimed by a goddess he'd never even heard of, Rakesh looked to Virin for help. His husband was staring at the table, frowning furiously, his face like a storm. Then Virin looked up.

"Why didn't he kill you?" he asked quietly. "You were there. He knew you were there. He had to, if he knew the religion. So why did he let you live?"

Raizi shook his head and smiled. "Too much of Gavir in you, Virin. Too much. He would have asked the same question."

"So will you answer?" Virin leaned forward. "Or maybe I should answer for you?"

Raizi looked amused, and for some reason, oddly relieved. He leaned back in his chair and spread his hands. "Tell me what you think."

Virin nodded and started counting on his fingers. "No record of a Dark Spider in the religion books. So this isn't a religion practiced by the common people, the ones who would actually have their religious works recorded and shared. The book that my parents bonded over, one of them was yours. No mention of the Spider in there, either. I know. I just re-read it. So, this is a secret religion. A religion of the upper echelon, since you mentioned a sacred bloodline. Who has sacred bloodlines? Rich, powerful, important people. Nobility." He paused, looked at Raizi. "How am I so far?"

"So far, you do well," Raizi admitted.

"All right. So, we have a religion of the nobility. Again, no mention of it in the records. No Spider temples in Felanore city, not even ruined or repurposed ones. Tarason might have been an idiot, but he was a very thorough idiot. He took a complete inventory of all buildings, both intact and in ruins, when he took command of the garrison. There was no ruined temple that didn't fall into the harvest god or fertility goddess mold."

Raizi snorted, made a twisting gesture with one hand. "The other way around, Virin. Harvest goddess, fertility god. But yes, go on."

"Fine. Switch the genders. So, the only place that he didn't inventory was the Imperial Palace. The ruins there are off-limits. So, where's the most likely place for a temple we can't find?"

"In the place we can't go into," Rakesh answered. "A royal religion?"

Virin was nodding. "Royal religion. How do you keep it secret? You keep it in the royal family. There... There are loads of religions like that, over the seas, according to the books. The head of state is also the head of the religion. The story is that they're descended from the gods, usually. They marry within the bloodline, to keep it pure. Which the history books say they also did in Aakar. Add to that the fact that there was a prince of the blood who vanished without a trace before the Palace fell, and..." Virin stopped, his eyes wide. Rakesh felt his heart hammering in his chest.

"*Aba*? You aren't... You can't be—"

"Finish, son of my heart," Raizi said softly. "Say the words."

"Creator..." Virin breathed slowly. "You? You're the missing prince?"

Raizi sighed, and it was the sound of a lifetime of secrets falling away all at once. "You have spoken the truth. I can therefore now speak of it. You ask if this is something dangerous, something to report to the Ran-ti-ar. I would say you must judge that for yourself. The truth of it is that when I was no more than a boy, I swore on the blood and body of my mother, the Spider Priestess, the Queen Saranja, that I was none of his. No longer the son of the King. I swore myself to the Spider, and gave an oath to keep Her secrets until She gave me a sign that it was time to reveal myself. The Mad One, he had me taken up, locked away inside the Palace, in order to provide my sisters with heirs. He was afraid that if I remained free that I would, in time, rally the people against him and raise up a rebellion. He thought to control that. To control me. He failed."

"You escaped. How?" Virin asked.

"There was a young guardsman, assigned to my prison." Raizi smiled slightly. "I bear his name, now. Raizi is not the name my mother gave to me. He felt pity on the young prisoner. I am not certain which of us seduced the other. But it was so. I cared for him, deeply. And he for me, though he risked his life to do so. Because he loved me, he saved my life, managed to get me out of my prison and out of the Palace in the madness that preceded the fall of the Empire. Outside of Felanore, we parted ways. They were hunting us, you see, and they did not think we would separate. They thought I would not know how to survive, alone outside the Palace for the first time as an adult. But I had learned much during my confinement, and Raizi taught me more. He went south under another name, to the crossing at the Trade City. I went north, through the Gap. If all had gone well, we would have reunited in safety." Raizi looked down and shook his head. "I never saw him again."

"He came through the Trade City crossing?" Rakesh asked. "We can find—"

"He never told me the name he would be using. He told me to use his name, told me that he would find me on the other side." Raizi smiled sadly. "And truly, after fifty years, I cannot believe that he would know this old man I have become. I prefer to think that he, as I, found someone that he was content to make a life with. I prefer to think of him happy, because the alternative is that he was discovered, and he died to protect me."

Virin nodded. "All right. I do have to report this. And Molari will probably want to talk to you."

"I will speak to him. I suppose that means you wish me to stay in the city?"

"You can stay here, *Aba*," Rakesh said. "And, I have questions. About this Spider Goddess. I don't know that I want to be a priest, *Aba*."

Raizi laughed out loud. "My son, my dear son. Do you not realize that you are one already?" He reached out and touched Rakesh's black-and-gold collar. "All who wear this are the priests of this country. And what we are called to do in the Arena, it is not so different from dancing in the webs. It is something that surprised me greatly, when I wore the white. I wondered then, if Mathias knew of the Spider, or if she snared him in her webs to give him the dreams that created the Swords. Think on that. For the rest, I will translate the scrolls. And..." He paused, looked thoughtful. "I wonder...."

"What?" Virin asked.

"Will you perhaps need a translator in your new garrison?" Raizi smiled, no doubt at the stunned look on Virin's face, and the matching one that Rakesh was fairly certain he wore. "I would like to see Felanore again. And to spit on the grave of the Mad One."

"I... I think they burned his body," Virin stammered.

"Then I will spit into the wind," Raizi answered. "I will laugh at the knowledge that his shade will never see peace, and that I live free, with a wife and children of my own, and all that he sought to deny me. And I will seek the Spider, and present to Her my son, who will follow me."

"I don't think that would be a good idea," Virin said. He leaned back in his chair, looking distant and thoughtful. "You said you're not the only one who remembers the old days. How many of them, do you think, would remember you?"

Raizi frowned. "I doubt there would be many. If any. When I was imprisoned, I was a boy of twelve. I was imprisoned for seven years, and the only ones who knew I lived were my sisters and the guards. All of them are dead. No one lives now in Aakar who has seen me as a man."

"What about family resemblances?" Virin persisted. "Do you look like your mother? Like Tragar? What about Rakesh? Does *he*?"

Raizi caught his breath. He turned and looked at Rakesh, until Rakesh felt his face grow warm. He fidgeted in his chair, looking at Virin, then at the framed portrait on the wall, of himself and Virin at their wedding. It was somehow easier to look at the portrait, to see himself happy. It made it easier to deny that, yet again, his entire world had been turned upside-down.

Raizi cursed softly, and Rakesh turned back as his father said, "Yes. Yes, he does."

"Who?" Rakesh barely recognized his own voice speaking the strangled words. "Who do I look like?"

"In profile, you are..." Raizi's voice faltered. Virin rose from the table without a word and went over to the bookcase. He studied the bound books for a moment, then picked one up and flipped through it before carrying it back to the table and setting it down.

Rakesh turned the book so that he could see it, then picked it up and looked at the cover. "Rin, why do we have a book on coins?" he asked.

"My father, the Sword-scholar," Virin answered as he sat back down, pulling his chair closer to Rakesh. "If it had pages and words, he'd read it." He took the book from Rakesh and set it back on the table, tapping on of the images. "Look at this one."

"What is it?" Raizi asked. He rose and came around to stand behind Rakesh, his hand firm and strong on Rakesh's shoulder. "Oh...."

"How accurate was this?" Virin asked, looking up at Raizi. "These coins, the book says that they were struck to commemorate his becoming a god. Did they enhance the image? I don't know...straighten his nose? Give him a better looking chin?"

"No, Virin," Raizi answered. "And I wonder that I have never seen the resemblance before. Perhaps...because I have not looked at that angle. And now Kesh-*na* is of the right age—"

"So I do look like him," Rakesh interrupted, reaching out to touch the picture of the coin. "What does that mean?"

"It means that you need to get dressed, love," Virin answered. "We need to go to the Ran-ti-ar."

"That wasn't what I meant," Rakesh said. He looked up at Virin, feeling himself starting to shake. "Crazy Collared, you used to call me. Am I? Or...will I? Go mad, the way that he did?" He reached out and closed the book, resting his hand on the cover. "I... I couldn't live like that, Rin. I've lost so much already—"

"You will not, Kesh-na." Raizi crouched next to Rakesh's chair. "His madness did not come from his blood. He attempted to take control of the webs, to subvert the power of Queen Saranja in her role as Priestess. That is what drove him mad—he was not the chosen of the Spider, and could not control the power. That was when he became convinced that he was a god. When the Dark Spider cast him off. There is no other madness in our blood."

"None?"

"None," Raizi said. He squeezed Rakesh's arm. "And you have shown already that you can dance the webs, and that the Spider accepts you. You are here. You are hale, save only that you bear the marks of her first kiss. That will not happen again. And you have not lost your mind."

"Except that I'm still thinking of going to Felanore," Rakesh added, forcing a laugh.

"That remains to be seen," Virin said, his voice grim. He got up and held his hand out to Rakesh. "Let's go get dressed."

———— ◉ ————

RAKESH SAT ALONE IN the sitting room of the Ran-ti-ar's palatial quarters in the main Garrison. Once Molari had heard Virin's initial report, he had called the Senior Councilor. Then he'd hurried Virin and Raizi both off into the secure meeting room that adjoined the sitting room. There was a young-looking ir-Zaan stationed at that door, and Molari's pretty attache had been assigned to see to Rakesh's comfort. Not that there was anything that Rakesh wanted. Except perhaps for Virin, and a very deep hole for them both to hide in until this all had passed.

"Sir?"

Rakesh looked up, and for a moment could not remember the Sword's name. He frowned, thinking hard. He'd never forgotten a Sword's name before.... "Listrel? That's your name, isn't it?" he asked.

The attache smiled. "Yes, sir. You haven't eaten or drunk anything since you've gotten here. And the Kian-ti-ar said you were to eat. He said you'd been hurt, too. Should I call a medic?"

Rakesh smiled, trying to hide the fact that her hovering was starting to grate on his nerves. "No, I don't need a medic. It's minor. And...if I ask for tea, will you stop asking me what I need for ten minutes?"

She pursed her lips, looking as if she were considering it. "For tea, that will be five minutes. If you want ten, you'll have something to eat, too."

Rakesh snorted. "You treat the Ran-ti-ar like this?"

"No, sir. He knows better."

"All right. Tea. And...if you have something sweet?"

"Three-berry tart?"

"That would be nice. Thank you, Listrel."

She smiled and walked away, out of the room. Once she was gone, Rakesh tipped his head back and closed his eyes. The welts on his skin where the ropes had made contact were alternately aching and itching, and if he'd asked for a pain-killer, Listrel would have called for the medics despite his protests. Better to wait. Virin would help him when they got home. Whenever that was.

He heard the door-chime sound, and then soft voices. Listrel, and another woman. He recognized the cadences in the newcomer's voice and sat up, turning to face the door as Iras walked in. Even though she was approaching seventy, she was still as beautiful as she had been when the portrait that hung in the Arena had been taken, back when she had been Taramar. She smiled when she saw Rakesh, coming over to the couch and sitting down with him.

"Virin called me," she said. "He thought you might need looking after, and he wasn't sure how long this meeting would take. Rakesh, what happened?"

"Mother, I'm not entirely sure I understand. Or that I want to," Rakesh said.

"And you're hurt? Virin was more than a little terse when I spoke to him, so I don't know much. I thought you just got out of regen."

In answer, Rakesh held out his wrist, pushing his sleeve back so that Iras could see the welts. Her eyes widened, and she took his hand in both of hers and peered closely at the damaged skin.

"This looks like a chemical burn," she said slowly. "Rakesh, have you had this looked at?"

"Not yet. There's been no time since I woke up. And it's been...well, insane." Rakesh dragged his other hand through his hair. "What do you know?"

"That you were hurt, that this involves Raizi in some way, that they're in with Molari now, and that my son seems to think you need looking after. That's all." She didn't let go of his hand. "Rakesh, what caused this?"

"Rope."

"Rope?" Iras's voice spiraled up in shock.

"Rope made from fidelis fibers. *Aba* called it spidersilk. And it's something to do with who he was in Aakar." Rakesh frowned, forcing his thoughts into order, and told Iras what he knew. While he was talking, Listrel came in with tea and bowls of berry tart; Iras made him stop long enough to eat.

"So, in the course of a few hours, I've gone from being Rakesh a'Raizi Tarkarin to being son of the Spider Priest and some flavor of heir to the Imperial throne of Aakar," Rakesh finished, and looked down at his empty bowl and cup. He leaned over and set them both on the table, amazed that his hands didn't shake.

"You're still Rakesh a'Raizi Tarkarin," Iras offered, her voice soothing. "You're still the same man you were when you woke up this morning. All of these outside forces can't change that."

"That's a pretty big outside force, Mother," Rakesh protested. "A goddess I've never heard of seems to think I'm her priest. That's what these mean, if my father is right. And now I'm having...prophetic dreams? Visions? I don't know what to call them."

"You never did before?" Iras asked.

"No!"

"Because I've heard some of the Collared say that in deep trance, they have visions," Iras explained. "I never did, so I never really believed it. You should read some of the records on trance-work in the Arena. They might help."

"I didn't realize there were records on trance-work," Rakesh said. He reached up and rubbed his forehead. "I can't remember ever seeing any in the library."

"Talk to Marga. I think they might be with the medical records." Iras rubbed his hand, then touched his wrist, being careful not to touch the welt. "How extensive are these?"

"Ah...the pattern runs from neck to hip, and then around my knees and ankles," Rakesh answered. For a moment, he felt as if he were back in training, and wondered if he were blushing.

"That must be interesting to look at," was all that Iras said. Then she looked up. The door to the meeting room opened, and Virin came out into the sitting room. He smiled when he saw them.

"I was hoping you'd be able to get here, Mother," he said, coming over and kissing her cheek.

"And a good thing, too," she answered, her voice tart. "When were you planning on taking Rakesh to the medics for these burns?"

"I didn't think they were that serious!" Virin answered. He sat down on Rakesh's other side, taking his other hand. "These.... Kesh, are these getting worse?"

"I don't think so. They itch. And hurt, a bit."

Virin arched an eyebrow. "How much is a bit?"

"If I stood up to walk, I wouldn't feel the marks any more."

"Ah. Low-grade hurt, then. They look more red than they were before." He kept his hand in Rakesh's, lacing their fingers together. "Molari wants some of the rope for analysis. I told him he's welcome to it. And Raizi will be here for a while longer, answering questions."

"And then?" Rakesh asked. "Are you still going to Felanore?"

"That depends."

Rakesh looked at Virin, who was smiling at him. "Depends on?"

"On if you're coming with me."

"Virin, is that wise?" Iras asked.

"Rakesh is going to be inside the new Arena. As he pointed out to me, he'll have the weight of the entire garrison between him and the rest of the world." Virin shifted, putting his arm around Rakesh. "The trainees we can find in Felanore, if we find any, will be too young to remember Tragar. And the older folks will probably think their eyes are playing tricks on them."

"Unless they know that *Aba* escaped from the Palace."

Virin nodded. "There is that. But Molari made a good point. We're going to be hiding you in plain sight, Kesh. Who would expect to find the heir to the Spider priest, and a potential heir to the mad Emperor, in a collar? If anyone even suggests it, no one would listen to them!"

"That ruse worked for me for five years," Iras said, her voice thoughtful. "But when it failed, it failed rather spectacularly. Do you have a back-up plan?"

"Not yet," Virin admitted. "I will, by the time we get to Felanore."

"And what about *Aba*?" Rakesh asked. "Is he coming with us?"

"That Molari won't allow. Nor does he want the scrolls leaving Tyese. So your father is making copies of them, translations that you can read and learn from. And we're to see if we can find this Spider Temple. I have a map that Raizi drew for me."

"Didn't we think it was in the Palace?" Rakesh asked. "And didn't you say that was off-limits?"

"Yes and yes. And yes, we're going to find a way in." Virin grinned. "It'll be an adventure."

Iras snorted. "Adventure. You sound like you're five years old again, tagging along with your father on patrol. Listrel, my dear, can you call ahead to the medical center and tell them we're coming in with a patient with unusual chemical burns?"

Chapter Four

The next several weeks were long and hectic, filled with administrative duties for both Rakesh and Virin. Rakesh spent long hours at the Arena, hand-picking two dozen of the fifth-year Tarken to serve in the new Arena, and a dozen of the more advanced Taramar to act as trainers. Then there was requisitioning equipment and supplies to be delivered to the embassy, and arranging for immersion hypnotic language training for everyone. He wanted to be sure that all of his trainers were fluent in Aakari, so there would be no misunderstandings. All of this had to be fit in and around his regular duties to the new novices—seeing that they were all settled and comfortable in their new homes, the introductory lessons in Discipline, and the inevitable crises as the new novices started to understand the path that they had chosen.

Sitting in his office, he stared down at the long list of requirements, and wondered again why anyone had thought this a good idea. A soft knock at the door made him jump, and he looked up to see Lela standing in the doorway. She looked upset, and Rakesh was surprised—out of all the novices, she'd seemed to be the one settling in to her new life with unbridled enthusiasm.

"Lela!" he smiled and waved her inside. "Come in, dear. You look troubled. How are you acclimating?"

"I'm doing well, thank you," she said, coming into the room and sitting down in the chair Rakesh offered her. "I like it here. But...I am a little upset. I have heard you are going to Felanore?"

"Yes, I am. I leave in five days, if I can ever manage to get all this paperwork done." Rakesh grimaced at the pile of hard-copy forms on his desk. "Bureaucracy at its finest," he joked.

Lela didn't smile. She wrung her hands and blurted out, "Do not go! Please! Don't leave us!"

Rakesh blinked, startled. "Lela!"

"You don't understand!" she insisted. "You have never been there, you can't understand."

"So tell me," Rakesh said gently. He moved his chair so that he was facing Lela, close enough that their knees touched. "You're afraid. I can see that. Afraid for me?"

She nodded, not looking up. "You don't understand," she repeated. "The people... My people... They will not see you for who you are. In Aakar, we know of the collars, of the Arena. They call it proof of the Tyesean depravity there. They think that those who wear the collar are worse than the dirt under their feet. They will not see you as an honored counselor and a great man. They will call you whore. And they will call you criminal. They will hurt you if they catch you, kill you if they can. You cannot go there! We need you here!"

Rakesh let his head hang and sighed, then reached across to take Lela's hands in his. "Thank you, Lela. For your concern. I know what I'm facing when I get to Felanore. Virin made certain I knew. But the new Arena will be inside the Embassy, and attached to the garrison. Do you understand how that works?"

"Inside the embassy walls, it is Tyese, even though the embassy is inside Aakar," Lela answered. "Although I do not understand how this is. How can it be Tyese, when it is an Aakari place, on Aakari ground?"

Rakesh grinned. "I know. Makes no sense to me either. But the provisional government of Aakar has agreed that the Tyesean embassy exists under our laws, not the laws of Aakar."

"And if you leave those walls?" Lela asked. "Then what?"

"Then he is considered an ambassador from Tyese, and if anything happens to him, the Tyesean government takes it out of Aakar's hide," Virin answered from the doorway. "Assuming I leave anything of the person who dared for them to take to trial. Hello, Lela. How are you liking it here?"

Lela turned and smiled, and Rakesh was pleased to see that she hadn't jumped at the sound of Virin's voice, nor did she seem afraid of him. Given what he now knew of her history, he'd wondered how she would ever be able to serve in a collar. But she had confided in him, was seeing the counselors, and she seemed determined to become a Tarken. "I am liking it very much!" she answered. "I would like it more if they did not take our *Aba* Rakesh away." Her eyes widened, and she blushed. "I... I did not mean..."

Virin burst out laughing. "*Aba* Rakesh? Kesh, did you know they called you that?"

"I didn't," Rakesh admitted. He squeezed Lela's hands. "Lela, sweetheart, thank you. I'm honored that you think of me like that. I think of all of you as my children, you know. So it's only appropriate."

Lela looked at him, a shy smile on her face. "You don't mind?"

"No, Lela. I'm flattered." And more than a little surprised, when Lela flung her arms around his neck and hugged him tightly.

"We will miss you!" she said in his ear. "You must come home to us!"

Rakesh hugged her, then let her go and nodded. "I'll be back, Lela."

"You promise?" she insisted. Rakesh smiled.

"I promise."

Lela nodded and rose, then turned and faced Virin, pointing at him. "You will take care of him!" she ordered. Then she turned red and fled the office. Virin watched her go, then looked out the door.

"Fierce one, that girl. Reminds me of Mother," Virin said as he came into the office and took the chair that Lela had abandoned.

"She'll go far," Rakesh agreed. "Maybe we should introduce her to Iras."

"What's her history? She's terrified of you going to Felanore. The place scares the actual fuck out of her."

Rakesh looked back at his paperwork, then sighed and leaned back in his chair. "Born on the streets, running with gangs since she was old enough to remember. Raped at the age of twelve—"

"What?" Virin gasped, sitting up straight. "And she's *here*?"

"The counselors are monitoring her carefully. Her and the half a dozen other girls like her. And the five young men. Apparently, the street gangs are considered...." Rakesh stopped, suddenly realizing the meaning behind what the trainees had told him.

"Considered what?" Virin asked.

"Prey," Rakesh said quietly. "Lela says that she was told she was prey."

Virin's eyes widened, and his face went cold. "You don't think...?"

Rakesh nodded slowly. "Control!"

Acknowledged.

"Novice Lela. Send her back to my office, please."

Confirmed.

"You didn't need to send for me," Lela said quietly. "I did not go far. I... I was listening. You learn, on the streets, to listen. It might save your life."

Virin turned in his chair, resting his hands on the back. Keeping them in sight, Rakesh realized. "And...was it a Sword, Lela? If it was, you can identify him, and I'll see him punished."

"You would punish them all?" Lela whispered. "They all hunt. It has been so since the Black Swords first came to Aakar. My mother told me that my father was one such."

Virin went still, closing his eyes, and Rakesh knew that he was fighting hard to keep control of his temper. He rose and put his hand on Virin's shoulder, then met Lela's eyes and nodded. "Lela, the other girls, anyone else who was hurt like this. Anyone else who might be the child of rape. Gather them up and go to the big meeting room. The one where we first met. I'll... I'll meet you there."

Lela nodded and fled, and Rakesh waited until she was gone before he squeezed Virin's shoulder. "Rin?"

"We were supposed to be there to protect them," Virin growled. "We were supposed to protect them all. That was our purpose. That was why we were created." He turned and looked up at Rakesh. "We're not supposed to hunt our own."

"You know there are those that don't follow those rules," Rakesh said softly.

"But these are Swords," Virin snarled back. "Not the rogues, not the ones who were trying to turn the Creator's purpose to their own ends. These are Ishkarin, sworn to protect." He looked down and rubbed his forehead with his hand. "I need to call Molari."

"You can use my sat-comm."

"I need a secure scramble. The fewer people who know about this, the better."

Rakesh nodded and reached for his canes. "You can do that here. And I'll leave you to it. Control!"

Acknowledged.

"Hush field on the door until the Kian-ti-os is done here."

Confirmed. The air in the open doorway started to shimmer.

"Take as much time as you need, Rin," Rakesh said. He leaned down and kissed Virin's cheek. "I'm going to go and tell Marga."

———————⊙———————

AN HOUR LATER, RAKESH was sitting in the lecture hall where he'd met the new training group, surrounded by twenty-seven young men and women in gray, and twenty-eight in white. When he'd realized that Lela had brought every new Aakari trainee with her, he'd at first thought that she'd misunderstood his instructions. Then he'd talked to them. At that point, he'd sent for all of the Collared who had originally come from Aakar.

"Why did none of you tell us?" he'd asked, distraught, when Linter came forward to join the ranks of the Aakari who had been preyed on by the Swords.

"What could you have done for us, Rakesh, that you have not already done?" Linter replied. "You have given us a new life, a new purpose. You have given us control of ourselves, our bodies. You have given us dignity and pride. This..." he touched his collar. "This gives us power over those who preyed on us. What more can we want? Revenge? To what purpose?"

"To stop them from hurting anyone else!" Rakesh looked around. "This could have been stopped!"

"How?" Linter asked. "There will always be those who prey, Rakesh. You know this as well as I!"

"Perhaps, but the predators will no longer be the ones who should be protecting you."

Rakesh grabbed at his canes and rose, turning to face Molari Ran-ti-ar. Molari scowled—he'd ordered Rakesh to stop standing every time he came into the room. But it was an impulse that Rakesh couldn't put aside. Molari had a presence to him that made Rakesh want to stand, want to follow. Virin had commented on it, too, in telling how Molari had never wanted to command, never wanted to take the position that should have been Gavir's. Thrust unwilling into the position when Gavir had been killed, Molari had excelled. His one failing, he had once told them, was that he'd never found the people responsible for Gavir's death.

"Sit down, Tarkarin," Molari grumbled. Behind him, Virin had a look on his face that told Rakesh he was trying not to smile. Rakesh bowed slightly and sat back down, and Molari looked around the room slowly. Counting, Rakesh realized, and watched Molari's face grow cold as he finished.

"Ladies, gentlemen, thank you for coming forward. I can only wish you older ones had come forward before, so that something could have been done to perhaps protect these novices. But there's nothing I can do about the past. What I can do is this—if you will help me to identify the Swords who attacked you, I will see them punished. And I will make certain that this does not happen again. Some of you have met Virin Kian-ti-os?" He looked around to see people—mostly the older Collared—nodding. "Virin will be taking command of the Aakari garrison. In addition to repairing what I now know has been a badly mismanaged outpost, he will be addressing the issue of Swords who hunt unlawful prey.

"Now, how many of you are certain that you were fathered by Ishkarin?" he asked, looking around. Hands went up, and he nodded. "All right. Each of you, please see the medics. We'll want a tissue sample from each of you, so that we can identify paternity. And so that we can register you as the children of Ishkarin, with all the appropriate benefits." He smiled, and Rakesh felt people around him relax. "I can see that you've all settled in here, but if any of you wish to be tested to see if you have inherited the abilities of the Ishkarin, please talk to Rakesh, and he'll make certain I hear of it. Does anyone have any questions for me?"

There was a soft wave of murmuring, but no one spoke up. When silence again fell, Molari nodded once more. "Very well. I am sorry, children. I will do my best to make certain that the people who did this to you are punished, and that it does not happen again. I'll leave my comm-code with Rakesh, so that if any of you wish to reach me, you can." He smiled, bowed slightly and left. Virin remained behind, moving to stand by the wall, away from the group surrounding Rakesh.

"All right," Rakesh said, turning in his chair to look around at the novices and Tarken watching him. "The ones of you who need to see the medics, go on. Anyone who needs to talk, or who wants to see a counselor, you should do so. And the rest of you, you have your duties."

They filed out in ones and twos, until the only people left were Rakesh, Virin, and Lela. She had been sitting on the floor at Rakesh's feet, and didn't move when Rakesh dismissed the others.

"Lela?" Rakesh asked, seeing Virin coming over and shaking his head. "Is there something I can do for you? Do you want to talk?"

"I... I wished to thank you," Lela said quietly. "For... For everything."

"Lela, sweetheart, you're welcome," Rakesh said. He held his hand out to her, and was shocked when she grabbed his hand and kissed it. "Lela!"

"Please, will you let me show you? How grateful I am?" she offered, moving to kneel in front of him. "I... I know I am not in a collar yet, but I am willing—"

There's always one, Rakesh thought ruefully. He leaned forward and kissed her on the forehead. "Lela-*sa*, I know how grateful you are. You don't have to show me anything. Especially not in bed."

"But I want to!" she insisted. Rakesh smiled.

"No, Lela. I am flattered. But it would be a betrayal of trust, and I will not take advantage of you like that. Now go on. You need to see the medics. And thank you, Lela. For trusting me enough to offer."

She pouted, but obediently got to her feet and followed the others out. Rakesh turned and watched her go, then looked over at Virin. "I think she might have forgotten you were there."

"And I think she was going to invite me to join in the fun," Virin said as he came closer. "That happen often?"

"There's one or two in every training class. For some of them, especially the ones who came from the streets, I'm the first male who has ever been anything approaching supportive to them. I try to keep myself as a father figure to them, but that never seems to matter. Which.... I don't know how I feel about that! Honestly, though, I'm surprised that it was Lela. I'd thought it was going to be one of the others." He smiled and stood up. "You leave tomorrow?"

"Yes. Serris is practically begging."

"And we'll be there in a week, I think." Rakesh took Virin's arm and they start towards the door together. "Rin?"

"Hm?"

"Do you think we'll do any good?"

Virin nodded. "We're certainly going to try." He fell silent, then stopped and turned Rakesh to face him. "Kesh?"

Rakesh smiled. He'd been expecting this since Virin had found out about what was really happening in Aakar. "Do you want a room, or do you want to go to the Floor?"

Virin smiled slowly. "You up to showing the novices what they have to look forward to?"

"If you don't mind the audience. And we will have one."

"Oh, I know," Virin answered, turning and steering Rakesh towards the door. "After five years? I've come to expect it. Any time we take the Floor, we have an audience. And it adds a bit of spice, doesn't it?"

Rakesh laughed. "When did you become an exhibitionist?"

"I learned from the best, love. Now, is that lift working properly?"

NEWS TRAVELED QUICKLY. By the time Rakesh had changed into his black Arena garb and he and Virin reached the Floor, there was a large crowd of novices and Collared alike waiting for them. Virin stopped as they came out of the lift and looked over his shoulder at Rakesh.

"Too late to change my mind?"

"Yes." Rakesh grinned at him, then took a deep breath. He slowly followed Virin out onto the Floor, carefully setting each foot down and making certain of his balance before taking another step. He'd changed from his usual supportive boots to a pair of lighter boots that had been designed for him to wear in the Arena. They still supported his damaged feet, and they had control bands integrated into the synth-leather. It helped, but Virin had chosen to lock Rakesh's arms behind him, leaving him with no way to catch himself if he fell, and no way to use his canes. So he moved slowly, and what he now lacked in balance and grace, he made up for in sheer, stubborn pride. So long as he wore a Collar, he would walk onto the Floor under his own power, or not at all.

"Are you sure about this?" Virin had asked him, just before the lift doors had opened.

"Yes. You need this." Rakesh assured him. He didn't mention that he needed this release as well, needed the assurance that even after the attack in the lift and the accident with the ropes, he could still trust Virin. Somehow, he suspected that Virin knew. And when Virin had halted the lift and kissed Rakesh, that suspicion turned to certainty.

"I love you," Rakesh told him.

"I love you, too. Let's go show the children what a real Tarkarin looks like," Virin answered with a grin.

Now here they were, a stately procession of two, making their slow way across the Floor. Rakesh wasn't entirely certain where they were going. Virin was certainly not going to use the disruptor. Not today. Perhaps the whipping frames?

He was right. Virin stopped outside the familiar enclosure, holding the gate open and standing back to allow Rakesh to enter. He closed the gate behind them, then moved over to the frame.

"Come here, Tarkarin." Virin called, his voice low, a wicked grin on his face. "I'm leaving you with something to hold you until you get to Aakar. If I do it right, you won't sit comfortably until I see you again in Felanore."

Rakesh smiled and walked forward until he was standing inside the frame. It was only them that he noticed the neat coils of rope laying on the ground. He frowned, confused, then looked at Virin. "You planned this?"

"I was hoping we'd have the chance, yes," Virin said with a nod. Then he laughed. "I was hoping we'd have the chance a few hours ago," he added. "I've been thinking about those pictures. And I have some ideas. Don't move."

Rakesh stood where he was, watching as Virin picked up the first coil of rope and walked around behind the frame. He felt a tugging at his waist, and the belt that held his loincloth released and fell to the ground. Rakesh heard a soft, dark chuckle, then felt Virin's arms encircling him. A moment later, a rope tightened around his waist; when he twisted to try and see, Virin slapped him hard on the ass.

"Stay still, or I'm going to blindfold you," he said, then stepped back. The control bands binding Rakesh's arms released, and Virin continued. "Hands on the overhead and don't let go, Tarkarin."

Rakesh reached up and put his hands on the horizontal bar over his head, which seemed to be set much lower than usual. He looked down though, watching as Virin's arms reappeared, wrapping the rope once more around Rakesh's waist. This time, Rakesh had seen that the rope was doubled. What was Virin doing? He looked at Virin, puzzled, as Virin came around in front of him, then yelped in surprise as Virin reached down, between Rakesh's spread legs, and pulled the ends of the rope forward. Behind him, Rakesh heard a wave of giggles.

"See, you can surprise an old hand at this, once in a while," Virin said aloud, and the laughter grew louder. Virin winked up at Rakesh, then wrapped some of the rope around Rakesh's right thigh. He did something that made the ropes tighten, and tied a knot at Rakesh's hip. He repeated it with more rope on Rakesh's left, then moved back behind the frame. When Rakesh craned his neck, he could see as Virin laced the rope into an attachment point on the side of the frame, pulled it tight, then came back and tied the rope off again to Rakesh's leg. He continued this all the way down both of Rakesh's legs, lacing him into the frame. When he finally rose and moved around to stand in front of Rakesh, he was grinning broadly, and Rakesh could see the prominent tent in Virin's trousers.

"Oh, this is going to be lovely," Virin murmured, picking up more rope. "Hands to the corners, Kesh. Then give me your left."

Rakesh reached up and grabbed the corner of the frame with his right hand, holding his left out to Virin. He watched as Virin turned a small coil of rope into a cunning rope cuff that he attached to the frame, something that he repeated with Rakesh's right hand.

"Pull on those a bit, while I get some more rope," Virin said over his shoulder as he turned away. "They shouldn't tighten."

Rakesh pulled hard on the rope-cuffs. "They're fine."

"Good." Virin came back with more coils of rope looped over his arm. "Almost done. You're not going to see this kind of set up, usual-ly," he said, raising his voice so the novices could hear him. "This is re-ally more elaborate than the standard. Most of the time, the Swords you'll see won't have the patience or the time for something like this. Probably, most of the time you'll be strapped in using your control bands. There won't be this kind of build-up. Consider this something to look forward to for special occasions."

"So why do you do this, if it is so much more complicated?" someone asked. With his back to them, Rakesh couldn't see who, and he made a note to ask Control.

"Because sometimes the buildup is worth it. It's more exciting, for both of us," Virin answered, moving back to the frame and shak-ing out another coil of rope. He knotted another cuff around Rakesh's bicep and bound the ends off to the top of the frame. "The anticipation makes it that much more erotic. And the dread—to slowly lose your mobility, to be completely at the mercy of someone else, with no idea what they're going to do to you and no way to stop it. In the right hands, at the hands of a person you trust, that loss of power is intoxicating." He looked at Rakesh and smiled slightly, but Rakesh saw the haunted look in his husband's eyes. He smiled at Virin, nodded slightly, watched as Virin relaxed.

More cords, around Rakesh's forearms and biceps, attached to each other and to the frame, until at last Virin stepped back and picked up the last coil of rope. This cord was easily twice as thick as any of the others, and only a few feet long. Virin picked it up, shook it out, and walked around behind Rakesh, who turned to try and see what Virin was doing. He saw Virin raise his arms and drop them, then saw something moving out of the corner of his eye. He turned towards it, and Virin pulled back on the rope, forcing it into Rakesh's mouth. Before Rakesh could spit it out, Virin had looped it around his head twice more, then knotted it tightly. The layers of rope made it impossible for Rakesh to close his mouth, and he almost immediately started drooling; he made a strangled, indignant noise, and Virin laughed.

"Now, once you're in this position, there's damn little you can do except take it," he told the novices. "Show them, love. Oh, right." He tapped a control on the side of the frame, and the frame rose, just far enough that Rakesh's feet no longer touched the ground. The sheer number of attach points made the bondage secure, if not completely comfortable. "There. Now show them," Virin said as he turned the frame so that Rakesh faced the novices. Rakesh groaned and tried to move, found that there was no movement that he could make, save only small shifts forward and back. He groaned again, wondering if this was what a fly in a spider-web felt like.

"Now, once you're in this position, what you're going to be taking might not just be pain," Virin continued. He looked up at Rakesh and smiled slowly, and Rakesh shook his head. *Oh, no. No, Rin, don't....*

His silent pleas and frantic grunting did nothing to stop Virin, who knew exactly where Rakesh was the most ticklish. Very quickly, Rakesh was shrieking and struggling futilely as Virin assaulted sides, armpits and inner thighs with his nails. There was no way for Rakesh to tell how long Virin toyed with him before finally moving off, no doubt to prepare for the next step. Whatever that was. Rakesh hung limp, breathing hard and gasping, feeling the ropes digging into his flesh. He'd look up in a moment. Once he'd caught his breath.

"Now, that's something else that probably won't happen to you at first," Virin was saying. "For some reason, tickling is very...intimate. More so than pain. You'll probably have to have a regular patron before that happens to you, and by regular, I mean one who knows you well enough to know that you are ticklish, and where, and just how long they can go. I'd been calling on Rakesh for nearly three years, I think, before I even knew he was ticklish." Rakesh felt a warm hand on his flank. "That right, love?"

Rakesh nodded. He'd still worn the white then, and he remembered how surprised Virin had been to see Rakesh's reactions to what had started as a simple massage after a beating. The tickling that followed had been almost as bad as the beating itself.

"For most of you, this is what you'll expect. A lot of Swords like the whipping frames. It satiates the hunting need easily, because it's simple, fast, and brutal. Which usually also describes what comes after, too. At least until they get to know you better."

Rakesh felt the frame turning, found himself looking at the rear wall. He heard Virin moving behind him, and heard a slight susurration that he knew all too well. He sighed and relaxed, and heard Virin laugh.

"See, he knows what's about to happen," Virin said. "After a while, some of you will come to crave this. Usually, those will be the ones who'll go on to take the red. Now, how many of you have ever seen one of these used before? Novices, I mean. No one? All right. This is a type of flogger. This one is made from a heavy leather. Real leather, not synth. This isn't the only kind you'll see. There are some with more falls, some with fewer. I've seen ones made from rope, ones made from synth-leather. I've seen ones made from chain, too, but that's a bit more brutal than I'm wanting today. You can find them with knots in the falls, like this one. Or with metal barbs or tips. This one delivers a solid strike, and leaves bruises. If you go at it long enough, it can break the skin—"

Rakesh heard Virin grunt, heard the swish-and-whistle, and jerked at the impact across his shoulders. Pain washed over him, and he whimpered,, dropping his head forward as the second strike fell, crossing the first.

"The safe areas are the back, the ass, the backs of the legs," Virin announced, placing the next strike across Rakesh's ass. "Inner thighs are good, too, but you have to be careful, especially on a man. Usually, I'll use something with a bit more precision for the inner thighs. If the Sword knows what he or she is doing, they might also work the chest, but that's risky. No one should ever take a flogger or a whip to your belly. Not enough padding, too many organs close to the surface." Another blow fell, this one across Rakesh's legs, and Rakesh wondered why Virin was going so slowly. Surely he wasn't going to just make this a demonstration lecture? Not after all this set up?

"Now, this is something you might see, but only with a more experienced Sword. It's a bit harder to master."

Rakesh howled around the gag as the beating began in earnest, the knots driving into his back like hailstones. He knew what Virin was doing—two floggers, used in tandem. It was incredible to watch, and excruciating to experience first-hand. There was nowhere for him to go, nothing he could do but fight the ropes and scream.

Then, without warning, he was somewhere else. The pain was gone. He looked around, confused, and realized that this was the same place, the same cobweb-draped room that he'd seen in his fidelis-induced vision.

Welcome.

Rakesh looked around again, turning slowly in a circle. No one else. Nowhere for that sensuous, sexless voice to come from. "Who are you?"

You know.

"You're the Spider, aren't you?"

You're quick. Good.

"What do you want?" Rakesh asked. "And why?"

What I want is what you are doing. Teach. Learn. And come to me. Find me, in the darkness. That is your mission, son of my son. That is why I have called you to come home. You must find me, and in doing so, find yourself.

"Find myself?" Rakesh asked. "That's.... I don't understand."

You will.

Rakesh nodded slowly. "Those doors. They're important, aren't they? What's behind them?" he asked. "I feel like I need to choose between them. What choices are you giving me?"

A good question. You will choose, son of my son. Love...or love.

Rakesh blinked. "That's...not much of a choice."

Is it so? You will learn. Now go back.

Something hit Rakesh hard in the center of his back. He jerked, and found himself unable to move, rough rope digging into the corners of his mouth. He gasped, feeling both of Virin's floggers coming down at once on his shoulders. His entire back felt like it was aflame, and Rakesh wondered how long he'd been in trance. Surely not very long, or Virin would have noticed.

"That's...enough of the public part of this display," Virin announced. "Control!"

Acknowledged.

"This frame, can it be moved to the large trysting room?"

Affirmative

"Then do so."

The frame shuddered, then turned, slowly rolling towards a gap that appeared in the enclosure. The novices moved back and away, forming a pathway through the crowd. All of them were staring at Rakesh with looks of mingled awe and disbelief. There was hunger in a few of those gazes, and arousal. And Rakesh saw, standing back and away from the crowd, the older woman in gold. Marga nodded once when she saw Rakesh looking at her, and he knew that she'd be reviewing the recordings of this session, finding among the faces those novices who reacted with eagerness, and who would need more attention. And those who reacted poorly, and who would gently be eased out of the Arena and into something they were perhaps better suited to. The frame turned, moving down the hall towards the rooms, away from the crowd, until all Rakesh could hear was the heavy footsteps behind him.

"If you sit down at all for the next week, I'll be very surprised."

Rakesh turned, craning his neck, unable to see Virin behind him. He mumbled behind the gag, an interrogative sound that made Virin laugh.

"Oh, I'll cut you down when I'm ready."

The frame stopped, then moved sideways and into one of the bedrooms that lined this corridor. Rakesh turned and watched at Virin followed him inside, letting the door iris closed behind him and locking it so that they would be undisturbed. Smiling, Virin came to stand in front of Rakesh, reaching out and running his hand down Rakesh's chest and stomach. Rakesh whimpered, pulling on the ropes, trying to thrust his hips and his cock forward. Virin shook his head and let his hand fall.

"I'm not done with you yet. Not hardly," he said. Then he stepped back and started unfastening his coat. He stripped off his clothes slowly, deliberately moving just far enough out of line-of-sight that

Rakesh couldn't see anything but the uniform pieces falling to the floor. Then he moved behind Rakesh, and strong hands started to knead Rakesh's aching ass. He groaned, tensing under Virin's touch.

"Oh, you will not be sitting at all for a while," Virin said with a laugh. He slapped Rakesh's ass. Then Rakesh heard soft beeping from the frame's control panel, and the frame started to tip forward. Rakesh yelped, then realized that the frame was pivoting, moving from vertical to horizontal. When it fell still again, Rakesh was suspended face down, his head hanging down far enough that he could see Virin's feet as he moved into position between Rakesh's legs. Warm fingers traced up the insides of his thighs, and he moaned. Tugging at the ropes set him to swinging, ever so slightly, and Virin grabbed onto his hips to stop him. He kept his left hand on Rakesh's hip, running the fingers of his right hand down between his legs, tracing the line between balls and ass.

"This is going to have to keep me until I see you again," Virin said, his voice low. "This is going to have to keep the both of us. So let's make it last." His hands moved away. When they came back, a single, slick finger slipped into Rakesh's ass, probing for a moment before sliding almost all the way out. Two fingers came next, pumping faster, making Rakesh grunt and try to beg around the gag.

"More?" Virin called out. "You want more? You want me?"

Rakesh tossed his head, nodding, tugging against ropes and setting himself swaying again. Once more, he felt Virin's hands on his hips, but this time, there was also Virin's slick cock pressing against his ass. Rakesh yowled as Virin entered him, feeling his fingers digging into his hip. There would be little round bruises there tomorrow, Rakesh was certain. Not that he cared. He clenched his ass, something he knew would drive Virin to the very brink. Virin groaned, then slapped Rakesh once more.

"You are not going to bring me off that fast, Kesh," Virin growled. "And just for that..." Virin pulled out, almost completely. And stopped. Rakesh whimpered, waiting for the next stroke. When nothing happened, he tried to make himself sway again, but Virin's hands held him still. And still Virin didn't move. Rakesh groaned, straining hard on the ropes, wanting more....

"Oh, no, Tarkarin. I said we're going to make this last, and I mean it." Virin shifted, slowly filling Rakesh's ass, then pulling out equally slowly. He did it again, and again, until Rakesh was biting down on the rope gag to keep from screaming with frustrated need. He heard Virin laughing, then the hard, pounding thrusts that Rakesh so desperately wanted began. He could feel the conflagration building, clenched his fists as he reached for it....

And felt Virin spend, heard him roar as he shot. He slowly went still, then leaned over Rakesh's back and kissed him between the shoulder blades. "I did intend to make it last," he murmured as he stepped back, leaving Rakesh feeling open and unfulfilled. "My body had other ideas."

There was soft beeping, and the frame slowly righted itself, settling upright with Rakesh's feet resting on the floor. He tugged at the ropes and whined softly as Virin walked into view.

"I thought not," he said, coming up to stand in front of Rakesh. "Sorry, love. Do you want me to finish you off up here, or take you down?" Then he grinned. "Oh, that's right. You can't answer. Well, I suppose it's my choice, then." Without another word, he reached out and wrapped his hand around Rakesh's cock, pressing up against his side as he started to pump. With his other hand, Virin reached up and grabbed a handful of Rakesh's hair, pulling his head back.

"They can look," he growled. "All of them, they can look. They can admire you, you gorgeous creature. They can ask. But you are mine. None of them can touch you, none of them can have you the way I have you. You are *my* Tarkarin, *my* husband, my very own. No one else, ever."

Rakesh whined, trying to nod with his head pulled back. In response, Virin pulled his head back harder, and Rakesh felt the sting of teeth against his throat. He closed his eyes, feeling Virin's hand tightening, pulling harder, his thumb rough against the head of Rakesh's cock, until at last Rakesh howled and thrashed and spent.

Virin cut the gag away first, and wiped saliva from Rakesh's chin and chest. "Think that will hold you for a week?" he asked, leaning in and kissing Rakesh before he could answer.

Rakesh snorted, grimacing at the feel of rope fibers in his teeth. "Will it hold you?" he countered. "And are you all right?"

"Me? Fine. I've just had a long day, and I can't keep going for hours the way I used to." Virin shrugged and knelt. "Hold still and I'll cut you free."

"You've been planning this for a while, haven't you?" Rakesh asked as Virin slowly cut the ropes binding his legs.

"Yeah, I've been thinking about it. Doing research. Found some references on advanced rope techniques in the Arena library. Someone named Foole. Mother says he was in her training group."

"And he was one of my trainers when I was a novice, back before he retired," Rakesh added.

"Was he?" Virin sat back on his heels and pointed with his knife. "He developed that cuff design. I like it. Of course, with the control bands, it's sort of superfluous, but still. I like it."

"So I imagine we'll be using this at home?"

"You imagine correctly." Virin ran the flat of his knife down the inside of Rakesh's thigh. "Let me finish this, then I'll take you home. Maybe we'll continue this there."

"Continue?" Rakesh echoed.

Virin grinned up at him. "I want you to miss me, love."

"You know I'm going to."

The grin grew wider, more wicked. "Every time you sit down."

Chapter Five

"No, I did not order six beds for the new dormitories," Rakesh snapped at the person on his screen. "I ordered sixty beds. I have the order right here, and your name is on the bottom as having received it." He held the printout up. "See? So, sixty beds need to be on the transport to Felanore tomorrow. You have twenty-six hours to fix this, or I'll see your ass in the sling on the Floor, and I'll be the one holding the whip. Out." He waved the sat-comm off and slumped in his chair, wincing as his still-tender back came in contact with the back of his chair. He closed his eyes and rubbed his forehead. Twenty-six hours until he saw Virin.

"Are you channeling that husband of yours, to be so aggressive?"

Rakesh jerked up. "*Aba*! How long have you been standing there?"

Raizi laughed and came into the office. "Just long enough to hear you threaten to beat a man. Truly, he is a poor influence on my gentle Kesh-*na*."

"Hardly," Rakesh protested. "It's just.... Well, you know about dealing with merchants. They want all your money, and don't want to deliver. Getting the supplies we need for the new Arena has been one long exercise in frustration. But enough about that. Come in, *Aba*. Sit. Have you eaten yet?"

"No. I came to have dinner with you before you leave, and to give you something." Raizi came into the office and sat down, setting a heavy bag down on the desk. "This, you must take with you to Felanore."

Rakesh opened the bag and took out a book. He opened it, and saw his father's cramped handwriting. "Are these the translations?"

"Yes. The first few books. It is all I have had time to translate for you. I will work on the rest while you study these. Learn your heritage, and your role, my son. Have you had other visions?"

"Not since the one I had on the Floor, no." *The one I haven't told Virin about*, he added silently. There had simply been no time that last night. No time that he hadn't been either gagged, sucking Virin's cock, or asleep. And it wasn't something he wanted to discuss over the sat-comm. He'd tell Virin when he saw him. Tomorrow.

"You will tell me, if you have another. And...there is also this." Raizi reached into his pocket and took out a woven bracelet. Rakesh recognized the shining, cream-colored fibers and shuddered.

"A fidelis bracelet?" he asked. "You want me to wear that?"

"While you study. It is traditional for the priests to wear spidersilk, to strengthen their bond with the Dark Spider. When you reach Aakar, do not wear it out where anyone can see. Only those of royal blood can wear spidersilk and live." Raizi held it out. Rakesh hesitated, then took the bracelet. The fibers were cool under his fingers.

"*Aba*, what do I do if someone recognizes me as Tragar's grandson?" he asked. "If someone decides I'm heir to the Empire?"

Raizi looked confused. "But you would not be. Even if I had remained in Felanore, become the Spider Priest, and been blessed with you as my son, you would not be heir. Those called to the Spider do not rule."

"You weren't the heir? Then...."

"Why did he not kill me? Because I was his only male child." Raizi shook his head. "No. I was not the heir. I had six sisters. My oldest sister Antaria was the heir to the Imperial throne, and my second sister Treala was her heir, until such time as she bore a child. And there were four others, all of them older than I." Raizi looked distant, thoughtful. "Now, it is possible that I sired children on them, but I do not know—"

"You what?" Rakesh blurted. "Control! Hush field on my office!"

Acknowledged.

"*Aba*, you had other children?" Rakesh asked, waiting until the shimmering field was in place over the open doorway.

"I do not know," Raizi answered with a shrug. "It is possible. My sisters were of an age to need an heir, and all of them came to me in my prison...and that, I think, is what disturbs you." Raizi sighed. "It was the way of kings, in Aakar. Virin mentioned that, I think? To keep the blood pure. I was the only male of my generation. If any of my sisters bore children, they were your half-brothers and sisters. But my sisters were murdered by the Mad One. I cannot but think that if there were any children, that they would also have been killed." Raizi frowned, cocked his head to one side. "I wonder if perhaps that was why you reacted so badly to the spidersilk? That your blood is not entirely royal."

"So, should I still wear this, then?" Rakesh asked, setting the bracelet on his desk.

"At first, wear it only while you are with Virin, so he can be sure you do not have another reaction. I imagine he will want to read the translations over your shoulder."

"Can he?"

"I am the Spider Priest," Raizi said, pitching his voice low. His stentorian pronouncement was completely undermined by the puckish grin on his face. "I declare that my son and heir to the Spider may share his knowledge with whomever he so wishes. Because when the time comes, he will be the last Spider Priest in all the world."

Rakesh stared at his father for a moment. "The last?"

"Unless you can someone figure out how to get a child out of Virin?" Raizi added. He smiled and shrugged. "I know that I will not have grandchildren from you, my son. Your sisters have more than made up for that lack. But your sisters and their husbands, they are of Tyese. Their children are of Tyese. There is nothing of the Spider in them, and so the Spider will not claim one of them."

"So, I'm it?" Rakesh asked. He looked down at the books and nodded. "I'll study, *Aba*. And...if I have any questions, I'll ask."

"Write your thoughts down, Kesh-*na*. As you learn, your thoughts, your understanding of the web, through eyes that that will see Aakar through a Tyesean glass, they will offer something to those who come in the future. A way for others to learn, so that what we are will not be forgotten."

Rakesh picked up the bracelet and looked at the intricacy of the weaving. "I hadn't thought of that. *Aba*, did you make this?"

Raizi nodded. "A skill I learned as a boy. I perfected it... Well, I had little else to do. You learn, when you are locked away, that there are things you will do in return for a touch, a word, any form of contact with the outside world. It is...why I consented, when my sisters came to me in the night." He sighed again. "There is...something else. Something I saved, through all these years. Your mother does not even know that I have it." Raizi reached into his coat and took out a small box. "I had thought, perhaps, that I would have to destroy this, that I would have no one to take it from me when my time came."

Rakesh took the box and opened it, drew out the square gold pendant that he found there. "*Aba?*"

"I was given this when my father acknowledged me as his son. It was the mark of the royal house." Raizi reached out and took the pendant, turning it so that Rakesh could see the design etched into the metal. "See here, the Dark Spider? And these dots? This mark, this is the mark of the seed. This means a son of Her blood. A daughter would have had a series of waved lines, the mark of the river. The seed and the flow, you understand? These were unique to us, the children of the royal blood. On our deaths, they would be destroyed. But I give mine to you, my son. Again, do not wear it where it can be seen. Now, come and have dinner, and we will talk."

"Good. I can practice my Aakari on you," Rakesh said, picking up his canes. Then he set them down, picked up the bracelet, and slipped it onto his wrist. The pendant he slipped back into its box, and put the box into his shirt pocket. "There. Now I'm ready," he said as he rose.

Raizi looked at him for a moment, then smiled broadly and put his arm around Rakesh's shoulders. "I love you, my son."

"I love you, too, *Aba*. Thank you."

———◦———

THE TRANSPORT RUMBLED, then shook hard as it grounded. Rakesh glanced out the small port to see tan stone walls and not much else. He turned and looked around the inside of the transport.

"All right, children. We're here. Until we have a better feel for how we're going to be welcomed, don't leave the compound without an escort. Understood?"

"You've said that already, Rakesh," Linter reminded him, grinning widely. "Twice, I think."

"And I've just said it again," Rakesh said. He rose as the transport doors opened. "Here we are. Our new home."

He started forward, then stopped in the doorway. The buildings were constructed of the same tan stone as the walls. The Tyesean flag flew over the largest building, one that towered three-stories above the courtyard. There were two Swords stationed at the doors. Behind that building stood another one, a single-story building with shuttered windows—barracks, Rakesh assumed. And that was all. Where was his new Arena?

"Tarkarin!"

Rakesh turned to see a familiar man coming towards them. He smiled and leaned on one cane so that he could clasp hands with Serris, Virin's aide. "Serris. Good to see you."

"And you, sir," Serris replied. He looked past Rakesh and nodded. "Glad to see all of you. Come inside, and we'll get you settled."

"Actually, Serris, we should get settled in the new Arena. We've got a lot of work to do to get things ready to start serving," Rakesh said as he fell in next to Serris, walking towards the taller building. "Is Virin here?"

"The Kian-ti-os is on patrol, and asked me to send his regrets for not being here to meet you himself. This whole mess with Swords going rogue.... We've sent so many north that it's left us short-handed." Serris sighed. "We're due a complement of ir-Zaans from the training school, but not for another month or so. So until then, we're all serving minimum eight-hour shifts, back-to-back."

Rakesh blinked. "I'd no idea it was so bad. Sounds like we're just in time. You all are going to need to outlet. Where do we set up, Serris?"

Serris blushed, stopped walking, and turned to Rakesh. "That's...part of the problem, I'm afraid."

"What is?"

"When we went to take out the rogues, there was a firefight. A big one. And...some of the surrounding buildings...well...they fell down."

"Serris!"

"No one was hurt!" Serris hurried to say. "But...well, one of them was the one that we'd marked for the Arena." He nodded towards the wall, where Rakesh could see what looked like a hasty patch-job on the stonework. There were broken beams visible over the wall. "So...we don't really have a place to put you."

Rakesh stood still for a moment, just staring at Serris. "And...I wasn't informed of this why?" he asked quietly.

"Because we really needed you to come now?" Serris offered weakly. "Because...we're starting to get close to the edge, and we need to hunt. Taking out the rogues, that did it for some of the men. But not everyone was on that squad, and... Damn. I'm sorry, Rakesh. Really. We've got a nice wing set up for you, here in the embassy——"

"We need more than a wing, Serris!" Rakesh said, his disbelief making his voice project more than he'd intended. "You know what our space needs were. You were our point of contact here. Now, what *do* you have that would work for us? I know there was a building inventory made. Virin told me about that."

Serris paled. "There's nothing that meets all the requirements, Tarkarin. Nothing that we can enclose and name as part of the embassy—"

"What about adjacent?" Rakesh interrupted. "The surrounding buildings, are they all occupied?"

"No, but—"

"Fine. Let's go take a look at them. Hopefully, there will be one that works for us—"

"You will not!"

Rakesh turned and smiled. "Virin!" His smile faded as he saw the stormy look on his husband's face. "What?"

"You will not be picking out a building outside these walls, Rakesh. Not yet. It won't be safe."

"And we can't function cramped in a corner of the embassy, Virin," Rakesh said, leaning hard on his canes. "Now, I'll ask you what I asked Serris: Why wasn't I told that our Arena was destroyed?"

"First, it happened yesterday. The ferro-cement on that wall isn't fully dry yet, and I haven't had a chance to send the reports in," Virin answered. "Second, my men need you. Badly."

"Kian-ti-os, we came here with the understanding that we would have a place that was ready to turn into a functional Arena," Rakesh said, his voice low. "Having us in the embassy proper will be disruptive to the diplomatic process, and highly inappropriate. We need to be a separate entity."

"I understand that, Tarkarin." Virin's voice was equally low. "Our main concern is your safety. The safety of all the Collared. If you leave these walls, the Ishkarin cannot guarantee your safety. We're too short-handed. There's a good place across the way, right over there." He pointed. Rakesh turned and looked, seeing the closed gate and another building, this one of light pink stone, across the road. "I've got that one earmarked for you. Once we have the men to guard it. Having you in the embassy is temporary, until we get our reinforcements from up north."

Rakesh nodded. "Serris didn't explain that."

"Probably because you still scare the piss out of him," Virin answered with a wry grin. "He still thinks you're going to turn around and lay him on his ass for grabbing you in the Arena."

"That was five years ago!" Rakesh protested, laughing. "And you could have told me."

"Not until I make my official report. Which I haven't had time to do. And I'm going to go and do right now. Welcome to the embassy, Collared. Come inside, and we'll get you settled into your temporary quarters."

Inside, Virin led Rakesh and the rest of the Collared through a side door, and into a large, airy room. "This will be your lounge, once we get it set up. All of the equipment and supplies you ordered are in storage, but we can pull out anything you need. There are smaller rooms off this one, and you can use those as enclosures."

"I'm more worried about dormitory space right now, Virin," Rakesh said. "Where do we sleep?"

"Top floor. You'll share medics with us, for now. And the floor above this one will be your working rooms." Virin turned and looked around. "It's not much, but I hope it will work until we can get you set up across the way."

Rakesh nodded, looking around. "This could work. For the short term. All right, children. Go on up and choose your spaces. Don't bother to leave a room for me." There was a wave of tired-sounding laughter, and the Collared filed out of the room behind Serris.

Rakesh sighed and leaned heavily on his canes, hearing Virin coming up behind him.

"I'm sorry, Kesh. I wasn't planning on keeping you in the dark. I just haven't had the time." Virin slipped his arms around Rakesh's waist, pulled him back to lean against his chest. "I missed you."

"I missed you, too. And speaking of keeping you in the dark, there's something I didn't have a chance to tell you before you left. And I didn't want to tell you over the sat-comm—"

"Not that we've had all that much time to talk that way," Virin interrupted.

"True. I had another vision, Rin. When you had me on the Floor that last night." Rakesh turned to face Virin, who looked stunned. "This time, the Spider spoke to me."

"You... you're serious? And you waited a *week* to tell me?"

"I wanted to tell you to your face." Rakesh ran his fingers through his hair and tried not to yawn. "Rin, it wasn't like I could tell you before you left. We didn't do very much...talking that night."

Virin frowned, then nodded. "Oh. Oh, yes. We... were rather busy, weren't we?" He put his arm around Rakesh's shoulders, turned him towards the door. "Come on. I'm just going off shift. We'll get a bite, and you can tell me about it. Did you tell Raizi?"

"Yes. He wants me to write down anything else that happens. He's also given me permission to share the translations with you."

"Oh, that will be interesting. All right. This way. We have to go back out through the courtyard to get to the barracks." Virin escorted Rakesh outside, and Rakesh noticed that the transport was being unloaded.

"Where are they taking the supplies? You said storage—" He stopped and looked around, seeing for the first time the crowd at the gate. "Rin, who are they?"

Virin sighed. "Some of the street children. They run like rabbits when we try to get closer. But they're curious about us." He smiled and waved, calling out, "Good morning!"

The crowd scattered like frightened birds, and Virin sighed again. "We've been trying to approach them, offering them food and medical attention. But, given what's been going on here, I'm not surprised that they won't let us help them."

Rakesh nodded, then looked at Virin. "Maybe they'll let us help them? The Collared, I mean."

"Kesh—"

"We're not Swords. We're not threatening. Creator, Rin, I'm probably the least threatening looking person in this compound. And it will give us something else to do."

Virin scowled, looked at the now-abandoned gates, then nodded. "Let me think on this, think about how we can make it work. We'll talk about it, see if Serris has any ideas. It's a good thought. All right. Come on. The commissary is this way and I'm starved."

<hr />

IT TOOK TWO DAYS TO convert one of the embassy buildings that had street access into a small clinic. Rakesh supervised the process, splitting his time between the ersatz Arena and the new clinic, and found himself pleased with the results on both fronts. Having the Arena inside the embassy meant fewer complications for everyone involved, and there was ample space for what they needed. Despite his initial misgivings, Rakesh had to admit that Virin was right. This was a good space for the Collared.

The clinic had also turned into a good space. The front room, where Rakesh or another Collared would wait and supervise, was welcoming and comfortable. There were four rooms at the rear of the building—a small kitchen, and three examination rooms staffed by female medics. Virin and Rakesh looked over the arrangements early on the third day, and Rakesh found himself nodding and smiling.

"This is good. I don't think you can tell that the rooms are all being monitored." He turned towards Virin. "I think this will work. Thank you."

"Thank you, Kesh. If this works, it will give us a way to start making peace." He looked down at his wrist-comp and nodded. "I'm on shift in ten. Kiss me, love, and I'll see you tonight."

Rakesh moved into Virin's arms and tipped his head back. "Be careful, love."

"I'm always careful. You be careful, too." Virin pulled Rakesh close and kissed him hard, then stepped back and smoothed the non-existent wrinkles from the front of his uniform. "Now. Where did I hide the stunner?"

"Second drawer down."

"And the panic button?"

Rakesh grinned. "Underneath the seat of the chair. Go on, Kian-ti-os. You'll be late. I'll be fine."

Virin kissed him again, then hurried towards the rear of the clinic and the door that fed out into the courtyard. Rakesh went and sat down behind the desk, picking up one of the translated books and opening it. He didn't expect to see anyone today, but you never did know....

———⊶⊷———

THE TRUEST FORMS OF visioning are those found deep in the web, whilst cocooned within the web itself. It is the method by which one may dedicate oneself to the Web and to the Dark Spider. On initiation, the seeker will be caught within Her webs, and seek Her in the darkest places. If She accepts the dancer's tribute, She will release them to become Her Chosen One in the world.

Rakesh frowned at the passage, then nodded, turning to his own journal. As he moved, he noticed the girl hovering in the doorway. Painfully thin, pale for an Aakari, with a braid of dark hair over one shoulder, and a long fringe of hair hanging into her eyes. Her clothes had seen hard use, but were carefully mended. She couldn't have been more than seventeen.

"Oh!" Rakesh gasped, then smiled. "I'm sorry! I didn't hear you come in!" He marked his place with a piece of ribbon and set the book down. Then he picked up his canes and rose, hobbling around the desk. "Come in. How may I help you?"

The girl looked as if she were ready to flee. Until she saw the canes. She looked startled, then relaxed slightly. "I have heard that there is... a healer here? A... a medic?"

"Yes. Come in. I'm Rakesh Tarkarin. I run this clinic. And you are?" He turned and moved back towards his chair. "Please, come and sit."

"I..."

"If you don't sit, I can't," Rakesh added gently. "I'm not going to hurt you, my dear. And trust me, you're a lot faster than I am. So come sit." He sat back down, propping his canes against the desk. The girl looked at him for a moment, then moved to sit down in the chair facing him. Rakesh smiled. "Thank you. What's your name?"

"Ah... Ayani, sir."

"Ayani. Very nice to meet you. Do you need to see the medic?" Rakesh picked up his datapad and typed in the girl's name.

"No... I was curious. What are you doing here?" She looked around, briefly met Rakesh's eyes, then looked down. "You are not one of the Black Hunters."

"Is that what you call them?" Rakesh asked. "We call them Swords. And no, I'm not one of them. I'm a counselor. And we're here to try and make up for some very bad things that happened. Because we weren't paying enough attention to what some of our own were doing."

Ayani frowned. "There is a new Hunter here. We've seen him. Silver hair. Quieter than the one he replaced, and the Hunters seem to listen to him more than the other one."

Rakesh nodded. "His name is Virin. And he won't be letting his men hunt you and your friends. Not any more. If he finds anyone doing it, they'll be punished. This..." Rakesh gestured, taking in the whole clinic with one hand motion. "This was his doing."

"And... it is not a trap?" She looked around and frowned. "There have been other traps."

"Would you be here, if you thought it was?" Rakesh asked. Then he blinked. "Oh... you're here to test and see if it *is* a trap. And if you walk out, alive and unharmed, then your friends know we're safe?"

She smiled slightly. "It is not quite that simple. But... you have been here for a week now. This door has been open to all, and people come and go. You've given work to people who need. You have offered food to all comers. You have told everyone about the medics, and about the help that you will offer. And you have given it all without hesitation. And without asking for coin. Now... we came to see."

"People come and go, but you're the first person I've seen over the age of ten and under the age of thirty. So either there aren't a lot of young people around here, or you're all hiding, trying not to be noticed. Which is it?" Rakesh shook his head. "I retract that question. I haven't done anything to earn your trust enough to get an answer, and I should know that. Have you eaten today?" Ayani blinked rapidly, then shook her head. Rakesh smiled and continued, "I was just about to have something to eat myself. May I offer you something?"

"I..."

"It's no trouble." Rakesh turned slightly and raised his voice. "Jiren? Is lunch ready?"

"Yes, Tarkarin!"

"Bring enough for two... no, make that three, please." Rakesh turned back and smiled, picking up his datapad. "So, tell me about yourself, Ayani? The Tyesean government is trying to make sure that everyone who was hurt by the ones you called Black Hunters is taken care of properly. Part of the punishment was confiscation of all their possessions, and the funds were put into trust for their victims. Anyone assaulted by them, or who had a child by a Sword—"

Ayani shook her head. "No. I was lucky. I was faster, hid better."

"Good. Your friends who weren't as lucky—"

"Not many survived."

Rakesh stopped, shocked. "I... I didn't know. Given how many ended up in Tyese, I thought there would be more survivors here, ones who didn't have the ability to leave."

Ayani shook her head again. "Those who survived, they ran to the border, to hide among the ones who sought new lives. They ran, because they knew that the Hunters would find them and finish what they'd started. There is safety in numbers, you understand?"

"And anonymity, yes. I do understand. And the ones who didn't run?"

"Died. Or are hidden, so far in the dark or in the depths that no one knows where they are. They will not come out, and they will not be interested in what you have to offer." Ayani shrugged one shoulder. "But the street packs, they will be interested."

Rakesh nodded, turning to see the young widow who they'd hired to work in the kitchen coming in with a laden tray. From the moment they'd met, Jiren had seemed to be insulted by how thin Rakesh was, and had taken it as her duty to, as she put it, put some meat on his bones. The meal for three would easily have fed twice that number.

"Jiren, you're going to make me fat," Rakesh teased gently as she set the tray down.

"Good. You're all bones," she answered, poking him gently in the upper arm. "Look at this. You'll blow away in a strong wind. Ayani. It's good to see you." She smiled at Ayani, then bowed slightly and turned for the door.

"Is Kestri awake?" Rakesh asked. Jiren had been forced to bring her two-year-old daughter with her on her second day of work, when her usual baby-tender had gotten sick. Rakesh had spent a good portion of that day entertaining the child, to the amusement of both her mother and the medics. Jiren had brought Kestri with her the next day. And the next.

"Not yet." Jiren smiled. "When she wakes, I'll bring her out, if you are not with someone. Now eat."

"Yes, ma'am," Rakesh said with a grin. Jiren laughed and left, and Rakesh started uncovering bowls. "You know Jiren?"

"A little. From the market. Her little girl is sweet. She would feed us when she could. Is that for me?"

"Not all of it. But as much as you like. Come eat, and you can tell me about the area between bites. I haven't had much of chance to explore, and I'm not as mobile as I used to be."

Ayani hesitated, watching as Rakesh served out two identical plates of food. He passed one to her and started eating, noticing that she watched him carefully, and only started to eat after he'd sampled everything on his plate.

"So... they used drugged food?" he asked softly, looking down at his plate.

"Yes. Was I obvious?"

"Only because I was watching. It's all right. If there's anything you want to try that I haven't had first, just let me know and I'll take a bite. Jiren really is a wonderful cook. Almost as good as my mother. So, what is in this area?"

"Not much, not anymore." Ayani paused while she took a bite. "I'm told this area used to be where the nobles lived, before Crazy

Tragar. Now... well, lots of ruins. Lots of places to hide. That's why we live here."

"Shops?"

"No. The shopping district is about a mile that way." Ayani pointed with her spoon. "There's a greenmarket a few streets over, though, where farmers set up tents and stalls. That's where Jiren buys her vegetables, and where we scavenge. Sometimes we work for some of the merchants, for food or coin. There is an artisan quarter. That's not far, and you might be able to walk there. Pretty things. And...ah...the palace ruins are half a mile behind you."

Rakesh almost turned to look at the wall behind him, but stopped himself. "That close? And I'd heard that those were off limits?"

She smiled. "Off limits to foreigners."

"Ah. That kind off off-limits. I see." Rakesh looked down at his plate, took another bite, and didn't look up when he asked, "I am full-blooded Aakari. But I was born in Tyese. Am I a foreigner? Or someone coming home?"

Ayani frowned, cocking her head to one side. "I...don't know. May I answer that when I come back?"

"I look forward to it," Rakesh answered, grinning. "And I'm glad to hear that I've passed the test."

"I didn't say that." She smiled slightly, then looked down at her now-empty plate. "May I have some more, sir?"

Rakesh laughed. "Help yourself."

They talked for nearly an hour before they were interrupted by a young mother bringing her children in to see the medics. To Rakesh's surprise, Ayani didn't leave. She lingered in the corner of the waiting room, watching him as he talked with the young woman and her two sons. When the medic came out and escorted them into a room, Ayani came back over to the chair.

"You're very nice to them," she said.

Rakesh looked at her. "Why shouldn't I be?"

"Because she can't pay you. Unless you want her to sleep with you. I know she sometimes pays her bills with that coin."

Rakesh snorted. "I wouldn't ask that of her. Or of you, for that matter. Or anyone I was trying to help." He paused, then shook his head. "Not unless they asked me first. And even then, only if I thought they needed that kind of help."

Ayani just stared at him. "You... are like no one I have ever met. What are you, Rakesh, when you are in Tyese?"

Rakesh leaned back in his chair, wondering how much of the truth to tell her. Enough, he decided. "What do you know about Tyese? Have you ever heard of the Collared?"

Ayani's eyebrows disappeared under her fringe of dark hair. "The whores?" Then she looked at him, and pointed at the gold and black collar he wore. "You're one of them?"

Rakesh smiled. "And I don't care for being called a whore. But your ways aren't my ways, so I'll let it pass. Yes, I'm one of the Collared. We're not whores, Ayani. We're counselors. Medics, of a sort. And... we're the safety valve on the Swords."

"I...don't understand." Ayani said slowly, clasping her hands in her lap.

Rakesh nodded, considering his words carefully. "We...volunteer to be their prey, so that they don't hunt innocents. And there are thirty-six men and women like me in the embassy now, helping keep the hunters sated. If we'd been here before, maybe things would be different." He signed and shrugged, reaching up to run his fingers over his collar. "I've worn this for fifteen years now, Ayani. I married a Sword. It's who I am. And I'm proud of my collar. This is... my calling. My purpose, if you will."

Ayani studied him for a long moment. "You don't sound like the whores I know," she said after a long silence. "You sound like one of the crazy mystics in the market who spend all day preaching about the coming of the Lost One."

Rakesh blinked. "What do you mean, the Lost One?"

Ayani shrugged. "It's just an old story they tell to get coins out of the gullible."

"Tell me? I'm curious." And worried, Rakesh told himself. The Lost One was entirely too apt a description for Raizi.

"Just... stories." Ayani cocked her head to one side. "The Lost One. He's... some of the street packs swear by him. He was supposed to be a great warrior, a hero who vanished under the rule of Crazy Tragar. He was champion of the people, protector of children, and rightful ruler of Aakar. Someday, he'll return and throw off the yoke of the oppressor. That's you, in case you didn't know. Tyese, I mean."

"Is that so?" Rakesh asked with a grin, and made a note to remember to tell Virin and Raizi about the Lost One.

"Yes. All shadow stories, to put little children to sleep, really. I don't think there ever was a Lost One."

"Too old for bedtime stories?" Rakesh asked. "And, am I oppressing you?"

"Only if you make me try to eat more. I don't think I've ever been this full. You're not a crazy mystic, are you?"

"Depends on who you ask, I suppose." Rakesh frowned, then shrugged. "My father says that what the Collared are really is a form of priest. And that we're all a little crazy. He would know. He wore a collar, too. That's how he met my mother."

"Is your mother a Sword?" Ayani asked. "I don't think I've seen a woman Sword. They let women do that, too?"

"Yes, they let women be Swords. But my mother? Creator, no!" Rakesh laughed. "Her name is Akesha, and she wore a collar, too. My father's name is Raizi. They were both born here, in Felanore."

Ayani nodded, then looked thoughtful. "Are you going to try and make me a who— wear a collar?" she asked. "Because this would be the strangest approach by a pimp I've ever seen. And, just to let you know, the last person who tried to make me a whore, I gelded."

"Gelded?" Rakesh repeated. "That seems...appropriate."

"So, are you? Because you're very nice, and I would hate to hurt you."

Rakesh grinned and shook his head. "No, I'm not going to force you into anything. Not if you don't want to try, and not just because you told me you'd geld me if I said yes," he answered. "It's not a life for everyone, and we're very particular about who we train. I'd thought about seeing if anyone in the area was interested, but it's a grueling life, and not many pass the tests to start training."

"Tests?" Ayani echoed, looking amazed. "Training? To be a whore?"

"I told you. There's more than spreading your legs to being one of the Collared." Rakesh stopped, thinking. "Do you want to see?"

She hesitated, and he watched as skepticism warred with curiosity. Curiosity won. "Yes."

He nodded. "All right. Do you know how to read?"

Ayani bristled. "I'm not ignorant!"

Rakesh held up both hands. "Sorry! Most of the women who have come in here to see the medics haven't been able to read, so I had to ask. I had some of the texts we use translated into Aakari, in case we did have any applicants. You're welcome to borrow one."

"And leave with it?" Ayani gasped. "Truly?"

"So long as you promise to bring it back. Or you can read it here. Your choice. If you read here, I'll feed you again. Later, though, when you're hungry. I'm not going to try to oppress you."

Her eyes widened. "Really? I can... stay here, and read?" She turned and looked at the overstuffed couch in the corner, then nodded. "All right. Will you help me if I get confused?"

"Of course." Rakesh picked up his datapad, called up the Aakari translation of the basic training manual, and passed it to Ayani. "You turn the pages by tapping the edge of the screen. Make yourself comfortable."

She did just that, curling up on the couch with the datapad, reading silently. She stayed there the rest of the afternoon; every time Rakesh glanced at her, she was focused on the screen, a small frown on her face, her lips moving slightly as she read. The only time she stopped was when Jiren brought in their evening meal, and even then, she bolted down her food and returned to her reading. Rakesh read his own book, making notes on his father's translation, and neither of them were disturbed until a soft chime sounded. Rakesh closed his book and rose, picking up his canes.

"Ayani?" She didn't move, and he grinned and walked over to the couch, stopping just out of arm's reach. "Ayani. It's time for me to close for the night."

She jumped, her face growing pale. "It's that late?"

"Yes. It's almost dark. Do you need an escort home?"

She shook her head, putting down the datapad and getting up quickly. "No. No, not while it's still light. I shouldn't have stayed this late. He'll—" she stopped, bit her lip, then smiled at Rakesh. "Thank you. That was very interesting."

"You can come back tomorrow, if you like. Read the rest." Rakesh stepped back, clearing her way to the door.

"I can?" Her grin made her look much younger than she was.

"I look forward to seeing you." He walked her to the door, holding it open for her. She smiled shyly and darted out into the gloaming, running down the street. As Rakesh watched, another figure came out of the shadows and joined her. The shadows joined, then parted again, and vanished around a corner. He nodded and closed the door.

"How was your day?" Virin asked that night.

"Promising. Very promising. And we need to start a lending library. Some of the street children can read."

Virin chuckled, pulling Rakesh into his arms. "Anything else?"

Rakesh smiled, yawning as he rested his head on Virin's shoulder. "Maybe...a school?"

Chapter Six

To Rakesh's surprise, Ayani was waiting when the clinic doors opened the next morning, and had brought with her two others, boys of about sixteen. "We would like to see the medics, please," she announced. Once she and the boys had seen the medics, and had eaten a good meal, the boys left. But Ayani stayed, taking her place on the couch as if she belonged there, asking questions about the reading she'd already done.

"You allow yourself to be hurt, to be assaulted, so that the Hunters will not hunt others," she said as she sat down. "I don't know if this makes you brave or insane."

Rakesh laughed. "That depends on who you ask."

"And... you like this? You like being hurt?" The look on her face told Rakesh clearly that she thought he was going to lie to her. He shook his head.

"I don't like pain, Ayani. I live with it every day, and honestly, I hate it. But that isn't the same." He stopped, considered her question. "This... When I'm on the Floor, what is done to me... That's more of an exchange of power." He propped his elbows on the desk. "Trust, and power. I trust the Sword to do no lasting harm. And the Sword trusts me not to take advantage of the power I gain."

Ayani turned to face him, drawing her legs up onto the couch. "Power? I... What power can you have, when they are hurting you?"

"More than you realize," Rakesh answered. "All Collared are more than a touch sensitive. It's one of the things we're tested for before we're accepted for training. Do you know what that means?"

"I think so," Ayani answered slowly."You can hear their thoughts?"

"Not quite. Or at least, not me. I don't think there have been any Collared yet who have actually heard thoughts. No, we can feel their emotions. When a Sword is on the Floor with us, they're...open. Raw. There are no walls to hide behind, no pretenses. Just them and their naked need."

"And naked other things," Ayani added, her voice dry. Rakesh snickered.

"That comes later," he said, then groaned when Ayani hooted at his inadvertent pun.

"So... you let them hurt you, and you learn about them that way. About what hurts them," Ayani said once she stopped laughing. "And then what?"

"Then you help them," Rakesh said. He picked up his teacup and took a sip. "Think about it, Ayani. These are men and women who have been fighting their whole lives. No matter what their drives are, what they've been made to be, they're still people. They can still be sick, still be tired, still be exhausted by everything they've done and everything they're supposed to do. We—I mean, me and others like me—we're there to give them a respite. We understand, and we make them feel... human, I suppose." Rakesh grinned at her. "I've never had to justify this before. Even our Aakari candidates know enough about who and what we are to not need this level of depth. So, did that answer your question?"

"I think perhaps." Ayani looked down at the datapad. "I will think of other questions."

The following day, she came in the late afternoon, with three young girls. Again, once the girls had been seen by the medics and had been fed, they left. And again, Ayani stayed, and read, and asked questions. This became a pattern. Ayani would never come at the same time of day two days in a row, but she would come without fail, usually with at least one other street child in tow. Then she would stay, reading anything Rakesh would give her, and asking questions.

"If you'd like to be tested, Ayani, I'd be happy to bring you in. You're smart, and I think you'd pass the empathy testing. And frankly, I'd love to have some local candidates," Rakesh said one morning. Ayani said nothing, but the next morning, she brought with her two young women, both of whom asked about testing.

"They are already whores," Ayani told him after he'd sent them in to the medics. "Perhaps they will be able to be more?"

To Rakesh's surprise, both girls passed the tests to enter training, as did the next two girls that Ayani brought with her. By the end of the clinic's first month, it was a rare day that Ayani wasn't there. She would share a meal with Rakesh, read anything he offered her, and help Jiren with the cooking. When Rakesh offered her a job, she refused.

"If I am working for you, then I cannot come and go as I please," she explained. "I will come when I come. Not when you tell me to be here."

"That's fair," Rakesh agreed slowly. Then he smiled. "And, to be fair, when you do come, I'll pay you for the time you spend helping Jiren."

Ayani laughed. "That is fair."

It wasn't long after that Ayani missed three days in a row, three days in which Rakesh saw none of the street children who had begun to come in regularly for food and to tell him the street gossip. He was about to ask Virin to organize a search when Ayani arrived before dawn, obviously disturbed by something. She went to the couch and sat down, looked at the datapad that Rakesh had labeled as hers, then shook her head and pulled her knees to her chest.

"Ayani?" Rakesh asked gently. She shook her head and looked down, so he let her be. She stayed silent until after Jiren brought in the morning meal.

"You said the Black Hunters will not walk the shadows any more, and they have not," she said slowly. "What about the Red ones?"

The plate Rakesh had been filling fell from his hands, smashing on the floor and scattering food everywhere. "Red? There are Red Hunters? Here?"

"Yes—" Ayani's voice broke off, and she jumped to her feet, hearing the commotion from the back of the clinic. "What?"

"Ayani, please. Sit. It's... it's not what you think." Rakesh tried to calm her. He picked up his canes and tried to walk, but his hands were shaking too hard, and his left slipped. His cane clattered to the floor, and he almost fell, catching himself on the edge of the desk. Then, Virin was there, catching him, calling his name.

"Kesh, it's all right," he whispered. "I'm here. It's all right."

Rakesh nodded, trying to slow his breathing. "I'm... I'm all right."

"Sure, you are, Tarkarin," Virin said, and there was both humor and skepticism in his voice. "Sit down before you fall down," Virin helped him into his chair, then turned. "It's all right, little one. I won't hurt you."

Startled, Rakesh looked past him, and saw Ayani, standing in the corner, holding a knife that she must have been hiding in her clothes. She looked terrified, but her voice didn't shake at all when she snapped, "Don't hurt him!"

"Ayani, it's all right," Rakesh said weakly. "It's... Rin, sit down. Let me explain to her."

"All right, if that's what you think best." Virin moved away, into the far corner, and sat down. Ayani watched him go, then looked back at Rakesh.

"The Red Hunters. You are afraid of them. As afraid as we are," she said. "Why?"

"Because they did this to me," Rakesh answered. "Five years ago, they kidnapped me, tortured me, tried to kill me—"

"Almost succeeded," Virin interrupted. "They had to resuscitate him twice. And he spent a week in a regen capsule."

Rakesh looked over at Virin, then back at Ayani. "We thought they were all gone. That we'd found them all. But you've seen them here?"

Ayani nodded. "Yes. They hunt here. They... They hunted the last few nights. That is why I was not here. We went underground. All the packs did. But last night they found us. They took our pack leader. Teren led them off so that they would not find us. He did not come back."

"And...why didn't you come to us?" Virin demanded. When Ayani didn't answer, Rakesh sighed.

"Ayani, this is Virin Kian-ti-os. My husband. Remember, I told you I was married to a Sword? I've told him about you, and he won't hurt you."

Ayani's eyes went wide, and she squeaked, "Husband?"

"Yes. Husband." Rakesh smiled. "So you understand why he came in like there was something on fire?"

"That was mostly because with Rakesh, something usually is on fire," Virin grumbled. "Now, tell me about this Teren. Where did the hunt start, and which way did he lead them?" Ayani froze, shaking her head, and Virin growled. "Do you want him back alive?"

"Yes!"

"Then tell me!"

"Ayani, the faster we can get out there and find him, the better chance of finding him alive," Rakesh added.

Ayani went pale, then nodded. "I... It would be fastest to show you where we went to ground. It...cannot be reached from the streets if you do not know the way."

"Understood." Virin raised his wrist and started barking orders into his wrist-comp. Rakesh staggered towards Ayani and put his hand on her shoulder, the first time he could remember touching her since they'd met.

"Virin will find him, Ayani. Or he'll find the ones who took him and kill them."

Ayani's eyes went wide. "He would do that?"

Rakesh nodded. "The Red Swords are under sentence of death in Tyese. And you are my friend. He'll help you."

"Right. We've got a squad outside. Kesh, close the clinic—"

"No!" Ayani blurted out. "I... I can send the rest of the pack here? For safety? If I show you our dens, we can't sleep there any more."

"Send them," Rakesh said immediately. "How many in your pack?"

"Seven. You've met most. Heri and Niri, that second day. Agati and Gira and Wishi are all mine, too. Teren is the only one you haven't met. And... I can send the others?"

"Send them all. Anyone you find who wants to come. Once you've shown Virin where he's going, then you come back, too. We'll find beds for all of you inside." Rakesh looked up at Virin, who nodded. "You'll be safe here, Ayani." Acting on impulse, he hugged her, and felt her shivering.

"Come on, Ayani. Let's go find him," Virin said gently, coming up next to her. He didn't touch her, instead leaning across and kissing Rakesh lightly. "Don't wait up, love."

"Like I ever listen to that!"

"I know. I just need to say it."

"Be careful."

Virin snorted, smiled, then looked at Ayani. She drew herself up and followed him out into the street. Rakesh watched as the door closed, feeling suddenly lost. He jammed his hands into his pockets, and felt the silken braid. Taking the bracelet out of his pocket, he looked down at it for a moment, then put it on and ran his fingers over the warm strands. Warmth and calm filled him, and he took deep breath and slowly started to relax. It would be all right.

"Will they find him?" Jiren said from behind Rakesh. He turned to see her standing in the doorway, a broom and dustpan in her hands, then looked back at the outer door.

"Virin will find him. Make sure the medics know that we'll have an emergency coming in. And probably an influx of children needing to be seen to."

"I will. And then I'll make some tea for us while we wait."

"We?" Rakesh turned to face Jiren.

"I remember what it was like. The waiting." Jiren looked past him. "My man, he was a peacekeeper. Until he didn't come home one night. We don't know what happened, where he is. If he's still alive. We did not find a body."

"Jiren, I didn't know."

She smiled slightly. "I didn't tell you. I... I didn't want to burden you, when you take so much on from everyone else. I didn't want to add my pain to theirs. But now...you need to share your pain. So we will wait together."

Rakesh nodded and smiled. "Thank you, Jiren."

"Thank you," she said in reply. "You have done a good thing here, Rakesh. All of you have. And...you are my friend." She came to stand in front of him, then stood on her toes and kissed his cheek. "Even if you exceedingly odd, and married to a man. Now, sit. I will get the tea."

By the time Jiren was back with the teapot, the first of the street children had arrived, two young girls that Rakesh had never seen before. Both of them were frightened and near tears, and by the time Rakesh and Jiren had calmed them down and surrendered them to the medics, three more were waiting. Two of the girls who had come with Ayani startled Rakesh by throwing themselves at him, almost throwing him off balance as they clung to him and begged him not to let the Red Hunters get them.

"It's all right, children. It's all right," Rakesh found himself repeating over and over. "You're safe now."

The stream finally tapered off late in the afternoon, and Rakesh sat down on the couch and groaned. "How many, Jiren? I lost count."

"Seventy-three, I think," Jiren answered. She sighed, leaning against the desk and tucking back a loose strand of hair. "Perhaps a few more. Where will you put them all?"

Rakesh nodded towards the door. "The building across the street was supposed to be the new Arena. I think it's now the new safehouse for the street packs. We've got the supplies, so it shouldn't be too much to set it up. I'll talk to Serris and to Linter. Keeping the Collared under the same roof as the Swords, I think that makes more sense now. Is there more tea?"

"I'll make another pot. What's keeping them, do you think?"

Rakesh sighed and leaned forward, resting his elbows on his knees, absently rubbing the bracelet with his fingers. "I'm not sure. Strange ground, more than likely. I'm more worried about Ayani. She should have been back here by now."

"Would they have kept her with them?" Jiren asked. Rakesh shook his head.

"She doesn't have the training—"

"She will."

Rakesh jerked, sitting up straight to see Virin standing in the doorway, looking tired and haunted. "Rin! When did you get back? Did you find him?"

"Just now. And yes. He's hurt, but he's alive. Serris took the young man straight in to the embassy. Our medical facility is more complete. He'll live. Thank the Creator, he'll live. And that girl..." he shook his head. "No weapons training. No discipline. No idea of what she was doing... and if we'd had another of her, we'd have been home two hours ago."

"She's that good?"

"I'm recommending her for the Ishkarin training camp, assuming the genetic tests prove me right," Virin answered. "I asked her on the way back, and she told me that she doesn't know who her father was. But she's got the instincts and the reflexes. That girl is a born Sword."

Rakesh started to laugh. "Damn it, Rin, I was sure that she'd make the choice for the Arena!"

"She'd have been wasted in a Collar, Kesh. Now, how many are we sheltering tonight?"

"Seventy-mumble. Something between seventy and seventy-five, I think. But maybe more. Jiren and I both lost count. Linter has them bedded down in the ballroom. And I have plans I need to discuss with you."

Virin nodded and sighed. "Later, Kesh. Lock the doors up. We're in for the night. Jiren, why don't you see if you can find a bed here tonight?"

"That's a good idea," Rakesh agreed.

"Are you sure?" Jiren asked, her eyes wide. "I don't live very far—"

"And everyone knows you work here," Virin interrupted. "We're not sure we got all the bastards. You and Kestri should stay here. We'll find you a proper bed."

"Thank you. I was going to ask for an escort, but staying here would be safer." Jiren frowned. "But I have no more clean diapers, no clothes for tomorrow. And Kestri's lambie is at home."

"Lambie?" Virin asked, sounding amused. "Let me guess. Some kind of bedtime toy?"

"Yes. She won't sleep without it. Her father made it for her."

"Sounds like Avira, then," Virin said. "One of our nieces."

"Oh, is that why you're so good with children?" Jiren asked.

"I have six older sisters," Rakesh answered. "So, we have sixteen nieces and nephews. At last count."

Virin nodded. "All right. Do you want one of us to go fetch?"

"Would you?" Jiren asked, her smile bright. "I'll make a list."

"Do that. Plan for several days. Come on, Kesh."

"Where are we going?" Rakesh asked as he closed the door and locked them, then set the alarms.

"Medical. This boy..." Virin looked at Rakesh, then looked away. "I want you to take a look at him."

———◉———

THE FIRST PERSON RAKESH saw in the medical facility was Ayani, sitting curled up in a chair that had been pulled up next to one of the regen capsules. She looked up as he came in, slowly uncurled herself and stood up.

"Rakesh?" she said softly, her voice quivering. Rakesh nodded and opened his arms. A moment later, he was holding a sobbing, shaking girl.

"It's all right, Ayani. He'll be fine. You saved him."

She hiccuped and nodded, her cheek rubbing against his chest. "He'll be all right, they said," she mumbled.

"You should get some sleep, Ayani," Virin said gently.

She sniffed and turned to look up at Virin. "I will. The medics said they'd find a cot for me. I... I want to stay here."

"Understandable. I spent a few nights sleeping next to regen capsules myself." Virin looked at Rakesh, smiled slightly, then reached out and patted Ayani's shoulder. "Have they offered you something to eat?"

"Yes."

"Good. Once you've eaten, get some rest. And if you need anything, tell the medics and they'll find one of us."

She nodded, letting go of Rakesh and moving to hug Virin. "Thank you."

He chuckled softly and hugged her back, kissing the top of her head. "You're welcome. And thank you. You did a fine job out there, Ayani."

She blushed, shaking her head. "And... you think I will be one of you? A Hunter?"

"I think you have potential, yes."

Ayani stepped back, clasping her hands behind her. "But... will I want to hurt people? Like... like *that*?"

Virin took a long breath, let it out, and Rakesh wondered why. Then Virin answered, "Not like that, no. Look... once Teren is out of the capsule, I'll take you down to the Floor myself. You can see what it's like for a real Sword. Not a perverted one like those Red bastards. We're protectors, Ayani. And you told me yourself that you've killed to protect your pack—"

"You have?" Rakesh interrupted. Ayani just looked at him as if he'd said something stupid. Perhaps he had, he realized. How else had she managed to survive so long?

"You never really know the ones you care about, do you, Kesh?" Virin asked, sounding amused. "Do you need anything now, Ayani?"

"No. Thank you." Ayani turned back to the capsule and went back to her chair. Rakesh turned to Virin, expecting Virin to take his arm. Instead, his husband nodded towards the capsule.

"Kesh... I want you to see him."

"All right." Rakesh walked over and peered through the clear hood of the capsule, seeing the young man inside. Despite the still-livid bruises on his face, Rakesh could see that Teren was very handsome. His thin face was all sharp angles, high cheekbones and a straight nose. His skin wasn't as dark as Rakesh's, not as pale at Ayani's. "How old is he?" he asked, turning back towards Virin.

"Nineteen," Ayani answered. "He says he's nineteen."

"He's sure?" Virin asked. "You weren't about yourself."

"That's because he was raised by his mother," Ayani said. "Not like the rest of us. Well, the rest of the pack. I knew her. She took me in off the streets when my mother disappeared. She took care of us, then we took care of her when she got sick."

"How old were you?" Rakesh asked.

Ayani shrugged. "I don't know. Three or four, I think? But she's the one who taught me to read."

"And his mother?" Virin asked. "Do we need to find her, tell her that he's all right?"

"She died, four years ago. That was when we took to the streets. We couldn't pay the rent on the house, and no one would hire a bunch of children. Teren says we have to take care of the little ones, the way his mother took care of us. That it was our responsibility to take care of our own." She frowned, then looked up at Virin. "And that's what you want me to do, too. Take care of the ones who can't take care of themselves."

"Exactly." Virin patted her shoulder. "All right. Tell the medics to call us if you need anything. Doesn't matter what time."

"Yes, sir. Goodnight."

Virin took Rakesh's arm and led him out of the medical facility. They walked silently through the embassy, then out into the covered walkway that led to the barracks. Rakesh looked at Virin, worried. There was a tension in him, something that felt to Rakesh as if it were going to shatter and break at any second.

"Rin?"

"Not yet, Rakesh," Virin answered, his voice tight. "Not here."

"All right." Rakesh let Virin set the pace, stumbling a little as Virin started to move faster as they reached their door. Inside, Virin let Rakesh go, walking over and sinking into his chair while Rakesh closed and locked the door behind them, then paused and engaged the hush field. He left his canes leaning against the wall, limping towards Virin and kneeling in front of him. Virin had slumped forward, his face hidden in his hands. He was shaking.

"Rin?" Rakesh rested his hands on Virin's thighs. "It was very bad?"

Virin nodded, taking a long breath. He dropped his hands, and Rakesh saw the traces of tears on his face. "... Kesh... they're hunting children. They're hunting babies. There were bodies in there, stacked like cordwood. And.. there... there was a girl in there... she couldn't have been older than four. Avira's age. She'd only been dead...a few hours, at most. They...." he stopped, shaking his head. "I... I think they did it in front of him. In front of Teren. Based on...on what we found, where we found him...that seems most likely."

"Part of his torture?" Rakesh asked. He shuddered. "Oh, Creator...."

"Right," Virin said. His voice was shaking. "Which makes you wonder how much they really know about the street packs, if they knew that much about him." He sighed and shook his head, leaning back in his chair. "We caught some of them. Ended sixteen of the red bastards. Ayani took down two, Creator love that girl. But there are more of them out there." He wiped his face with rough hands, looked at Rakesh. "I am going to end these bastards, Kesh. All of them."

Rakesh nodded, meeting Virin's eyes, seeing the determination there. And the desperate pain. Virin adored children, loved their nieces and nephews with his whole heart. Rakesh couldn't even imagine what it had been like for him. He swallowed hard and nodded again. "I know you will, love. Should you call this in to Molari?"

"I will. I just need...to get myself together. I... Creator, Kesh. I've never been...afraid before, of what I am. Of what I was made to be. Ashamed, yes. Especially after I hurt you, in the lift. But never...never *afraid*. Now...knowing that the Ishamar... They're Swords. Like me. This is something... I don't know. Kesh, this is something I'm capable of—"

"No," Rakesh snapped. "No, because you are not like that. Not like *them*. You know that. You tell everyone that. You are a protector, not a predator."

Virin stared at him for a moment. In a dull voice, he whispered, "We're all predators, Kesh. All of the Swords—"

"No, you are not!" Rakesh interrupted again, almost shouting as he pushed himself upright, feeling a surge of energy as he planted his feet. He pointed at Virin, who was staring at Rakesh as if he'd never seen him before. "Listen to me. Everything you've ever told me about the Swords, everything Iras has told me, everything I've ever read, it all says that what Mathias did was take your strength, your ruthlessness, all the abilities that you would have had naturally, and enhanced it. He made you more. You missed something, though. He didn't just enhance your abilities. He enhanced everything."

Virin blinked, looked confused. "I'm not sure I follow. And Kesh—"

"Listen to me first," Rakesh interrupted again. He turned and started to pace. "Look. People are light or dark. They either help or hurt. That's the way things are, the way things have always been. People who live in the light, those people, they try to help, they try to make the world a better place. The dark ones... well, they want what they want, and they don't care who they have to hurt to get it. When Mathias made the Swords, he enhanced that, along with everything else. So the good people, the protectors, the helpers, they became better. Men like you, love. Like Delan. Like your father, and Molari. And the ones who live in the dark...they got darker. Worse. The rogues, the Ishamar. Martiri. They are not like you, because you don't have that...that darkness. And the fact that you can ever worry about that shows that you never will."

Virin frowned. "I... I understand. I've never heard it put like that before. And...it explains why there are so damned many of them."

"Because darkness is easy to fall in to, and very, very hard to escape," Rakesh said. He took a deep breath and smiled slightly. "Now, you wanted to say something?"

"I..." Virin stammered, then rose and pointed at Rakesh. "Kesh, you...you're not limping."

Rakesh blinked. "What?"

"You're not limping!" Virin repeated. "You haven't, not since you stood up. You've been walking... Damn it, you've been pacing! And you haven't limped. Not once. I haven't seen you move like this in five years!" Virin shook his head, then stopped. "When did you put that on?"

"What?" Rakesh looked down at himself. "Put what on?"

"The bracelet. The one your father made. You told me you weren't going to wear it without me around to keep an eye on you."

"I..." Rakesh frowned, trying to remember. "I've been carrying it in my pocket, since I've been reading when the clinic is quiet. I... When you left to go after Teren, I put it on. It... It made me feel better."

"And now...you're not limping." Virin looked at Rakesh, wonder clear on his face. "Kesh, are you in any pain at all?"

Rakesh looked down at himself. "No. I...didn't notice. I was so...." he stopped, shaking his head. "I don't know."

"Angry," Virin filled in. "You were angry. Honestly, I can't say I've ever seen you that angry, Kesh."

"Was I?" Rakesh asked. He frowned, shaking his head. "Creator, Rin, I'm tired."

"Angry? Oh, yes. And I understand the tired, too. Come on." Virin put his arm around Rakesh's shoulder and steered him towards the bed. "It's been a long day. And you're not usually this close to the action. And... I wonder. Take it off."

"The bracelet?" Rakesh sat down, looked at his wrist. Then he looked back at Virin, his eyes wide. "Rin... this thing shrunk!"

"What?"

"It wasn't snug when I put it on before!" Rakesh held his arm out. "I could fit it over my hand. Now...look at it!" He turned his wrist, showing the bracelet that now looked as if it had been woven in place on his wrist. "That is not coming off!"

Virin took Rakesh's hand, picking at the edge of the bracelet. He hummed softly, then looked at Rakesh. "You're right. That isn't coming off. And I have a feeling that if I try to cut it off you, I'll hurt you badly. So it's staying where it is."

Rakesh pulled his arm back, ran his fingers over the bracelet. "I wonder what She's up to."

"Who?"

"The Spider."

Virin looked thoughtful, then put his arm around Rakesh's shoulder. "You said the Spider talked to you? Has that happened recently?"

"Not since we before we left Tyese. What are you thinking?"

Virin shrugged. "I'm not sure. Right now, my head is spinning. I think you might find out tonight."

"When I dream? Probably. I'll try not to wake you."

"Thanks. And thank you." Virin's arm tightened. "You always know what to say."

Rakesh smiled and leaned his head on Virin's shoulder. "You're a good man, Virin, and I love you. You're never going to be like them." He looked up at Virin. "Do you want anything tonight?"

"Creator, no!" Virin protested with a laugh. "I've had the hunting need purged for at least the next several days, and I'm too tired for sex. No, love. Tonight, I want to be held. That suit you?"

"That's fine." Rakesh yawned, then remembered something. "Why did you want me to see Teren?"

"Oh, I never did say, did I?" Virin dropped his arm. "He remind you of anyone?"

Rakesh turned and faced Virin. "Should he have? He's very handsome. But I can't think—" he stopped when Virin started to laugh. "What did I miss?"

"You don't have a drop of vanity, do you, Tarkarin?" Virin asked. "Love, how old were you when I had you the first time?"

Rakesh blinked, startled by the question. "You know that as well as anyone, Rin. I was two days short of my twenty-first birthday, and you were the best birthday present I've ever gotten. Why?"

"Because when I saw that boy, it was like looking at you, fifteen years younger," Virin answered. "Kesh, he looks just like *you*."

———◉———

THE DEEP VOICE SEEMED to come from the shadows of the ruins, and said a single word only: "And?"

"Sixteen down, sir," the young woman in red synth-leather answered. She looked down at the ground, knowing better than fidget, or try to see into the gloom. Perfect discipline was the key to success among the Ishamar. That, and knowing when to be the knife in the dark. She'd killed three rivals to get to this place. She was not going to lose it to laxity. "And the quarter is cleared of prey. As you anticipated, they've all been moved into the Embassy."

"All?"

"All, sir. Our surveillance showed seventy-three children entering via the clinic."

"Plus the two. And are there any signs that they suspect?"

"None, sir."

A long, low chuckle. "I knew the that son would be no better than the father. Blunted idiot. No real Sword would be so careless about the enemy. And what news from the north?"

"Tonight, sir."

Another low laugh. "Excellent. Keep me informed."

"Yes, sir."

Chapter Seven

Despite his expectations, Rakesh didn't dream, passing the entire night in quiet sleep, curled up with Virin in his arms. He woke before Virin and just laid there, warm and sleepy, his eyes closed, thinking of going back to sleep—

You are wondering why.

Rakesh grinned. *There you are. I was expecting you.*

Were you? I am pleased that you've taken in my children.

Did you think I'd have turned them away? Rakesh asked silently. *You're in my head. You should know me better than that!* Beside him, Virin sighed in his sleep and pulled closer, and Rakesh rubbed his cheek against Virin's short hair.

Others have. Are you pleased with what I have done?

If you mean fusing the bracelet to my wrist, not really. My father said to not wear the spidersilk in public. It might give me away.

It will not. This kind of weaving is common to my people, and I will obscure the fact that it is spidersilk. Until it is time.

What does that mean?

The time will come when you must be known, my own. But the bracelet was not what I meant. I meant taking your pain. So long as I am part of you, you will not feel the pain. If you had not been so timid, you could have been pain-free much sooner.

Rakesh blinked, flexing his feet. First the left, then the right. There was no pain at all. *Now, for that, I do thank you. Why, though?*

You will not be able to come to me on two sticks. And you must come to me, to do what you must do. But first, you must listen, my own. There is a traitor in your midst—

"What?" Rakesh said aloud, and felt the mental link snap, the shock leaving behind a hint of a headache. Next to him, Virin jerked and woke up.

"What is it?" he asked, scrubbing his hand over his face. "The medics call?"

"No," Rakesh answered. He closed his eyes and listened, then sighed and kissed Virin. "No, I was talking to Her."

"Her," Virin repeated. Then he coughed. "You mean the Spider. Again?"

"Yes. I think I should be worried at how...normal it's starting to feel, to have Her in my head." Rakesh slowly sat up. "She said that we have a traitor in our midst. And that's when I lost Her."

"A traitor?" Virin sat up. "Can you get Her back?"

Rakesh snorted. "I don't think it works like a sat-comm, Rin."

Virin scowled at him. "Right. A traitor. Inside the embassy. And you've no idea who?"

Rakesh shook his head. "None. But...I can guess."

"One of the older children." Virin let out a long sigh. "We can't turn them all out."

"No, we can't. But I never told you what I was thinking," Rakesh said. "We can move them to the building you set aside for the Collared. Use the supplies we brought for the Arena, set up a safe-house. And if we have them all under one roof—"

"We can watch them. Find out who. Good idea. We can't keep them all here, in any case. How do you feel this morning?" Virin asked as he got out of bed. Rakesh didn't answer immediately, enjoying the sight of Virin's naked ass as he walked across to the terminal. He stood there for a moment, looking at his messages. "Well?"

"I'm fine. She's responsible, by the by. For me not being in pain. Says that I need to come to her, and I can't do it on canes."

"Lovely. Next time you talk to Her, ask Her for plain answers." Virin turned, leaning against the table. "Nothing of import. Except for a pillow fight in the very early morning in the ballroom.... and apparently I spoke too soon," he said as the terminal chimed. He turned back, and went very still.

"What?" Rakesh asked, getting out of bed. "Rin, is something wrong?"

Virin turned slowly, his face pale. "There was an attack. Last night. On the training camp. Molari says that..." Virin stopped, closed his eyes. He shook his head. "He says total loss."

"No!" Rakesh gasped. "How many?"

"Not counting instructors? Four hundred twenty-nine children between the ages of ten and eighteen. Almost our entire next generation." Virin growled softly. "I... I need to talk to the men here. Some of them had children in the camps."

"Let us do it," Rakesh offered. "That's what we're here for."

"Thank you, but I need to make the announcement. Tell the Collared to be ready, though. They're going to be needed. And... Molari says he's going north, to see what he can find out. He's hoping that they might find survivors, cadet corps out on night maneuvers."

"You think it was them, don't you?" Rakesh asked. "The Ishamar?"

"I don't know. I think so. This fits what they've been doing here. And I haven't given my report on yesterday, not yet. I'll tape it now, zip it off to Molari." Virin folded his arms over his chest and frowned. "How many of them must there be, to be able to take down the entire school? And with what kind of arms?"

Rakesh shook his head. There was no answer he could offer for that question. In silence, he moved to Virin's side, kissed his cheek, and went off to get dressed.

"Don't forget your canes," Virin said absently as he sat down at the terminal.

"What? Why?"

"Protective coloration. And weapons. We don't want whoever this traitor is to notice you suddenly without your canes. And that reminds me. Do not open the clinic, Kesh. We need to take care of our own today."

"Yes, sir."

———⬥———

RAKESH WENT TO THE Collared dormitory first, waking Linter up and having him go roust the Taramar. The Tarkin were Rakesh's duty, and he walked down the corridor knocking on doors, hearing grumbling and cursing as Tarkin who had been kept up late the night before complained about being awakened far too early.

"Sorry, children," Rakesh called. "It can't be helped. I need you all dressed and ready and on the Floor in ten minutes."

"Rakesh, what's wrong?" someone called.

"Something bad. I'll tell you all at once." Rakesh leaned on his canes as he turned and made his way back up the corridor. "On the Floor in ten."

He didn't need to wait ten minutes. Linter came in with the Taramar only a few minutes after Rakesh reached the Floor, and the Tarkin came in as a group a moment later. Rakesh looked around, then nodded towards the door. "Someone close that?"

"Tarkarin, what is it?" Linter asked.

Rakesh took a deep breath. "We're going to be needed today. It's bad, children. Last night, the training camp was attacked. The Ranti-ar called it a total loss."

"Total?" one of the Taramars gasped. "Total as in... all the children? They're all dead?"

"Yes, Esha. All of the children. All of the instructors, and all of the cadets. How many of you have patrons here that have... that had children in the camps?" Rakesh looked around at the raised hands. "All right. You especially, you're going to be needed. They'll want the familiar. Don't be afraid to ask for help, though. I don't want to see any of you in medical for more than routine aftercare. Now, we're to be there when Virin tells the others. Go to them, do what you can. Help them. Understood?"

Linter raised his hand. "What happened yesterday, Rakesh? I heard a lot of commotion, then a patrol went out. Then there were children everywhere."

Rakesh nodded. "They... may be related. We found out yesterday that there are Ishamar here. The street packs call them Red Hunters. They've been hunting the street children. Ayani — the girl who has been helping out at the clinic — she came to us for help."

"Ishamar?" Linter murmured. "And... are you all right?"

"I'm not happy," Rakesh admitted. "But they can't get to us in the embassy. Now, let's go take care of our own. We can worry about the red bastards later."

Rakesh led the Collared down to the large meeting room where Virin had gathered the embassy staff and the Swords. They stood at the side of the room, watching, as Virin rose.

"My brothers and sisters-in-arms," he said slowly. "There is no gentle way of telling this. Last night, some unknown force attacked the Ishkarin training camp. The Ran-ti-ar is on his way there as we speak, but his preliminary report is that the camp was completely destroyed, and that loss of life was total." Even from where Rakesh was standing, he could see Virin swallow. "I... I am sorry."

"Total?" One of the older Swords stood, his face crimson. Next to him, Rakesh heard Linter hiss. "Total? I have two boys there! What do you mean, total? They can't... not my boys!"

"Linter, go," Rakesh murmured; Linter was already moving, pushing through the crowd to the Sword's side, pulling the older man into his arms as he collapsed, weeping over his sons. Other Collared followed him, and the crowd parted to allow them access to the grieving parents. Rakesh made his way forward, going to stand at Virin's side. Virin looked at him and nodded.

"Brothers, sisters, there isn't anything more I can say. Except that until further notice, we are on highest alert."

"What about the children, sir? The Aakari children?" Serris asked.

"Yes," Virin said with a nod. "Some of you may have noticed the additional personnel that we... acquired yesterday. I'm sure that those of you who were on the attack force with me have told the others what we found? I've made my report to the Ran-ti-ar, but given what happened, I don't expect any instructions any time soon. Until I hear otherwise, those children are under our protection. We may be moving them to the facility across the way, but for right now, they should be fine where they are. So long as there are no more midnight pillow fights." Virin tried not to smile at the ripple of uneasy laughter. "All right. Dismissed. Those of you who are on duty, report to your stations."

The Swords filed out. Several of them stopped to talk to Virin, to volunteer to take duty shifts over for the mourners.

"Will you send them home?" one Zaan-ti asked.

"If I can," Virin answered. "If I can get replacement troops here. We're short-handed as it is, and the men we were expecting were to be fresh from the camps. So we're on our own. Sending nearly a dozen men and women back to Tyese would cripple us. I'll know more once I hear from Molari."

"Understood, sir. And I'll take Hafer's duty shifts."

"Thank you, Kylier. Dismissed." Virin sighed as Kylier turned and walked out of the room. "Kesh, I wish I could send them back. But there's no way I can hold the embassy without them."

"Putting the children in the other building will be a security risk, wouldn't it?" Rakesh asked.

"Probably. But keeping them here will be a security risk, too. Which is less of a risk? I'll let you know. Come on. Let's look in on them. And they're decanting Teren now. He should be awake in an hour. I want to be there."

"All right." Rakesh fell in next to Virin as they walked out of the room. "Rin, have you eaten?"

"No. Have you?"

Rakesh snorted. "You know I haven't."

"Breakfast with the children?"

"I don't even know if someone saw to them!" Rakesh admitted. "Come on. Before they start climbing the walls."

When they walked into the ballroom, they found the room full of happy laughter, and all the children sitting on the floors and their pallets, eating. A table had been set up along one wall, and Jiren stood over a large pot, armed with a ladle, with Kestri asleep in a carrier on her back. She looked up and smiled as Virin and Rakesh walked in.

"Good morning!" she called. "Have you two eaten? There's porridge, and some fruit. Bread and jam, too. And tea."

"Jiren, you are a goddess," Virin said with a laugh. "We neither of us have eaten yet. How did you manage this?"

"I pointed out to your kitchen staff that seventy-three hungry children could easily do as much damage as one hungry Sword," Jiren answered. "After that, they were very helpful." She smiled and served them both, then brushed her hair back with the back of her wrist. "Eat while it's hot."

Rakesh took the bowl from her and had just turned away to find a chair when he was hit from the side, knocking him off balance. Something hit him from the other side, and a moment later, he was surrounded by children, all of them clamoring for his attention.

"One at the time!" he gasped, laughing, trying to juggle his bowl with one hand and two canes with the other. "One at the time, and back up! Or you'll all be wearing my breakfast!" Before the children could move, the bowl was taken from Rakesh's hands; he turned to see Virin, a bowl in each hand and an amused grin on his face. Rakesh smiled back, shifted one cane to his now-free hand, and raised his voice. "All right. Back up a bit!"

The children shuffled back far enough that Rakesh could go to one knee. Immediately, he was engulfed with hugs, and it took his a few minutes before he had the children settled and sitting on the floor around him.

"Did you all have a good night?" Rakesh asked as Virin handed him back his bowl. "I did hear about the pillow fight."

"That was fun!" one of the younger boys crowed. "Never done that before. Never ever had a pillow before!"

"Well, don't do it too often," Rakesh chided gently. "The guards need their sleep, too."

There was a wave of giggles, and Rakesh looked up at Virin. "What did I miss?"

"The fact that the guards were in on it," Virin answered. "Hafer and Serris and Myrte."

Rakesh grinned. Two of the three were had young children themselves, and Serris had grown up the youngest of three. All of them knew how to handle children... then he sobered, remembering that Hafer's sons had been in the training camp. Myrte's daughter, thank the Creator, was too young for the training camp, and lived with Myrte's husband in New Amali.

"*Aba* Kesh, is somethin' wrong? You got a sad?"

Rakesh shook his head. "Never you mind, Gira. It's... well, something bad happened last night."

Gira's eyes widened. "Where's Teren an' Ayani?"

"In medical. Teren will be fine, Gira," Rakesh answered. "And Ayani is with him. She slept there last night."

Gira smiled broadly. "Ayani is sweet for Teren. Did she tell you that? It makes her turn red."

Rakesh fought the urge to laugh. "I had actually figured that out, Gira."

"*Aba* Rakesh, what happens to us now?" one of the older boys asked. Rakesh frowned slightly, and the boy smiled. "Jetro, sir."

"Well, Jetro, it isn't safe to let you go back to your dens," Virin answered. "Kesh, eat. I'll talk." He turned back to the children. "You can stay here. All of you. We'll get proper beds, and we'll either make room here, or we'll move you across the way to one of the other buildings we've been preparing. As of last night, you are all fosterlings of the Tyesean government."

"What does that mean?" Jetro asked.

"It sort of means that you've been adopted," Rakesh answered. "If you have no objections and want to stay, I mean. We'll take care of you, provide food and clothes and medical care. You'll be able to go to school. And if you don't want to stay, we'll still help you—"

"You mean, you'll really be our father?" Gira asked. "Really really-ly?"

Rakesh blinked, looked up at Virin. They'd talked about adopting, had decided that between Virin's duty schedule and Rakesh's time in the Arena, it wouldn't be fair to the child. But now....

"Yes, Gira," Virin answered. "Rakesh will be your father. So will I. So will any of the Swords here. And Jiren here is your new mother." He grinned at Jiren, who looked stunned. "You don't have to call all of us *Aba* or *Ama*, though—*hey*!" Virin yelped as Gira scrambled to her feet and threw herself at him, hugging him hard around the waist. Then he knelt down and hugged her back, smiling as she kissed his cheek. "We'll take care of you, Gira-*sa*. All of you. I promise."

Gira smiled and poked him in the chest with one finger. "An' we'll take care of you, too. 'Cause families take care of each other, Teren says."

"Teren is right," Virin said. "So we'll all take care of each other. Now, if you'll excuse us? I wanted to go look in on Teren." He rose and rumpled Gira's hair, then came over to Rakesh and held his hand out. "Finished?"

"Yes. Thanks." Rakesh let himself be helped to his feet, then handed the bowl to Jiren. "All right. We'll be back later. If you need anything, you ask *Ama* Jiren or one of the Swords."

"Yes, *Aba* Rakesh!" The chorus of voices made the room ring, and Rakesh found himself grinning from ear to ear as he and Virin walked out into the hall.

"That wasn't what I had planned, Rin," he murmured.

"I know. It wasn't what I had planned, either. But there wasn't any way I was going to say no to her."

Rakesh leaned into Virin's arm. "You, my love, are a pushover for a little girl with big, dark eyes," he teased.

"You say that like it's a bad thing." Virin stopped in front of the lift doors. "And...I don't know. Maybe we can take that fortune you've let accumulate and actually have that family."

"You, me and seventy-three children?"

"And Jiren."

"Oh, of course. You, me, Jiren and seventy-four children," Rakesh said. "Rin, that's insane."

"And it will give every single one of those children a choice. And a chance." Virin walked into the open lift. "Not all of them will take it. You know that. Some won't want what we can offer. There's probably half a dozen of those older boys who will be gone tomorrow. I can see it in them. Some of the others will test into Sword training, and right now, we desperately need them. And some may find others they want to be their parents."

"Maybe. But that still leaves us with a very large family." Rakesh took a deep breath and leaned against the rear wall of the lift. "So...are we buying a farm?"

"Near your family?" Virin asked. He shrugged one shoulder. "Maybe. We could. Get them out of the city entirely."

Rakesh stared at Virin in shock. "Rin, you're talking about the both of us retiring, aren't you? Retiring and raising these children?"

Virin looked thoughtful. "We'd have to, wouldn't we?" Then he shook his head. "I don't know. And I shouldn't be thinking this now. I shouldn't be making these kinds of plans now. Not when I might be called into battle at any moment. So we'll keep them here. Keep them safe. And we'll see what happens."

Rakesh nodded and reached out to take Virin's hand. "Have I told you yet today that I love you?"

Virin frowned, then shook his head. "Don't think so. I can't remember. I love you, too."

"We'll be all right. And it will be one wonderful farm."

Virin nodded, then smiled slightly, starting forward as the lift doors opened. "It will, won't it? All right. We shelve this for now. Let's go see Teren."

———— ◉ ————

AYANI LOOKED UP AS they walked in. She was clean, her hair pulled back into a tail, and she was wearing new, clean clothes. She smiled and stood. "They're waking him up now. Did you come to see?"

"Yes. How are you doing this morning?"

"I'm fine. I slept well, and the medics gave me breakfast. And I had a real bath, and they found clothes for me." She held her arms out to show off her neat tunic and trousers. "I've never had clothes like this before. I like them."

"Good. We'll have to make sure that Teren has something to wear," Rakesh said.

Ayani nodded. "They salvaged what they could of his clothes, but really, there isn't much." She looked over at a small table, where

Rakesh could see a pitifully small pile. There was a knife, what looked like a belt, and...

"Ayani, what's this?" Rakesh asked, reaching out and picking up a small, square gold pendant. He studied it for a moment, trying to stay calm.

"Oh... that," Ayani murmured. She fell silent, and when Rakesh looked at her, he was amazed to see just how red her face had turned. "I was surprised that he still had it, that he hadn't lost it when they took him. He guards it very carefully."

"It's lovely. Where did he get this?"

"He did not steal it!" Ayani snapped. "It was his mother's. It's the only thing he has left from her, he told me. And he told me that when I am old enough, that it will be my promise."

"A promise?" Virin came over and looked at the pendant. He nodded, glancing at Rakesh. "You mean, like a pledge gift?"

Impossibly, Ayani turned even more red. "Maybe. I'm not old enough, he says. Not until next year. I do love him, though. And he loves me. So when I'm old enough...." she stopped and looked down, and her eyes widened. "Oh... I like your bracelet, " she said, reaching out to stroke Rakesh's wrist with one finger. "I had one like this. It fell apart, though."

"You did?" Rakesh forced the words out past the knot in his throat. "Who made it?"

"I don't know." Ayani shrugged. "Who made yours?"

"My father," Raizi answered, and had to bite his lip to keep from saying anything more. He met Virin's eyes, and Virin nodded.

"Kian-ti-os?" a medic said, coming towards them. "He's awake."

Ayani brushed past them and ran into the next room. Virin came closer and hissed, "Is that what I think it is?"

Rakesh nodded slowly. "It's the royal pendant. Female line. This came from one of my father's sisters."

"Which one?"

"Does it matter?' Rakesh asked.

"I suppose not. I'll have the medics check for genetic matches in the blood test. We'll know later today if he is related to you, Kesh. It could be no. It could be that someone stole that pendant, or found it in the ruins."

"I know." Rakesh laid the pendant down on top of the pile. "And the bracelet?"

"Could be nothing," Virin said. He took Rakesh's arm and started towards the door. "Raizi isn't the only one who can weave bracelets. Come on, love. I think we've given them long enough."

"Long enough?" Rakesh started to ask. Then he stopped, realizing what Virin meant as he caught a glimpse through the door of Ayani leaning over the bed. Virin looked at him, clearly amused, then tapped on the door-frame.

"May we come in?" he asked. Ayani squeaked and straightened, and didn't look up. Teren looked at them, then tried to sit up, only to wince and fall back.

"I... afraid... I.. not... not... stand... yet," he said in very slow, heavily-accented Tyesean. Rakesh coughed and looked at Virin, who looked startled.

"Don't try," Virin answered in Aakari. "Just because you're out of regen doesn't mean you're healed. It's nice to finally meet you."

Teren smiled. "Does having you save my life mean we've been introduced?"

"Not really, no." Virin moved to the side of the bed, held out his hand. "Virin Kian-ti-os."

"Teren," Teren replied with with a wry smile. He clasped Virin's hand, then let his own hand drop. "No surname that I know of." He looked over at Rakesh and smiled wider. "You, I know. You are Rakesh. I've seen you, the few times when you come outside of the clinic and into the street. You should not be standing."

"Thank you. And you're better than I am," Rakesh said as he sat down in the bedside chair. "I think I may have seen you once. That first night that Ayani came in, when she stayed late."

Teren grinned. "Yes, that was me. I was worried." He frowned and looked around. "And the pack?"

"They're all safe. We can bring them up to see you, a couple at a time. So we don't make the medics mad," Rakesh answered.

Teren smiled slightly. Then he sobered. "And what now, Kian-tios? What happens to us now?" he asked.

Virin nodded. "Let me raise that bed. I imagine you don't want to have this conversation lying down?"

"Thank you. I would rather sit up."

Virin picked up the controls and used them to raise the head of the bed so that Teren was sitting up. He handed the console to Teren, then backed away, standing at the foot of the bed. "Now what?" Virin repeated. "For right now, you're staying in that bed. Until you heal, at which point, you have the same choice that every other street child that came in here last night has. To stay, or to go."

"You're letting us go?" Teren asked, sounding shocked. "All of us?"

"Once it's safe, yes. And if you want to go. I can tell you right now, I think Gira's adopted me and Kesh, and I don't think she'll want to leave." Virin smiled slightly. "And, I've no objections. But that's the choice. Whoever wants to stay, can stay. You'll be considered fosterlings of the Tyesean government, possibly granted dual-citizenship, if I can get the Ruling Council to agree to that. If any of you prove to be the children of Swords, then you will be automatically granted citizenship, and the benefits due to any child of ours, and will be welcome to test for training."

"What sort of testing?" Teren pointed at Rakesh. "Will you push my girls into *that*?"

"No!" Rakesh answered. "We only take willing volunteers into the Arena, only over the age of eighteen, and there is a testing process they have to go through first. We only take two or three out of every ten. None of the girls that Ayani brought in were accepted, so we helped them find other places off the streets. Didn't Ayani tell you that?"

"He did not believe me," Ayani murmured.

"Regardless," Virin continued. "If you want to leave, then when you are able to, you're welcome to do so."

Teren nodded, then looked thoughtful. "I am nineteen. Too old to be considered a fosterling."

"But not too old to start training," Rakesh said thoughtfully. "I can bring up copies of the books that I gave to Ayani. If nothing else, it will help pass the time."

Teren stared at him for a moment. "Training?" he sputtered. "Training?" He pointed at Rakesh again. No, Rakesh corrected himself. At his collar. "Do you have any idea what they did to me in there?" Teren demanded.

"Probably something very similar to what they did when they took me," Rakesh answered quietly. He held up one cane. "There's a reason for these, Teren. They crushed my feet, so I couldn't run. Broke all of my fingers, so I couldn't fight them. They—"

"Kesh, enough!" Virin snapped, just as Teren whispered, "Don't...." His face was pale, and he swallowed and looked away. He looked back after a moment, frowning. "You... You understand, then. But I don't. You still wear a collar. You still let them hurt you. Darkness, *why*?"

"Well, yes and no—" Rakesh started to answer, stopping when Ayani groaned.

"That is your favorite way to answer a question!" she said with a giggle.

"It's true, though!" Rakesh protested. "I do still wear a collar. But I no longer serve. I train. The only person who is allowed to touch me is Virin. That is what the Black means. One person, and one person only."

"It would be a long while before you would be able to take the Black, if you went that route," Virin added. "A year of training. Five years in the White. And for you, Ayani, we'd be looking at at least that long in training before you made ir-Zaan. You're starting years late. Then perhaps that long again before you had sufficient rank to be allowed to marry."

"What?" Teren gasped. "You? Ayani.... You? A Hunter?"

"He says I might be able to be that. To be something more that prey. To be a protector. Like him." She looked shyly at Virin. "Like the others here. I could protect more than just our pack."

"She's got the instincts. She killed two Ishamar yesterday to get to you," Virin added. "The hard part would be the waiting. Trust me, I do understand that part. I waited seven years for Rakesh. So, could you wait five years or more, Teren?"

Teren scowled. "I've already been waiting that long.... My pendant!" he gasped, looking down at himself. He groped at his naked throat, a look of near panic on his face. "Ayani, it's gone!"

"No, it isn't. It's in the other room," Ayani told him. "I found it."

Teren relaxed, closing his eyes. Without opening them, he asked, "And if I choose not to enter your training, Rakesh?"

Virin answered, "We're testing you and every other child to see if you've the genetic markers of a Sword. If you do, you can enter training with Ayani. If you don't, you could still enter training, to become a peacekeeper or a general guard. You could go to school, or apprentice for a trade. We'd help you with whatever you wanted. So the real question, Teren, is what *do* you want?"

Teren didn't answer the question. Instead, he opened his eyes and looked at Virin. "My father was a Sword. My mother told me that. He was stationed here, and she was his housekeeper. And she was...other things. She told me that when he found out about me, he promised to marry her. But he didn't have the rank. Then he went away, and never came back."

Virin nodded slowly. "Do you know his name? We can find out from the tests, but if you know...."

"*Ama* told me that she named me for him. But I don't know if his name was Teren, or if she did what your people do and changed it."

"All right. Some twenty years ago, and possibly Teren or some variant of the name. I'll check."

"Teren, do you want to talk?" Rakesh asked. "If not with me, then with someone?"

Teren looked at him, his eyes wide. He shook his head slowly. "Not... Not yet. I... Not yet."

"Whenever you're ready," Rakesh said. He stood up slowly, leaning on his canes. "We'll let you be now. Ayani, he's going to sleep, a lot. If you want, Jiren could use your help with the children."

"I'll come when Teren sleeps."

"Thank you." Rakesh turned towards the door, and was halfway there when Teren's voice stopped him.

"Rakesh?"

"Yes, Teren?"

"May I have those books?"

Chapter Eight

True to Virin's prediction, eighteen of the older boys and girls were gone by the next day. Rakesh wished them all well, made sure that they had food and clothes, and warned them that the clinic was not going to be opening again until the crisis was over. He didn't have any say in the matter—orders from the Ran-ti-ar came in, sealing the embassy, recalling all non-essential personnel and closing the clinic until further notice. He also requested any and all potential Sword trainees be sent immediately to Arena City. On the transport that was set to take the non-essential personnel away, there would also be twenty boys and twelve girls who were confirmed as the children of Swords, and who had expressed interest in the training.

But not Ayani. She refused to leave Teren, who had not been released from medical. When Rakesh arrived, bringing a datapad loaded with the training books that he'd promised, he found Teren chafing at the orders to stay in bed.

"I thought your advanced healing technology meant that no one had to stay in bed to heal!" Teren complained.

"Depends on how badly you're hurt, and how well you respond to regen," Rakesh answered, sitting down in the chair next to the bed. "After they decanted me, I was still confined to my bed for over two weeks. But I was in bad shape. I don't think you were as bad as that. What have they told you?"

Teren frowned. "Not much."

"So?" Rakesh turned in his chair and raised his voice. "Medic?" He heard footsteps, then a young man in a medic's jumpsuit appeared in the doorway. His rank pins showed that he was a very junior medic, and Rakesh frowned.

"Yes, Tarkarin?" he asked.

"What's the status on this patient?" Rakesh asked, nodding towards Teren. "Diagnosis, prognosis, all that? He says you haven't been telling him much."

"Ah..." he colored slightly and didn't answer. Rakesh blinked in surprise and slowly got to his feet.

"Medic, are you honestly telling me that you're not giving a patient information on his own injuries?"

His eyes widened, and he swallowed before answering, "Sir, he's—"

"A guest of Tyese?" Rakesh supplied, letting a hint of chill show in his voice. "As are the children who remain. Have you not been informed of that?"

"We have, Tarkarin, but we thought that meant he was...well...in custody."

Rakesh rolled his eyes and glanced at Teren, who had gone very still. "He is not, medic. When we said guest, we meant *guest*. As soon as he is able, he will be allowed to leave, if he chooses. Furthermore, he is the acknowledged son of a Sword, and a Tyesean citizen—"

"He is?" he squeaked. It was enough to push Rakesh's temper to the breaking point.

"Find the senior medic. Now," he snapped. The medic scurried from the room, and a few minutes later, an older woman came in. Her rank pins showed that she was the senior medic.

"Tarkarin?" she said.

"Medic...Danila, is it not?"

"Yes, Tarkarin," she said, bowing slightly.

"Danila, it appears that your information about your patient and the children that we are fostering is inaccurate. There is no one in custody here. There are no prisoners here."

Danila arched an eyebrow. "Is that so?"

A voice came from behind her: "Yes, it is."

Danila went pale as Virin spoke, turning around to face him as he entered the room. "Where are you getting your information, Senior Medic? Who told you that this young man was a prisoner?"

"I... he's Aakari!" the medic insisted, as if that explained everything. Rakesh bristled, but stopped when he saw Virin glance at him and shake his head. So he sat down on the edge of Teren's bed and waited.

"I see. He's Aakari, and therefore must be a prisoner?" Virin said softly.

"There are no good Aakari," Danila said, her voice firm. Rakesh growled softly, but Virin didn't seem to notice.

"I see," he repeated. "There has been no one looking in on the rest of the children who came in last night, and I know I gave orders for them to be examined. And the tests that I ordered run have not yet been delivered to me for a paternity check. Is this all your doing?" The woman didn't answer, and Virin nodded. "Yes. I do see. Who is your assistant, Senior Medic?"

The medic frowned. "Ah...that would be Makara, Kian-ti-os."

"Makara? Kesh, why do I know that name?"

"She's been on duty in the clinic almost every time you've come down. She's been a huge help to me," Rakesh answered. "I hadn't realized that she was that senior."

"Yes. Thank you." Virin nodded, then looked at his wrist-comp. "The transport back to Arena City lifts in twenty minutes, Danila. Pack."

"What?"

"You're leaving. I won't have a bigot in my embassy, especially not one who thinks that she can countermand my orders, ignore them outright, or keep information from me that I requested. So get yourself packed and get yourself out." Virin looked at his wrist again. "You have nineteen minutes. Don't take anything that belongs to the embassy. Now move!"

She opened her mouth to say something, looked at Virin, then turned and hurried from the room. To Rakesh, it looked like she was trying to maintain some measure of dignity, while at the same time running for her life. Virin scowled at her retreating form, then shook his head and turned towards Rakesh and Teren.

"Teren, I apologize. She was a legacy."

"A what?" Teren asked.

"I inherited her with the embassy. I should have realized that Tarason's people would all be narrow-minded bigots—"

"Not all," a calm voice said from the doorway. Makara walked in. "Some of us were trying to do the right thing, regardless of the opinions of our superiors. How may I serve, Kian-ti-os?"

"Start by accepting a promotion."

"Excuse me?" Makara gasped. "A promotion?"

"You are now the embassy's Senior Medic," Virin said. "So say thank you, and I'll ask my next question."

"Thank you, Kian-ti-os," Makara stammered. "And the next question?"

"Diagnosis and prognosis for Teren? Also, are the genetic tests back?"

"I haven't been involved in his case. So I'm not sure. Let's see." Makara went to the corner terminal and started typing. "Goodness, child. Someone does not like you."

"I think I figured that out," Teren said, his voice flat. "When can I get out of bed?"

"Ah... I'll have to run some scans to be completely certain you're healed enough. You seem to have a bit of regen resistance. But there were no broken bones. A few cracked ribs, but that's not terrible. Otherwise, mostly just deep muscle damage and tearing. So... tomorrow soon enough for you?" She turned and looked at him, then grinned. "No, I see not. I can offer you a hover-chair."

Teren's grin was small, but it was there. "I can get up?"

"So long as you stay off your feet. I don't want to have to put you back into a regen capsule because you pushed too hard."

"Senior Medic, what was the extent of the injuries?" Virin asked.

"Deep muscle damage, as I said. Mostly in the legs and lower back. Internal bleeding from ruptured organs, cracked ribs. Lacerations to the wrists and ankles, and to the face." Makara turned back to the terminal. "On the whole, young man, you were lucky. They didn't have you long enough to do life-threatening damage. You'll hurt, but you'll heal. If you weren't resistant, you'd have been discharged already."

"That... makes it sound like they were playing with him," Rakesh said softly. "Like...."

"Like they didn't want to kill him," Virin finished. He folded his arms over his chest. "Teren, did they say anything while they had you? What do you remember?"

Teren licked his lips and frowned. "I.... I'm trying to think. It's... Honestly, it's all a blur. I knew that if they took Ayani or the children, we wouldn't even find pieces. So I made them hide, and I led the hunters away. I didn't expect them to catch me, but...I think they knew where I was going." He looked up. "How could they know where I'd go?"

"We think they were watching you," Virin answered. "Still not sure why. I'll ask them before I kill them Now go on."

"Yes, sir. They grabbed me as I came out from under..." he paused, then shook his head. "You wouldn't understand. You don't know the pack roads. After, I'm not sure where they took me."

"A ruin outside the palace walls," Virin answered. "At least, that's where we found you."

"If you say so," Teren said. He reached up and rubbed the back of his neck. "They... Do you really want to know what they did?"

"No, son. Just what they said. If they said anything."

Teren nodded, then leaned back and stared at the ceiling for a long moment. "Most was in Tyesean. Which I really am not very good with. *Ama*, she wanted me to learn, but..." He shook his head. "I don't know. They did a lot of talking. A lot of laughing. But I couldn't really tell you what they said. I didn't understand it."

"That's all right, Teren," Rakesh said. "We'll find them, and then we'll find out. Now, do you want that hover-chair? Because I brought the books."

"Books, or out of bed?" Teren grinned again. "That's a hard choice to make. Show me the books first?"

"Before you start, I have something else I want to show you, Teren." Virin took another datapad out from under his arm and turned it on. "This was why I came. Not to deal with Danila." He passed the 'pad to Teren. "When I didn't get the test results, I overrode Danila's security and pulled the information. She did run the tests on Teren and Ayani, but she was in the process of erasing the data when I grabbed it. We'll have to redo Ayani's tests. I ran Teren's through the Sword database and got a paternity match. Teren, your father's name was Tarant Zaan-ti-ar. And I should have recognized the name. You should have, too, Kesh."

"I do," Rakesh gasped. "That was Akera's intended!"

"Who's Akera?" Teren asked.

"My oldest sister," Rakesh said. Teren's head jerked up. "She's almost twenty years older than I am. She took a Sword for a lover, had two children by him before he was murdered. I was small when this happened. I barely remember him."

"He was murdered along with my father and the Ran-ti-ar," Virin added. "He was the driver of the aircar they were using when someone planted a bomb in the 'car."

Teren frowned. "He had a woman already. So... he lied? He wasn't going to marry my mother? He was already married?"

"He wasn't married, Teren," Rakesh said "What he told your mother about not having the rank was true. He didn't. I imagine that he was going to break the engagement with Akera to marry your mother."

"He was. He left personal papers behind, journals where he acknowledged that he had sired a child in Aakar, drafts of the letter he was going to send to Akera breaking off the engagement. I found reference to them in his records. But he never identified your mother, Teren. Not even as his housekeeper. He just said that he met a woman in Aakar. That he fell in love. That she was having his child. Nothing more. So no one knew where to look for her and for you." Virin leaned on the foot-board of the bed. "I can contact the archives, get those journals for you if you like. And... the pledge bracelet that he bought for her. He was expecting a promotion. From his records, he was due for one."

"I... Yes, please," Teren said slowly. "And...now what?"

"Now, you're a Tyesean citizen. A rather high-caste one, at that. You have a pension as the surviving child of a Sword. And two half-siblings, a brother and a sister. Kesh?"

"Keran and Tara. Keran is a farmer. Tara is a medic, and she's married to another medic and lives in Maryst," Rakesh answered. "Neither of them was really old enough to remember their father. Keran was three when Tarant died, and Tara was an infant. Akera's second husband is the father they know."

"So, you have a family. Of sorts," Virin said. "What you do now is entirely up to you."

Teren looked down at the two datapads on his lap, then looked up. "I'd like that hover-chair, please?"

⸺⊙⸺

"WHERE ARE WE GOING?" Rakesh asked, walking alongside the chair as he and Teren left the medical unit.

"I'm curious about my options," Teren answered. "Why don't you use one of these?"

"Pride," Rakesh said immediately. "I imagine I'll have to have one eventually. But for now, I'm going on my own two feet."

"I understand that," Teren said. "Where can we see the Swords training?"

"There's a training area at the back of the embassy, behind the barracks. We can go there now, if you like."

Teren nodded. "And...what about the Collared?"

Rakesh glanced at him, saw the flush on Teren's face. He ignored it. "They're here, in the Embassy."

"Can we see them first?"

"If you like," Rakesh said with a smile. "It's late enough that there should be someone on the Floor. We can watch. This way."

He led the way to the lift. Teren followed silently, and Rakesh looked back at him quickly before pushing the call button for the lift. "Ayani said you didn't believe what I told her," he said.

"I didn't. It seemed impossible. That you put yourself in the way, to keep others from being hurt?" Teren said. "Then...I was thinking, last night, after you left. And...that's just what I did, wasn't it? I was the target, so that Ayani and the pack wouldn't get hurt. That's what you do."

"That is just what I did," Rakesh agreed, stepped into the lift. "What the others still do."

"And...it's something I could learn to do well."

"If you're accepted for training."

Teren nodded, looking thoughtful. "What happens when you're done? When you've served your five years?"

"You're granted a lifetime pension and high-caste status, if you leave the collar. If you stay, you become a Taramar, a Red-collar. Your earnings are banked for you, and you basically become one of the elite of the Arena. You also start teaching the novices at that point."

"Your collar is black. Black and gold. You said the black means only one person can touch you. What does the gold mean?"

"That I'm Senior Trainer, and second to the Chief Trainer. She wears all gold." The lift doors opened, and Rakesh nodded. "Here we are."

Teren hesitated for a moment, then drew himself up and drove the hover-chair out onto the Floor. Rakesh followed him, coming to stand next to Teren as he stopped and stared.

"Not too busy right now," Rakesh commented, looking around. "That's Serris, over at the whipping frame. And... oh, hello, Hafer," Rakesh turrned as the Sword came towards them. "How are you?"

"I'm... managing, thank you, Tarkarin. Have you seen Linter?"

"Not today, no."

Hafer grimaced. "I'm afraid I went at him a bit hard last night. You understand... I'm sure he's all right. I made sure of that before I left him. But I was still worried about him."

Rakesh nodded. "I do understand. And I haven't seen him." He looked around, saw a pretty, delicate-looking girl in a white collar coming towards them. Rakesh grinned when he saw her.

Petite, blonde Janera had been a no-caste girl when she'd tested into training, and no one had thought she'd make it through the first day. They were all wrong. Now a third-year Tarken, Janaera had been a joy for Rakesh to train. Her enthusiasm was unbridled, her capacity for both pain and pleasure rivaled Rakesh's own, and her skills as a counselor far exceeded anyone's expectations. She often spoke of how much she was looking forward to taking the Red, and Rakesh privately expected her to someday succeed him in the Gold—she was good enough that he had contracted her for Virin's last birthday, presenting her as a gift, much to the delight of his husband.

She came to him and hugged him tightly, then smiled at Teren. Rakesh kept his arm around her shoulder as he addressed her, "Janera, my dear. Your room is next to Linter's, isn't it?"

"Yes, Tarkarin," the girl answered. She smiled up at him, then slipped out from under his arm and went to Hafer. "Kian-ti, Linter was looking for you this morning. He offers his regrets, but he's been taken off the Floor for the next three days. He asked me to take care of you, if that meets your pleasure?"

Hafer looked at her, then nodded. "That does. Thank you, Janera. I'll look in on Linter later, make sure he's doing all right. How do you feel about knives, my dear?"

Janera smiled. "That was why Linter asked me to see to you." She took Hafer's arm, smiled at Rakesh, and led the Sword away.

"He's really going to use knives on her?" Teren asked, his voice cracking slightly as it spiraled up.

"Janera's a bit notorious with her preferences. She likes edged weapons. Well, she likes everything, but especially knives." Rakesh turned towards Teren. "Linter usually doesn't, but Hafer had become a regular for him, and last night...." He stopped, grimaced. "I can't break confidences. Suffice it to say that Hafer needed careful handling last night."

"I heard something. That medic was gossiping outside my room, and she's louder than she thinks she is," Teren said. "Something about an attack? A training camp?"

"The Sword training camp. Over four hundred children killed." Rakesh sighed. "A good number of the pack children who showed up as having Sword potential have been sent off to Tyese for further evaluation and training. Did Ayani tell you?"

"Yes. And she told me that Hagari and his pack are back on the streets," Teren said. "That's good. He'll keep you informed, so long as you keep feeding him and his pack."

"I'll tell Virin," Rakesh said. "Now, is there anything in particular you want to see?"

"I wouldn't know what to ask for," Teren admitted. "What do you think I should I see? So that I understand?"

"We can start with the whipping frames." Rakesh smiled, remembering the training session in Tyese. "It's the place most people start, Collar or Sword." He stopped, frowned. "Actually, you said you want to see what we do. What we really do. Right?"

"Yes."

"Then let's go and watch Hafer."

⸺⬤⸺

TEREN LOOKED AROUND the room where Rakesh led him, one that was empty save for electronics. "I thought we were going to watch?"

"We are. Just not overtly." Rakesh sat down at the terminal and touched a button. "Control."

Acknowledged.

"Video and audio on Hafer Kian-ti. On screen." Rakesh turned to look at Teren. "Come on. We can watch them from here."

The screen brightened, and showed another room. Hafer was bent over a table, lighting a candle in a low bowl. He turned to Janera, who was standing near the wall, her arms behind her back. She was already naked except for her control bands.

"The bracelets and armbands she wears—that all Collared wear—those can be used to bind her," Rakesh said. "I would imagine that her wrists are bound right now, the way she's standing. Some Swords like rope or chain. Some just use the control bands. Depends on who you're with."

"And, they all do that. Tie you up?" Teren asked, maneuvering his chair in next to Rakesh.

Rakesh nodded. "Usually. It's freeing."

"Freeing isn't how I'd describe it. Terrifying as hell, maybe."

Rakesh grinned. "The situation is different here. Remember, this is something that you want. Being tied up, putting yourself completely in the hands of someone you trust implicitly, that is one of the most erotic things I've ever encountered."

"If you say so," Teren said, and the doubt was clear in his voice. "What's he doing now? And what's the candle for?"

Rakesh studied the screen. "Blindfold. It heightens sensation. Now, let's see. What is he...? Ah. I see why he picked that room."

"Because of that thing?" Teren asked. Rakesh nodded, watching as Hafer led Janera forward, released her arms, then strapped her into a frame. Unlike the whipping frames, this one forced Janera up into her toes, with wooden stocks that locked her ankles into place. She was bent at the hips over a padded surface, and her arms were drawn down and locked into place with similar stocks.

"Yes. That. It's not bad once you're strapped in. Fairly comfortable, since the surface takes your weight, and it's really well-padded. Now watch. Remember you wanted to know about him using knives? What do you think he'd going to do?"

Teren looked at Rakesh. "He's going to cut her," he said, his voice flat.

"No, he isn't. Watch." Rakesh turned back to the screen, watching as Hafer picked up the bowl, now filled with liquid wax. As they watched, Hafer held the bowl up and dribbled the wax over Janera's naked back. She tensed and gasped, squirming in place. Hafer laughed, and ran one hand over her ass while pouring more wax with the other.

"Doesn't that hurt?"

"Not as much as you think," Rakesh answered. "That wax is specially made—it melts at a much lower temperature than the candles you might use at home. All it does is sting a little. And it goes solid very quickly."

Teren leaned forward, watching until Janera's back was almost completely covered in thick, dark red wax. As the Sword set aside the empty bowl, Teren shook his head. "I don't see the point. And what about the knives?"

"Keep watching."

Teren nodded, then gasped; Rakesh turned back the screen and saw Hafer, a knife in each hand. He ran the blades down Janera's sides, making her giggle.

"Wait... Why is she laughing?"

Rakesh laughed. "She's ticklish. Keep watching, Teren."

Hafer stood behind her, close enough that his groin was pressed against Janera's ass, and slowly ran the knives over her skin once more. This time, Janera moaned. Rakesh touched a control, and the camera zoomed in enough that they could see a narrow welt rising along Janera's side. Hafer shifted the blades, turning them so that the edge was resting along Janera's wax-covered back. He drew the knives towards him, shaving a thin layer of wax from her skin. He continued, tracing patterns into the thick wax with the point of a knife, then erasing it with the blade, slowly peeling long curls of wax from Janera's skin, then delicately tracing more patterns in the heat-reddened skin underneath. When Hafer finally stepped back and started removing his uniform, Janera's skin was covered in ornate welted traceries in a design as intricate as any tapestry, and she'd had two orgasms.

"Control, cease transmission." Rakesh turned towards Teren as the screen went dark, noticing Teren's flush. His quick breathing.

"That... That is counseling?" Teren demanded after a moment.

"I expected him to be more aggressive, actually," Rakesh admitted. "He must have worked enough of his anger out on Linter last night. But yes. This is counseling. After this, he'll be able to work through his grief."

Teren looked up sharply. "Grief? Oh, Darkness... That training camp?"

"Hafer had two sons there," Rakesh said softly. "He'll take Janera now, and he'll probably end up in tears by the time she's done with him. Tonight, maybe tomorrow, Hafer will ask to sit down with me, or with one of the senior counselors here who isn't in a Collar. For a Sword, for a lot of people, release is the first part of healing."

Teren leaned back in his chair, rubbing his upper lip with his fingertips. "I never thought about that. About the Hunters having families of their own. How many...? I don't even know what I'm asking."

"How many have families?" Rakesh asked. Teren nodded. "Swords who earn the rank Kian are allowed to marry. Some of them marry other Swords. Others marry retired Collared. We understand them, you see." He stopped, thinking. "How many have families? Maybe about half of those with sufficient rank. The four hundred children who died the other night, they were almost the entire next generation of Swords. The only ones left are those under the age of ten."

Teren looked sick. "That's why you sent the ones who came from the packs off?"

Rakesh nodded. "They're needed. They're desperately needed. The attrition rate for Swords is still far too high, and only six in ten of their children become Swords themselves. If the Sword marries someone who isn't a Sword, that number drops to two in ten. The genes are recessive."

Teren looked thoughtful. "A good thing, I suppose. That means that the Swords won't overrun everyone else. If they need people so much, why is Ayani still here?"

"She wouldn't leave you," Rakesh said with a smile. "But that doesn't mean that she isn't already in training. That's our next stop." He stood up. "Then I'll leave you alone to think for a while. Unless you want to think out loud, in which case I'm willing to be a sounding board."

In the hallway, Teren cleared his throat. "That didn't look so bad. The wax and knife thing, I mean."

"It isn't. I rather like it. But Virin would tell you I like most things." Rakesh leaned against the wall next to the doors to the lift. "The hot wax makes the skin more sensitive. And the knife blades aren't sharp enough to cut. The tip is, though. And Hafer likes tip work. That's why you saw the marks. But he's good. I've never had a lasting scar from him."

"You've done that? With him?" Teren's jaw dropped. "If I did this. Let you train me. Then...would I be expected...with a man?"

"Most Collared do, yes. But it isn't required. You'd be tested for aptitude," Rakesh answered. "If your preferences are for females only, then that would be noted in your profile, and the Control Computer would refuse requests from males on your behalf."

"Oh," Teren said softly. "That... That's good." He didn't say anything else. All the way down on the lift, and out into the courtyard, he was silent, with a small wrinkle between his brows that Rakesh found amazingly endearing. He didn't break his silence until they were more than halfway down the walkway, almost at the barracks.

"Rakesh?" Teren asked quietly. "Why do you carry the canes if you don't need them? You keep forgetting to use them." He looked around, and pitched his voice lower. "If you mean to make people think you still need them, you need to actually use them."

Rakesh looked down, realizing that he had indeed forgotten to use the canes, reveling in the simple ability to walk without assistance. "Thank you. And...I'm not sure how much I should explain to you. How much I can explain. But we'll talk after."

"You don't have to explain anything, Rakesh. I'm in your debt. I will keep your secrets." Teren pointed. "Is that where we're going?"

"Yes," Rakesh answered. He followed behind Teren and wondered what Virin's reaction would be when he found out that Rakesh had taken Teren into his confidence. Because he'd decided that was exactly what he was going to do. And somewhere in the back of his mind, he could hear the Spider laughing.

You have something to say? Rakesh asked silently.

Tell the boy. Tell him everything.

Chapter Nine

"What are we doing here?" Teren asked. Rakesh closed the door to the quarters that he shared with Virin, then engaged the hush field.

"I wanted to show you something. In confidence. And explain about these," Rakesh answered, setting the canes aside. "I wasn't lying to you about my injuries. I can bring up the reports, if you want to see."

Teren frowned. "You use the canes sometimes, but then you forget. So...you need them usually. But not now?"

"No. Because...." Rakesh hesitated, sitting down next to the table. "Teren, I'm going to tell you something. And I want you to tell me if you recognize it. All right?"

Teren looked completely mystified, but he nodded. "Yes. Go ahead."

"The Dark Spider."

Teren's eyebrows shot up into his hair. "Be good, or the Spider will eat you?" he asked. "That Spider?"

Rakesh blinked. "Now you've confused me. I don't know what you're talking about."

"Sorry. Thought your mother might have used that on you. When I was very small, my mother would tell me to be good, or the Dark Spider would eat me. I have no idea where she got that from. None of the others know it."

"Interesting. Tell me about her?"

"My mother?" Teren asked. He frowned slightly. "Her name was Tiva. She was a house-servant for the garrison. Then, after she had me, she took in washing. We never had much, but...it was enough. The only thing of value she ever had was this." He fished into his shirt and pulled out the gold pendant. "And she gave it to me when she died. Told me never to sell it."

"Yes. That pendant. Do you know what it means?"

"It means something?" Teren looked down at the pendant. "It's pretty. That's all I know."

A buzzer sounded, and Rakesh got up and let Virin in, reengaging the hush-field. Virin looked at them both, then cleared his throat. "Kesh, is there something I should know?"

"Nothing like that, Rin."

"Good. Because I'd want to watch." He grinned at Teren, who groaned.

"Behave yourself, love. Teren pointed out that I keep forgetting to use my canes."

Virin winced. "Not good, Tarkarin. And...that doesn't require a hush-field. So what else are you doing?"

Rakesh took a deep breath. "She wants me to tell him."

"Oh," Virin breathed. "I see. I wondered why I suddenly needed to be here in the middle of the day. All right."

"Who wants you to tell me what?" Teren asked.

Rakesh looked at him, then went to the desk and took a small box out of a drawer. He handed it to Teren. "Open it."

Teren frowned, then opened the box. His jaw dropped. "This... This is like mine!"

"Only not quite. Look closer."

Teren picked Raizi's pendant out of the box and held it up next to his own. "Yes. I see the difference. But...how did you get this? Is this Tyesean?"

"No," Rakesh answered, taking the pendant from Teren. "No, this is Aakari. This belonged to my father. Teren, these pendants were made for the children of the royal house."

Teren's pendant fell from his finger to thump against his chest. "Royal house?"

"My father is, quite probably, the one you call the Lost One," Rakesh said. "He was the son of Tragar and the Spider Priestess Sarjana."

"That... That's a really odd joke, Rakesh," Teren said, his voice shaking. "I mean...I'm not laughing."

"I'm not laughing, either, Teren. Father told us he was a boy when Tragar murdered Sarjana because she wouldn't turn from the Dark Spider to worship him as a god. *Aba* was imprisoned inside the Palace, and kept as...as a breeding stud for his sisters."

Teren looked down at his pendant, back up at Rakesh. "My mother...was your sister?"

Rakesh nodded slowly. "I think it might be possible, Teren."

"More than possible," Virin said. "I looked at the test results again. And I had Makara run them against your genetic pattern, and against Raizi's. He's definitely Raizi's bloodline. So yes, Teren. You have royal blood. And, if it came down to it, you'd be considered heir to the Imperial Throne."

"But...Rakesh is older!" Teren protested.

"*Aba* wasn't in line to inherit. He was sworn to the Spider, to become the next Spider Priest. I'm not in the line to rule. You are."

"Later, we can sat-comm Raizi and introduce him to his new grandson." Virin grinned slightly, then crossed his arms over his chest. His face went slack, and Rakesh frowned.

"Rin? What else?"

"Ayani's tests are back, Kesh," Virin said.

"And?"

"And you're not going to like it." Virin hesitated a moment, then said, "I've confirmed paternity. She's definitely a Sword, Kesh...and her father is Martiri."

Rakesh sat down hard on the bed. "Martiri? You're sure of that?"

"Yes." Virin came over and crouched down in front of Rakesh, putting his hands on Rakesh's knees. "Do I need to send her away?"

"What?" Teren blurted out. "Why?"

"No. No, I like Ayani. And what her father did...that's nothing to do with her. She's fine," Rakesh answered. "And...Teren? Martiri was the one...."

"The one... Oh." Teren's eyes widened, and he glanced over at the canes leaning against the wall. "Oh."

"I'm not going to treat her any differently. She's still Ayani. She's still my friend," Rakesh said firmly. He glanced at Virin, who had gotten to his feet. There was a question in his eyes, one that Rakesh was fairly certain he knew. *Was Ayani the traitor?* He refused to believe it. But they'd watch her now.

"Now what?" Teren asked. "Either your father is the Lost One, or you are, it sounds like. Or I could be. What do I do now?"

"You keep it secret, unless you want there to be riots," Virin said. "Teren, look at it from the angle of the person on the streets. Rakesh told me that the stories say the Lost One is going to liberate the people, right?"

"Yes," Teren said. Then he grinned. "I don't think you need to worry, though. I don't know anything about liberating anyone."

Virin grinned back. "Good. We'll work on that later. Outside the gates, to them, this is going to look like you've been taken into custody, and the children are all hostages. They'd go mad."

Rakesh cleared his throat. "Assuming they didn't go for your throat. Tragar's own people tore him to bits and burned the pieces when they found his body."

"I knew that. I just... do you think they would?" Teren asked, his voice weak. "I mean...I'm nobody. I don't know anything. I don't want to be Emperor. Or King. Or... Or anything like that."

"We don't know, Teren. We can't guess, either," Virin said. "What if we guess wrong?"

Rakesh nodded, tucking his pendant into his pocket. "All I know is that the Spider ordered me here," he added. "She told me to tell you everything. And... he wants me to come to her. She says that it is important, but I'm not sure where I'm supposed to go."

"That I can answer!" Teren brightened. "I know that!"

"You do?" Rakesh asked.

"Yes! There isn't much of the old Palace left standing, but there's a temple. I never knew what it was, but there are carvings of spiders everywhere." Teren frowned. "I can't get there in a hover-chair. And it isn't safe. The ruins belong to the mystics."

"Ayani mentioned something about mystics in the marketplace," Rakesh said. "Why would it not be safe?"

"Because the mystics...." Teren's voice trailed off. "They were always trying to recruit me. They wanted me because I can fight, they told me. But why does a mystic need to fight?"

"Mystics looking for the Lost One?" Virin mused. "I...wonder."

"You're thinking some kind of resistance?" Rakesh asked. "There hasn't been an uprising in a long time."

"Because they went underground, years back. I'd wondered where they went. I'll report on that to Molari when I make my report. For now, it will keep. We keep this all among the three of us, understand?" Virin asked, looking from Rakesh to Teren and back. "Teren, no telling Ayani. Not until this is all over. Because now... Well, I have a theory."

"What?" Teren asked. "If I come forward, say who I am—what do you think would happen?"

"I think that you'd become a figurehead, the rallying point of a very short, very bloody war," Virin answered, his voice flat, as if he were giving a report. "I think that if the Aakari forces won, then in a very short period of time, you'd disappear. And these mystics you mention would take over. I wonder how many of them are descendants of former noble houses?" He shook his head. "No. We go on the way we've been going. And...we've still got twenty-three children downstairs, and they're wondering why they haven't seen their *Aba* Rakesh yet today."

"You've been to see them?" Rakesh asked, standing up and going to fetch his canes.

"Yes," Virin said with a grin. "Twenty-three children is a lot of noise. Teren, they were looking for you, too. Everyone wants to know how you are. Especially Gira."

"May I come visit?" Teren asked.

Rakesh nodded. "Come along. Oh, Virin? Teren says that the pack that left this morning will be a good source of information, so long as they get something out of it."

Virin nodded. "Good. That will be useful. Teren, once you're released from medical, which I have on good authority will happen right after breakfast tomorrow, will you coordinate with me on that? Help me figure out the best way to contact the pack, what they would want in return?"

Teren looked shocked, then smiled. "Yes, sir. I'd be happy to help."

"Thank you. Let's get on with our day, shall we? I need to get back to work."

———◉———

"TELL ME ABOUT GIRA," Rakesh said as he and Teren left the barracks and started back towards the embassy. Virin had left them at the door, heading towards the training area. Teren glanced at him, smiling.

"Gira. She's our sunshine. I have no idea how she manages to be so happy all the time. Even on the days when we had nothing to eat, she was always smiling."

"How old is she?"

Teren shrugged. "No idea, really. We—Ayani and I—we found her three years ago, I think. She was alone, crying in a cellar. Only time I've ever seen her cry. And there was a body in there with her. Her mother, I guess, but we didn't stay to see who she was or what happened to her. We just took Gira and left. If I had to guess, I'd say she's about six now. She didn't really talk much when we found her, and she only had a few teeth. Her teeth are just starting to get loose." Teren stopped, turning his chair to face Rakesh. "Rakesh? Virin said something about Gira adopting you. Was that serious? Are you going to be adopting her?"

Rakesh nodded, forcing himself to remember to lean on his canes as he stopped. "Virin wouldn't have said it if we weren't. We've been talking about adopting for a couple of years now. And he's really taken with her. We both are."

"She's a good girl," Teren agreed. "Smart, too. I've been teaching her to read, and she soaks it up like a sponge. Anything you can teach her, she wants to know more." He looked down, then back up. "You'll take care of her?"

Rakesh smiled. "We'll take care of all of them. Now come on. They want to see you."

Twenty-three children did make a lot of noise, Rakesh thought when he entered the ballroom. There were toys and books every-where, and the children were laughing and running around. Jiren was standing near the door—she saw him and Teren, and came over to greet them.

"Where did all of this come from?" Rakesh asked.

"Some of the Swords went out to the market. They said that chil-dren need to play."

"Teren!" It was Gira's high voice that pierced the din. Then other voices took up the call, and Teren was surrounded by a crowd of chil-dren, laughing and chattering and demanding rides on the hover-chair. Rakesh took advantage of the mayhem to draw Jiren away.

"How are they doing, Jiren?" he asked, watching the children. "They had a big upheaval, with us taking them all in like this. Are they all right?"

"I think so," Jiren answered. "Children are a lot more resilient than people given them credit for. I think they're handling this wonderfully well."

"Good. I don't know a damned thing about counseling children." Rakesh looked at her. "And how are you? Settling in all right? Is Kestri all right with the change?"

Jiren smiled. "She's fine. She's over there, playing with the girls. They've been marvelous with her." She nodded towards Teren. "How badly was he hurt?"

"The hover-chair is to keep him from pushing himself too hard. He'll be discharged from medical tomorrow."

"He'll be all right?"

"He'll be fine."

Jiren sighed. "Good. He's a good boy. I knew his mother. I tried to take care of him after she died, but he's so proud. He had to make his own way. He and Ayani, and all the lost ones they collected and cared for."

"*Aba* Kesh!" Gira called, and came running towards him. He knelt down and hugged her.

"How are you, Gira-*sa*?" he asked.

"I like it here, *Aba*!" she answered, her joy infectious. "We have lots to eat, and people to play with. And I have a doll! Come and see!"

"Coming, sweetheart. Not so fast! I can't keep up!" Rakesh followed her, laughing, letting himself be dragged into games free of conspiracies or hunters in red. He saw Teren across the room. There were several of the smaller boys surrounding him, waiting none-too-patiently their turns for rides. Jiren, with Kestri in her lap, was reading a storybook to some of the others. He could live like this, he realized. A family of his own. Children. Would they have room, be able to find room, for all of them? Rakesh snorted, turning his attention back to Gira. No matter. They'd find a way.

"SO, WHERE IS THIS FARM going to be?" Virin asked that night as he got into bed. Rakesh looked up from the book he was reading and smiled.

"You're in my head again, Rin. Near my parents, I should think," he answered. "They'll adore Gira. And the rest of the children, too. We'll have to build, you know. We're not going to be able to find a place pre-built for as many as we'll have."

"I was thinking that." Virin lay down on his side, facing Rakesh. "Twenty-three children. That's not a family, that's a squadron."

"That's a family," Rakesh said firmly. "The family we'll make. How many of them will come, do you think?"

"Most of them," Virin answered. "Just one I'm not sure of. What do you think about Teren?"

"I don't know. He was so quiet over dinner. I think we gave him too much to think about today. I'm glad we decided not to sat-comm *Aba* tonight. I think Teren's head would have exploded. But he'll make up his mind, and then we'll know." Rakesh set the book aside. "He won't give up his Ayani. You know that."

"I know. I'm looking forward to the wedding in about ten years. No, what I'm wondering is what will happen if the Aakari people ever find out that their Emperor's great-grandson is wearing a Collar."

"I'm thinking it would probably be the same reaction to the fact that their Emperor's son and grandson also wore Collars," Rakash said. He stretched out next to Virin. "Rin, I doubt that there's anyone who cares, except for those mystics, who may or may not be revolutionaries. Everything *Ama* told us indicated that Tragar was roundly hated by everyone who wasn't getting handouts from him. Did you send your report?"

Virin hummed and shook his head. "First thing tomorrow. I wanted to report directly, but Molari was busy when I sat-commed." He flopped back onto the bed and stared at the ceiling. "Kesh... what would you say to taking all the children and Teren and Ayani, and going back to Tyese? Getting a head-start on that farm?"

"I'd say no. I'm not leaving you, Kian-ti-os. And as Senior Trainer for the Arena here, I'm essential personnel."

"Thought you'd say that. You can always see right through me." Virin looked over at Rakesh and smiled. "I'll ask Molari for permission to reopen the clinic. Not that there's much need right now. Practically everyone who needed those services is either in Tyese or under our roof tonight!"

Rakesh chuckled and nodded. "There is that. What's really on your mind, Rin?"

Virin scowled and looked up at the ceiling again, his eyes moving this way and that as he silently traced the lines of the staring pattern over the bed, obviously trying to put his thoughts into words. Rakesh let him be, knowing that the answer would come. Finally, Virin snorted. "Nothing I can put my finger on," he said. "Just... a feeling. Things have been quiet for over a month. Then, within the space of a few days, we've got Ishamar and possible revolutionaries."

"Just when you were getting bored?" Rakesh asked, then yelped when Virin poked him in the ribs with one finger.

"Why now?" he asked. "Why show themselves now? And does the attack on the camp have anything to do with it?"

"You think it does."

"I think it's likely," Virin admitted. "And so does Molari. By the way, I forgot to tell you: three cadet squads were out doing night training. They turned up this morning." He stopped, and Rakesh poked him.

"And? There's an 'and' there. I can hear it."

"Perceptive Collared. Yes, there's an 'and' there. Molari decided to check on the other camps in the mountains. The confinement camps. There are three of them. One of them was deserted. Completely abandoned. No bodies, no prisoners. Nothing."

Rakesh sat up slowly. "That isn't possible! I know enough to know that!"

"Yep."

"Don't they have to make regular reports? Check in daily?"

"Yep." Virin stretched the word out, popping the last letter. "And there hasn't been a report missed. Not one. And every inspection had turned up fine, until Molari showed up unannounced. Which means that this conspiracy is... pretty far-reaching. So, what happened to those prisoners? Where do you run, when you know that you'll be shot on sight in your home country?"

"They're here, aren't they?" Rakesh shuddered. "The Ishamar?"

"I'm willing to bet that camp was the Ishamar base and training facility. Right under our noses and we never knew it. So yes, they're here. As themselves, or as the revolutionaries," Virin said. "Not sure which. Does it matter? They're going to show themselves soon. Molari is sending reinforcements tomorrow."

Rakesh licked his lips, then shook his head. "Let's talk about something else."

"Let's not talk at all." Virin rolled back towards Rakesh, running one hand up his husband's side. "Let's not think at all. Not anymore."

Rakesh smiled. "You have something in mind, Kian-ti-os?"

Virin grinned, his hand traveling up Rakesh's chest, finger tracing the line of his collarbone. "Why, yes. Something involving you, that hook up there, and about half your weight in rope. Interested?"

"Where do we start?"

Virin rolled off the bed and went to the cabinet where they kept their personal supplies. "Kneel on the bed."

Rakesh got up onto his knees. "Here?"

"Turn around. Back to me. And a bit closer to the foot...yes, there." Rakesh heard Virin come closer, heard the soft slither of the ropes. "Wrists behind you, love."

Rakesh did as he was told, feeling the smooth rope sliding and tightening around his wrists, then around his upper arms, drawing his elbows together. The bed shifted, and Rakesh nearly tumbled to one side, glancing to see Virin had climbed onto the bed and was standing underneath the hook, running a length of rope over it. Then he jumped down, and helped steady Rakesh back into position.

"There. Now we're set," he said as Rakesh felt something else tighten around his wrists. He heard hissing from above, and his wrists were pulled up, higher and higher, until his hands were nearly pointing towards the ceiling and his upper body was parallel to the bed. Virin chuckled, running one hand over Rakesh's thigh. "Very nice, Tarkarin. Very nice. But I forgot something." The hand fell away, and Rakesh heard the cabinet open and close once more. Then Virin came over and sat on the bed. He had in his hands two lengths of cloth.

"We'll keep it simple tonight," he said as he used one to blindfold Rakesh, and the other as a gag. The bed shifted, and Rakesh heard him moving around. "Simple," Virin repeated, his hands settling almost delicately on Rakesh's hips. "No toys. No tools. Just me." He laughed. "I'm going to enjoy this."

Helpless, Rakesh whimpered as Virin's nails raked against his ribs, long, slow strokes that dug into his skin, hard enough to sting. Not hard enough to draw blood. Not yet. That would come later. After the tickling. After the pressure points. After Virin had, as he so-often described it, turned Rakesh inside out. Rakesh whimpered again, setting his knees and tugging at his bonds, his cock already bouncing up against his belly. He shifted, pushing his hips back, hearing Virin's laugh just before his hand connected with Rakesh's ass in a solid smack. Rakesh jumped, then moaned, closing his eyes behind the blindfold.

He was going to enjoy this, too.

Chapter Ten

There were rocks digging into Rakesh's back. Big ones. He had no idea where they'd come from—there hadn't been rocks in their quarters before the attack. And there wasn't anything he could do about them, either. There was something heavy resting on his lower body, pinning him down, and his arms were still bound behind him, his hands long since gone numb. The alarms had fallen silent, and now, as hard as he strained to hear anything, there was no sign of Virin.

When the alarms had started sounding, Virin had given up on making Rakesh scream in pain, and was working on making him scream for another reason. He'd been kneeling on the bed behind Rakesh, fucking him hard and fast, every stroke hitting in just the right place. His orgasm only a heartbeat away, Rakesh had been so fragmented by pain and pleasure, so lost in what was being done to him that he did not immediately hear the alarms. Virin did, and cursed, pulling out and diving off the bed. He must have grabbed his knife, because the next thing Rakesh knew, he was face down on the bed, the rope holding him strappado gone. He yelped, then grunted through the gag.

"Hold on, Kesh," Virin called. "I'll cut you loose—"

Then the room shook as something exploded. Rakesh heard Virin cursing. He tried to rise, but another explosion threw him off the bed. He landed against the wall, probably in the bed's blast shadow. And that had saved him—the third explosion drowned out Virin's voice, rocked the room and sent things crashing and clattering all around Rakesh. He drew his knees up to try and protect himself from flying debris. Then something landed on him, and he knew no more. When he woke, he was pinned. Trapped on his back, unable to move, still blindfolded and gagged, and hearing voices nearby. Voices speaking in Tyesean.

"He's so nicely wrapped. We should take him with us, too."

"No time to dig him out. And we have a full load already. He's not going anywhere. We'll come back for him later."

They'd walked away, their feet making heavy crunching sounds that faded into near silence, punctuated only by the distant sound of fighting. Once he was sure they were gone, Rakesh started to struggle, trying to work his way out of the ropes. But pinned as he was, he couldn't find the leverage he needed. Nor could he work the tight gag out of his mouth. He tried shouting, but no one heard him.

Spider? Can you hear me? Spider?

No answer. He whined in the back of his throat, fighting back panic. They'd come back for him. They'd take him away and Virin would never find him this time. Assuming Virin was still alive....

No. Stop that, he silently chided himself. *Stop panicking. Think.* An attack. An attack on the embassy. Who was obvious—the voices were Tyesean. It had to be the Ishamar. But why? Rakesh tried to think, tried to force himself to stay calm. Someone would find him. Someone would help him. In the meantime, he wondered why. And in the distance, he heard more voices, coming closer. Shouting in Aakari.

"Freedom!"

"The sacred blood of Tragar will rise again!"

"Kill them all!"

Sacred blood of Tragar? Rakesh blinked, wondering what they knew. He heard them coming closer and held still, hoping that they didn't see him. They must not have come into the room, because the voices slowly faded away, leaving him in dark silence once more. And with a theory.

The Ishamar were helping the mystics. They must have convinced the revolutionaries that the Tyeseans had found the Lost One. How,

Rakesh couldn't imagine. But they'd incited the revolutionaries to rise up, helped them. Armed them, most likely. And now....

Now there would be war. The Ishamar would make sure there was no evidence of themselves in the ruins. So the Tyesean Ruling Council would see this as Aakar attacking the embassy. And they'd retaliate. Rakesh grunted softly. Virin. Where was Virin?

For what felt like a long time, there was nothing. No more voice, no more sounds of fighting. Rakesh felt his arms growing numb, and tried to ignore the rocks digging into his back. At least they made it harder for him to fall asleep.

Why was no one coming?

Then he heard it. The distant sound of someone calling his name. As the voice came closer he recognized it—Teren! He grunted, started to struggle again, hearing Teren coming closer. He could hear Ayani now, too.

"Rakesh!" Teren shouted, sounding as if he were right outside the room. "Virin! Where are you?"

"Are you sure?" Ayani asked. "Is this the right room?"

"This is the right room. I was here this morning. It was late when the alarms went off, they both should have been here," Teren answered, and footsteps came closer. "Rakesh!"

Rakesh grunted again, and heard Ayani gasp. "Teren! He's here!"

"Darkness! Yan-*sa*, get that end. We have to get this off him!" Rakesh heard them grunting, felt the weight being moved off of his body. There was a loud crash, then warm hands on his shoulders, helping him to sit up. "Ayani, your knife. Cut him loose," Teren said. "I'll get these. Rakesh, close your eyes."

Rakesh did as he was told, feeling his arms falling free, feeling tugging at his head. The blindfold fell away, then the gag. He blinked, wincing at the bright light, then looked around the ruins of the room.

"Are you all right?" Ayani asked softly. "What... why—"

"Where's Virin?" Rakesh interrupted. "I'm fine. My arms are numb, but I'm fine."

"We haven't seen Virin. But the mystics and the Red Hunters took prisoners," Teren answered. "Can you stand? We can't stay here."

Rakesh let them help him to his feet and looked around, wincing at the sight of the destruction. How close had that bomb been? And where had Virin been when it went off? "Prisoners?"

Teren nodded. "Some of the Collared. I'm not sure how many. We... We haven't found everyone."

Rakesh looked at Teren's ashen face, then at Ayani's pallor. "How many dead?"

Teren looked at Ayani, then swallowed. "I'm not sure. Makara... She's alive. She's trying to get a count. But some people were buried in the embassy—"

"Buried?" Rakesh gasped. "I... I need clothes. Teren, can you find something? My trousers, they were over... over there. To your left."

"I'll find them. How are your arms?"

"I've got pins and needles starting, but I still can't move my hands." Rakesh looked at his arms, at the furrows in his wrists. "Do you know what happened?"

"No," Teren answered, turning over the broken table and tugging Rakesh's trousers out from underneath. "I can't see a shirt. Did you have boots?"

"They were near the door." Rakesh looked over at the gaping opening that had once been their door. "And never mind the shirt. They're coming back. They said they would be back for me."

"Darkness," Teren murmured. "We... Ayani, get back downstairs. Tell Makara we're going to move. We can't stay here if they're coming back. We'll be slaughtered."

"Where are we going?" Ayani asked.

"Red... Red twelve. That big cave."

Ayani nodded. "All right. I'm gone." She turned and ran from the room, and Teren held up the dusty trousers. He frowned, then looked around, picking up a toppled chair and setting it upright.

"This...might be awkward," he said slowly. "Are you still numb?"

"Yes."

"We don't have time to wait, then. Sit."

Rakesh sat down and let Teren put his trousers on him. "Do you think they took him?" Teren asked.

"I think so," Rakesh said. "He was still here when the bombs went off. And...the two I heard planning to come back, they said that they wanted to take me, too. I think they took Virin."

"Why?" Teren rose, helped Rakesh to stand, pulling the trousers as far up as he could. Then he stopped, his face going red. He took a deep breath, gently tucked Rakesh's cock in, then tugged the trousers into place and buttoned them. Only then did he looked at Rakesh. "Sorry."

"You're saving my life. I'm not complaining about you being overly familiar."

Teren grinned. "Good point. Boots." He dug through the rubble, found Rakesh's boots and came back. Once he'd gotten both boots on, he rose and took Rakesh's arm. "Your canes?"

"I don't think we'll find them." Rakesh let Teren pull him to his feet, and heard something metal hit the floor. His pendant lay on the ground at his feet.

"Your pocket's torn through." Teren said as he picked up the pendant. He reached up and looped the cord over Rakesh's head, letting the pendant fall onto his breast. Rakesh nodded.

"Let's go."

———— ◉ ————

WITHOUT FULL USE OF his arms, it was hard for Rakesh to balance, and Teren had to help him down the crumbling stairs.

"Did anyone search for survivors?"

"Yes. Ayani and I came in again after we realized that you and Virin weren't outside."

"How many?"

"Survivors? I don't know. They were still looking. When I left, there were fourteen Swords, three Collared, and five of the staff."

"That's it?" Rakesh gasped, stopping at the bottom of the steps. "Twenty-two people? Wait... the children. How many children?"

Teren turned and looked at him, his face bleak. "We...hadn't found the children yet when I left."

"Hadn't—"

"We're not sure if they took the children before they blew up the embassy," Teren said softly. "Or... Or if they're still in there. Anyone who can is digging—"

Rakesh didn't wait to hear more. He pushed past Teren and ran out into the courtyard. Then stopped. The walkway was gone, nothing more than splinters on the ground. The tall tan building had been reduced to a pile of scorched and smoking rubble. All he could do was stare. A hand slipped into his right hand. Then another into his left. He looked and saw that Ayani and Teren were standing on either side of him.

"Everyone they've found so far has been an adult," Ayani said, leaning against Rakesh's side. "Makara says there haven't been any children, and they've been looking at where the ballroom was."

"So they took the children," Rakesh said. He forced himself to look away from the ruins, to look down at the ground. Mixed in with the rubble was someone's wrist-comp. "Why? Why take the children?"

"Torture?" Teren suggested.

"A child wouldn't last long enough for them." Rakesh knelt, picked up the wrist-comp in clumsy hands. He checked to see if it was functional, but the control board had been smashed, so he threw it away and stood back up. "Where are the survivors? We need to clear this area."

"Behind the barracks. The training grounds." Ayani answered.

Rakesh turned and started back the way they'd come, seeing someone come around the building. He stopped, and heard a familiar voice, "Kesh?"

"Linter?"

"It is you!" Linter cried out, stumbling through the shadows to throw himself into Rakesh's arms. There were thick bandages around his head and his arm, and he was limping. Rakesh hugged him tightly, then held him at arms length and looked at him.

"Are you all right?" he asked, his voice low.

"I... I'm fine. Hafer... He's dead. He came in to see me, and...they... they cut him down. I don't understand, Rakesh. Why attack us?"

Rakesh shook his head. "I have a theory, but not now. It's not safe. They're coming back. Teren and Ayani know a place, and we're going there as soon as we can get the wounded mobilized."

"What?" Linter looked over Rakesh's shoulder, as if he expected someone to be there. "Are you sure?"

Rakesh nodded. "They said they were coming back for me. So let's get everyone who can move moving."

"What about the building?" Teren asked. "There are still people in there, we think."

Rakesh turned and looked back at the ruins. His chest felt tight, and it took him a moment before he could answer. "We have to go. Virin told me that we'll have reinforcements here tomorrow...later today. We'll have to put a sentry here, to keep watch for them. Someone who knows how not to be seen. But we have to go. We're all dead if we stay."

———◉———

IT TOOK SOME YELLING to get Makara to agree to pack up the wounded so that they could move out. Rakesh went through the small group of survivors, searching. No sign of Virin. No signs of any of the children. No sign of Jiren either. Then he went to the other end of the grounds. To the rows of recovered dead. There was nothing to cover the bodies, so Rakesh walked down the line of black-clad bodies, silently naming the dead. When he reached the end of the last row and found Serris, his calm shattered; he sat down on the ground and wept.

That was where Teren found him. He said nothing, just crouched down next to him and waited until Rakesh sniffed and scrubbed tears from his face.

"We're ready, *Aba*," Teren said quietly. "We've scavenged weapons, and we've taken what supplies are left. All we need now is you."

Rakesh nodded. He stood up, wiped his face once more, then looked at Teren and cleared his throat. "All right. Let's go."

It was Teren who led them out of the compound, through the surprisingly-untouched clinic and out into the deserted street. They didn't stay on the main street for long—they were still in sight of the embassy walls when Teren turned into an alleyway, leading through the dark, narrow passage into another street. They pressed on, and Rakesh wondered that no one had come to see what the explosions were. Surely someone had to have been curious? There was no time to ask, though, as Teren led them into another alley. He stopped by a boarded-up door and knocked, a complex pattern that Rakesh knew he'd never be able to replicate. The door opened, and Teren whispered with the person inside. Then he looked back at them. "This way," he said. "Inside."

"Is this where we're going to hide?" Makara asked.

"No. This is the way in."

Rakesh followed the others in, catching a brief glimpse of a small room that was neat as a pin, and an old woman who smiled as he went past. Her eyes widened, and she pointed at him and made a sign with her fingers.

"You...!" she gasped.

"Is something wrong, *Ama*?" Rakesh asked. He looked down at himself, thinking that it was his half-naked state that had alarmed her. Then he saw his chest and caught his breath—the marks from the fidelis rope were back, crossing his skin in that elaborate pattern.

"Spider Priest. There is a Spider Priest, in my home!" the woman whispered. "Dark One, will you grant your blessing to an old woman who still remembers?"

"How do you remember?" Rakesh asked, stepping out of the flow of people and stretchers. "*Ama*, how did you know me?"

"I was only a girl, but I saw the body of Sarjana when they brought her out of the Palace for burning. I saw the marks on her. The same as the marks on you. We weren't supposed to know, but the ones who lived in the shadows of the Palace, we knew. My mother, her mother, they served in the Palace. We served the Spider, in our own way." She shook her head, laughing. "A Spider Priest. Bless me, Dark One! Protect me from Her webs!"

"I... of course," Rakesh answered. He had no idea what to do, though. So he stepped forward, took her face in his hands and kissed her, first on the forehead, then on the lips. "Thank you, *Ama*, for helping us," he said softly. She sighed and smiled, patting his hands.

"Some of us, we still serve. We still remember," she said. "You still have your servants, Dark One."

Rakesh nodded, his mind racing. The Spider wasn't as secret as Raizi had thought, apparently. "I'll remember that, *Ama*. Thank you."

Teren came up next to him. "Rakesh, we have to go."

The old woman's eyes widened. "Your... Your son, Dark One? He is your son?"

Rakesh looked at Teren, then back at the woman. "Yes." He leaned down and kissed her cheek. "We have to go. Her blessing on you, and your house. Goodbye."

He let Teren hurry him out, hearing the woman behind them wishing them luck and the Spider's blessing.

"You told her I was your son," Teren said as they started down a steep set of stairs.

"Yes, I did."

"But I'm not. I'm your nephew."

Rakesh waited until they were at the bottom before stopping and turning to Teren. "You're my son. If you want to be. Remember, we told you that you had the same choices as the others."

Teren didn't say anything for a moment, but Rakesh could feel the confusion and disbelief rolling off of him. Then he answered, "No. Thank you. I do appreciate it. And...if it were different, but...no." He took Rakesh's arm. "This way. The path isn't very good, so be careful where you step. Ayani took the others on ahead."

"All right. May I ask why not?"

"Because Ayani wants to. She told me last night."

Rakesh frowned, confused. Then he realized why. "Oh. If we adopt you both—"

"She'll be my sister," Teren finished. "Siblings can't marry here, even if they're adopted. I don't know what the laws are in Tyese, but I can't think it would be approved of there either. So I can wait for her to be free to marry me, but I can't let you adopt me." He paused. "As much as I'd like it."

"You're still my nephew, you know. You're still family." Rakesh touched Teren's hand on his arm. "You're still the closest I'll ever have to a son of my own blood. And I'm proud to call you that."

Teren stumbled, and Rakesh heard his breath hitch. He stopped, pulling Rakesh to a halt next to him. Teren said nothing. Instead he turned and hugged Rakesh tightly. Rakesh could feel him shaking.

"We'll find them, Teren," Rakesh said softly, wrapping his arms around Teren. "We'll get out of this."

"I'm scared, *Aba*," Teren said, his voice shaking. "I've never been this scared."

"I know. I'm scared, too. But we can't let them know. We have to be strong." Rakesh patted Teren's shoulder, then kissed him on the forehead. "Let me tell you what I know, and what I think. You can poke holes in it."

"All right. Watch your step here."

"There was a traitor in the embassy. I know that for a fact."

"Who?" Teren demanded.

"That I don't know. But someone shut down the defenses. No one should have been able to get within the walls without alarms going off."

"The alarms went off after the first explosion," Teren said quietly.

"Exactly. The explosion set off the alarms. Not someone coming through the defense shield. Which means that the shield was down," Rakesh said. "Virin and I found out last night that one of the confinement camps up in the mountains was empty. That means that all of the rogue Swords who were imprisoned there, they're all on the loose. We think they're the Red Hunters. And they're here, and helping those mystics you told us about. Possibly trying to incite war. And now...that woman knew who I was."

"The marks on your skin," Teren said. "There are carvings, in the ruins. Images of the first Spider Priest. He had markings like you do. But...you didn't have them before. I mean...I saw all of you. You didn't have anything but some old scars."

"Because I'm heir to the Spider Priest, Teren. If She's put her mark on me, that might mean I am the Spider Priest. How did you see those carvings?"

"I went into the ruins," Teren answered. "We all do, at one point or another. Or we did, until the mystics took over."

Rakesh frowned. "When was that?"

"Five years ago? Maybe less?"

"Oh..." Rakesh cursed softly. "And...Teren, is there any way that they could have guessed? At your bloodline?"

"You think that was why they were trying to recruit me," Teren said. He hummed softly as they walked. "It's...possible. I thought of that, after you told me. I don't know, *Aba*. Maybe. I don't know if *Ama* knew who she really was. And I never knew her mother."

"You look like me," Rakesh said. "Virin said so. And my father says I look like Tragar. Someone may have noticed the similarity."

"All right. So we have targets on our backs, the both of us. If they get their hands on us, we're figureheads until we're not convenient any more. Then we're dead. That sum things up?" Teren asked. "Not far now."

"That's a good summary. And that's all I've figured out so far."

"I have something," Teren said after a moment. "An idea. I think I know why they took the children."

"Why?" Rakesh asked.

"You said that the Red Hunters are on the run, and the Swords have probably killed a lot of them. That they're criminals in Tyese. That makes it hard to have children of your own, " Teren said. "Almost all of the children you took in were sired by Swords."

"Creator," Rakesh breathed, suddenly cold all through. "You think they took the children to turn them into Ishamar?"

"They'll kill the ones who fail. But yes. So think about that. Gira... \as a Red Hunter."

"Never," Rakesh growled.

"Right," Teren agreed. "Turn left here. See the light?"

They made a sharp turn, and the passage opened up into a large cavern. There were torches set into slots, the flames making the walls glitter and shine.

"Where are we?" Rakesh asked, looking around. There were far more people here than there should have been. "And who else is here?"

"Ayani?" Teren called out. Ayani appeared and came towards them.

"Hagari and his pack are here. And a bunch of packs from the far side of the city," she said. "There are Red Hunters everywhere up there, Hagari says. They're picking up anyone they can grab. And there are riots in the streets. Anyone from Tyese is a target."

"And you know all of them?" Rakesh asked.

Ayani looked confused, then nodded. "Yes, I do. I've known all of them since we were all children."

"Have any of them started acting odd?"

Teren looked at Rakesh, frowning. "You think one of them might have turned?" he asked, his voice pitched low. His frown deepened. "Ayani, find Hagari and...Neesa. Sound the others out."

"Right." She disappeared in a group of people. Rakesh watched her go, and saw movement out of the corner of his eyes. He turned, and saw more people coming into the cavern—his age, some of them. Some of them older still.

"Teren, who are they?" he asked.

Teren looked and nodded. "Them. They're Helpers. Street pack members that grew up, found a place in a trade. They help us when things get bad. Jiren was one of them, once. *Ama* Takayla...she's the one who recognized you. She's another. They know the roads under as well as any of us. And they know to come here when it gets bad."

Rakesh nodded. "All right. They can be trusted?"

"They're Helpers."

Rakesh scowled at him. "That's not an answer."

"That's the best I've got, *Aba*."

"All right." Rakesh closed his eyes and tried to think. *What do we do now?*

You come to me. It is time.

Rakesh jumped at the sound of the resonant voice, echoing inside his head. *Where were you?* he demanded.

I could be of no help to you. I could not free you. I have been watching. They have my children.

All of them?

All that survived. The child of your heart, she lives.

Rakesh let out a shaky breath. *Thank you. And Virin?*

Is not mine. I cannot see him unless he is with you.

Rakesh nodded. *All right. Why now?*

If you do not come now, there will be no later.

What does that *mean?*

No answer. Rakesh growled softly and opened eyes he hadn't realized that he'd closed. Teren was staring at him.

"You...weren't here. All of a sudden you were gone. What was that?"

Rakesh smiled slightly. "I... This is going to sound crazy."

"Oh, like anything else the past few days is sane?" Teren folded his arms over his chest. "Tell me."

"I was talking to the Spider."

Teren's jaw dropped. "You... You're serious? What you told *Ama* Takayla, that's true? You're really the Spider Priest?"

"You didn't believe me?" Rakesh asked, amused despite everything. "I just told you I was, and you see the marks. And you still didn't believe me?"

"I...." Teren waved his hand for a moment and shook his head. "I don't know what to believe anymore. There's just been too much."

"I understand that," Rakesh said. He rested his hand on Teren's shoulder and squeezed. "Look, go see what we have to work with. Who can fight. Who has weapons. What information people have. Let's find out what our resources are."

Teren stared at him. "We're going to fight?"

"Did you think we were just going to give them up? That I was going to let them take Virin and my Collared and the children?" Rakesh shook his head. "Go find out what we need to know. I'm going to check on the wounded. And let the people see me."

Teren licked his lips, then nodded and walked off in the same direction Ayani had gone. Rakesh turned, looking for Makara. He saw someone in dirty whites, and headed in that direction. He found a makeshift infirmary, and stood out of the way, counting heads and waiting for Makara to see him. He finished counting long before she looked up and hurried towards him, alarm clear on her face.

"What happened to you?" she demanded. "Your skin... you didn't have these scars before!"

"It's a long story, Makara, and we have no time."

"And where are your canes?"

"That's part of the long story," Rakesh said. He looked past her. "What are the numbers, Makara?"

"I have ten wounded Swords, two badly enough that I don't think they'll survive the night," Makara answered. "Two wounded Tarken, only one of those badly. And I'm fairly certain that the embassy was empty when they blew it up."

Rakesh nodded, then looked at Maraka. "And where were you?"

"Going to fetch your boy," she answered, a small smile on her face. "He was in the barracks, and it was long past time he was asleep."

"In the barracks?" Rakesh looked around. "I never thought about it, but he should have been in medical at that house, shouldn't he?"

"Yes, he should have. And he actually wasn't in the barracks. He was in the storage shed back behind the barracks. And he was with that young woman. I embarrassed them pretty badly, I think."

"Oh." Rakesh fought back a wave of near-hysterical giggles. "Oh."

"Yes. And I'm afraid I embarrassed them more when I gave them both a lecture on how she's not physically mature enough for anything more than the petting they were doing. But, I think they'll forgive me. It saved all our lives."

"Thank you, for that." Rakesh sighed and looked around. "How many Swords in any shape to fight?"

"None," Makara answered, her voice sharp. "The bastards hit the barracks first. That's why there were so many killed outright. The injured I have... Broken bones, some of them so badly crushed I might have to amputate. None of them is able to stand, let alone fight. I'm sorry, Tarkarin." Then she looked at Rakesh and her eyes narrowed. "Why?"

"Because those bastards took my husband, my Collared and my children. I'm going to get them back."

Chapter Eleven

Virin groaned. The pain in his head was excruciating, and he wondered for a moment what had hit him. Then he remembered the explosion, seeing Rakesh go flying off the bed. Virin had been turning to go to Rakesh when the next blast caught him. Now everything hurt. How badly was he injured? And was Rakesh all right? He groaned again, blinking to clear his vision. He tried to turn his head and felt the straps around his forehead, holding his head in place. That woke him up enough to notice the rest of the straps—wrists, ankles, knees, waist, chest, arms. He couldn't move at all. Even his hands were immobilized, caught by something that had been wrapped tightly around his fists. He blinked once more, swallowed, and felt the weight at his throat. A collar?

Claustrophobia hit hard, and he had to force himself to think, to notice what had been done to him. Creator, where *was* he? It was dark, but not so dark that he couldn't tell that this wasn't the barracks. And he was pretty certain that he wasn't even in the embassy anymore. He was naked, and had been bound upright, sitting in a straight-backed chair, in a room that was barely larger than the chair itself. He tried pulling in the straps, felt them biting into his skin, and realized that they were metal. Where was he? And what had happened?

"Oh, the blunted fool is awake." A light outside the room flared, dazzling Virin and blinding him. Footsteps, coming closer, and the light was blocked by a tall figure, followed by a smaller one. As the tall one came closer, Virin squinted and saw an unfamiliar older man in a blood-red uniform.

"Who are you?" he asked.

The Ishamar laughed. "How soon they forget. Really, Gavir? Have you forgotten me so easily?"

"Gavir?" Virin repeated. "I'm... I'm not Gavir."

"Don't be ridiculous—"

"Sir, this is Gavir's son." The smaller figure, a woman, said. Her voice was familiar, and there was a note to it that seemed to indicate she was reminding him of something that she'd already told him several times.

"Oh. Oh, yes." He steppped closer, reached up out of Virin's line of sight, and a light came on. Now Virin could see them both clearly, and it was the woman who shocked him to the core.

"You!"

She smiled. "Me. Hello, Kian-ti-os."

"You were the traitor?"

She looked surprised. "You knew there was a traitor? I'm impressed. How—"

"Not now, my dear. Gloating is over-rated," the older man chided. "And it doesn't matter how he knew. The fact is that he didn't know in time. He failed, and now we have what we wanted." He smiled, leaning down slightly to look in Virin's eyes. "And now I'll have what I want."

"And what would that be?" Virin demanded.

The man smiled. "Revenge, my dear Kian-ti-os. Do you know what this chair is, Gavir?"

"I'm not Gavir!"

The man continued as if he hadn't heard Virin. "This is what they use in the confinement camps when you've been in solitary confinement just long enough to turn on yourself. This is what they use to keep you from hurting yourself, so they can keep you locked away. So they can forget about you. This..." he chuckled, reaching past Virin shoulder and knocking on the back of the chair. "This was mine. I saved it, Gavir. Saved it for the man who put me in it."

"I don't know what you're talking about!" Virin insisted. "My name is Virin. Gavir was my father. He's been dead for over twenty years."

The man frowned, looked at the woman. "Dead? The blunted idiot is dead?"

She nodded with an air of long-suffering patience. "A bomb, sir. Placed in the aircar on your orders. It killed him and the Ran-ti-ar."

"Ah, yes." He nodded. "Yes. I remember now. Well, then. I supposed I'll just have to be satisfied with taking my revenge on the son." He smiled. "There is a gag for this chair, you know. So they don't have to listen to you when you scream. I'll show you what I mean. But I may not use it on you later. I will enjoy hearing you as you break. I will greatly enjoy hearing you beg for death."

"Why?" Virin demanded. "I don't even know who you are!" The older man laughed, reaching past Virin and bringing the gag forward. It was a cup-like affair that looked as if it would fit around Virin's jaw like a muzzle and would hold his mouth closed. He tried to pull away, a ridiculous reflex, considering how he was bound. The Ishamar just laughed again, settling the gag into place and attaching the end to something behind Virin's left ear. Then he rose, reached up towards the light... and stopped.

"No. No, I don't think I'll leave you in the dark, Gavir," he said softly. "I want you to see. I want you to see what kind of torture I faced every day, ever since you sent me to the camps. I want you to understand."

He backed away, and the door swung closed with a heavy thud, A moment later, Virin heard the sound of a bolt shooting home. He was locked in. Trapped, in a room that felt as if it were getting smaller by the second. He tried to shout, to call someone back in, but all that came out were grunts.

It wasn't long before the grunts turned to screams.

———◉———

RAKESH MADE HIS WAY slowly through the cavern, looking for Teren. It was surprising how easy it was to get used to people staring, to them wanting to touch his arm, or beg his blessing. Not that different from home, he realized. Except for the blessing part.

"Teren!" he called out, and heard his name being shouted from somewhere off to his left. He headed in that direction, and found Teren in an alcove, along with Ayani and several others of the older street children.

"This is insane," Teren said. "Have you talked to them? There are people being slaughtered above. By men dressed as Swords."

"What?" Rakesh asked. He turned around and looked back at the crowded cavern. "There are more newcomers, aren't there?"

"They've been coming in all night," Ayani confirmed. "Someone is going to be followed. We need to get people out of here, off to the smaller, more hidden places."

"Right. Can you delegate that?" Rakesh asked.

"If you tell me what delegate means."

Rakesh grinned. "Get someone else to do that. I need you, and Teren, and anyone else you think can fight."

Teren frowned, then his eyes widened. "We're going in after them? After Virin and the children?"

"Yes. But we need a strike force, and the Swords are all down. Makara thinks I'm insane. Maybe I am." Rakesh turned and looked around. "We'll have reinforcements soon, though. Real Swords. But we need someone to go and watch the embassy and wait for them."

A voice came from behind him. "I can do that."

The speaker was one of the ones who had left with Hagari, a slightly-built boy with hands and feet that seemed to large for his frame. He'd be tall when he had his growth, but for now, he reminded Rakesh of a half-grown puppy.

"You're Cazz, right?"

"Yeah. Look, I'm not much in a fight. But I know the hiding places up above. I can wait, tell them where we are. But they won't believe me."

Rakesh nodded. "Right. They won't. How do I...?" he paused, then reached up, ran his fingers over his collar. He licked his lips, then reached back and unbuckled it, passing it to Cazz. "Whoever is in command, give him this. Teren, I need something to write on. I have to make a report."

"I can do you one better," Cazz said. He reached into the satchel that hung at his side and pulled out a battered wrist-comp. "These things have a recorder, don't they?"

"Yes! Cazz, this is perfect. Thank you!" Rakesh took it, then looked down at it. "Where did you get this?"

"Took it off one of the Red Hunters," Cazz answered, looking smug. "They might be supermen, but if you drop a brick on them from the top of a building, they still die."

Rakesh opened his mouth, closed it again, then smiled slowly. "How many of the packs can do what you do?" he asked. "Get up without being seen, I mean. How many can hunt the hunters?"

Cazz frowned, then shrugged. "I can ask. But I can't hunt and wait at the same time."

"Can you coordinate? Get them out hunting?"

"Yeah, I can do that."

"Good man. You do that. Let's take the fight to them." Rakesh held on to the wrist-comp and looked at Teren. "Where can we meet?"

"There's a smaller cavern. Umm... I can't really tell you how to get there, though."

"Right. I'll stay here, then. I'll record my report, and wait for you to come get me."

"Right." Teren nodded and headed out, Ayani on his heels. The others spread out, too, leaving Rakesh alone. He sat down on the ground and turned on the recording function of the wrist-comp.

"This is Rakesh a'Raizi Tarkarin of Tyese. Voiceprint ID should confirm that, I hope. The embassy was attacked. There was a traitor there. We don't know who..."

———◉———

BY THE TIME RAKESH finished with his report, Cazz was waiting for him.

"Teren says to come get you. You all done with that?"

Rakesh handed the wrist-comp to him. "All done. Give whoever is in command that comp, and my collar. They'll know you're one of mine, then."

Cazz grinned. "I'm one of the Spider's pack now. Ain't that something?"

Rakesh smiled slightly and rose, following Cazz out into the main cavern, which didn't seem as crowded. "Have they started moving out?"

"Yep. Ayani, she went to each of the pack leaders. They put one of their younger children to taking groups out to the safe caves, out under the walls. Gets the little ones out of harm's way, gets the job done." Cazz pointed as a small group disappeared down one corridor. "There's another group gone."

"Good. Very good." Rakesh was about to say something else, but the thought was lost in the distant sound of an explosion. "What was that?"

"They're getting closer, Teren says. He doesn't think they found a way in, but we need to get out here soon."

"Good plan."

"Yes, sir," Cazz answered cheerfully. They went the rest of the way in silence, down another corridor in the caves, and into a smaller cave that was filled nearly to bursting. Rakesh looked around, seeing young faces he knew, older faces he didn't. Teren came out of the crowd to meet him.

"Everyone here wants to fight. They've all seen the good you and Virin have done. They don't want it to end," he said.

"Good. What do we have for weapons?" Rakesh asked.

"Homemade, mostly. Slings, rocks, a couple of bows. A few of us have pistols we picked up in the embassy."

Rakesh nodded. "Cazz, you still here?"

"Yes, sir!"

"Tell your hunters to save any weapon they liberate. They can each keep one, but we need the rest. Now, get your people together and get out."

Cazz grinned, reached out and touched one of the marks on Rakesh's arm, then kissed his fingertips. As he headed back down the passage, Rakesh heard him shout, "Right! Spider Hunters, let's go!"

"Spider Hunters?" Teren whispered.

"They need to believe in something. It's unnerving that they picked me, but if it helps, I'm all for it. I wonder, though. *Aba* said that the Spider was secret, known only to the royal family. Why do so many people know? I mean, *Ama* Takayla knew exactly who I was."

"*Ama* Takayla always said that she was born in the Palace. That her mother and her mother's mother served the queens of Aakar," Teren said. "Maybe they knew? And...well, I told you. We've all gone to the ruins."

"It doesn't matter right now." Rakesh shrugged. "We can worry about that later."

"They want you to speak to them, Rakesh," Teren said, looking out at the crowd. "They need to know what we're doing."

"We're starting with reconnaissance."

"Re... what?" Teren asked.

"Taking a look," Rakesh answered. "We need three people who can get in and get out without being seen. We need to know if they're in the ruins."

"That's easy," Teren scoffed. "There are tunnels all under the ruins. Parts of the cellars, some of them. Part of the prison, others. Some were washed out by a big flood when I was a boy. But the rest are passable. And there's never been any sign the mystics know about them."

"Good. Get three or four people in there, so we know what we're up against."

Teren nodded and walked off into the crowd, and Rakesh watched as he pointed to a young girl, a slightly older man with an odd pallor to his skin, and boy who couldn't have been more than fourteen. He drew them all off to the side, spoke to them for a minute, then came back to Rakesh as the trio headed out.

"Tarsis will take care of the children," he said. "He's a tunnel-rat. He lives down here all the time. I was surprised to see him, really. Usually, he hides when we come down."

"I'm glad he didn't. All right. I need to talk to everyone. Then...we need to plan." Rakesh looked around, then raised his voice. "Can you all hear me?"

There was a rumble of conversation that quickly died out, and Rakesh closed his eyes and nodded. "Thank you," he said. "I am Rakesh a'Raizi Tarkarin. My father is the son of the Spider Priestess Sarjana. I have been chosen by the Spider to stand as Spider Priest."

"You? But you... You're a—"

"A whore?" Rakesh finished, looking in the direction that the voice had come from. "Perhaps, by your thinking. But my father said no. My father said that the ways of the Arena are similar to those of the Spider. From what I have read of the sacred scrolls, I know this is true. And..." he held his arms out. "You can see that She has marked me."

A hush, a hiss of whispers ran through the crowd like the sound of approaching rain. Then a woman stepped forward. "May I see? May I touch?"

"You may," Rakesh answered. He held still as she came up to him, her fingers running lightly over the marks on his chest, on his arm. She stopped at his wrist.

"He...he wears spidersilk!" she called out. "And he does not die!"

"Spidersilk?" Teren whispered.

"The bracelet is fidelis fiber." Rakesh whispered back. He raised his arm, showing the bracelet. Then he raised his voice again. "Does that convince you?" he asked.

"What would you have of us, Spider Priest?" someone called out.

"The mystics in the ruins, they have joined forces with the ones you call Red Hunters. In Tyese, they are called Ishamar, and they are under sentence of death for their crimes. The chaos in the streets now is their doing—they seek to cast both our nations back into war. And they have taken hostages. People under my care. Children under my care. The daughter of my heart. And my heart himself, my husband, who you all know as Virin Kian-ti-os, the leader of the embassy. Teren tells me that you all approve of him, that you like the changes that he's made. Is that so?"

"It is," a woman near the front said. Rakesh recognized her from the clinic, and smiled at her. She blushed and smiled back. "The others did nothing except treat us as prey. And you put a stop to that. You've given us food, and medicine, and you've tried to help us. "

"And I'm trying to help you now," Rakesh said. He looked around. "How many of you would prefer things to keep getting better? Want to raise your children in safety, knowing that no one will steal them away from you in the night, that no one will hunt you in the shadows? How many of you want peace?"

Hands went up throughout the crowd. Rakesh nodded and raised his own hand. "So would I. So I ask you. Please. Help me to defeat them. Help me save those lives. If they keep the children, they will turn some of them into Red Hunters, and murder the rest. That cannot happen." He lowered his hand and looked around. "There will be Swords coming. Real ones, who will help us. But until then, we're alone. They know that. So they won't expect us to attack. Not yet. That may be to our advantage." He paused, then shook his head. "It may be our only advantage."

"Can we beat them, *Aba*?" Teren asked. "How?"

Rakesh frowned, thinking. "They are men and women. They are faster then we are, stronger than we are because they were made to be that way. But they are men and women. If you hit them, they'll fall. If you hurt them enough, they'll die. And..." he paused, his eyes wide. "And they won't come down here. None of them. They all have a terror of being closed in. It will drive them mad, if they're trapped. That may also be to our advantage."

"They can still blow up the tunnels!" someone shouted. "They can still kill us down here."

"They can kill you down here or they can kill you up on the streets," Rakesh answered. "Would you rather die fighting, or die on your knees?" He looked around again, then shook his head. "I kneel to one man only, and I will die fighting so that I might have that chance again. If any of you will join me, I'd be glad of it. But if not, then I will go alone."

He turned, feeling suddenly tired and sad. A hand caught his arm, and he looked back to see Teren. "I'm coming with you, *Aba*," he said, his voice carrying.

"So am I!" Ayani's clear voice rang out.

More voices, rising to the point that all Rakesh could no longer hear the words, only the vast wave of sound. When it finally died down, he looked around and softly said, "Thank you. All of you."

"It is past time we stood for ourselves," the woman who had touched him said. "We will follow you, Rakesh of the Spider. And we will take back what it ours!"

The roar that answered her words was even louder than the first. As the people shouted and argued, Teren led Rakesh out of the crowded cave and into the passage, down into a smaller cavern that was blissfully silent.

"You look like you're going to fall on your face, *Aba*," Teren said. "You need to rest. Tarsis and the children won't be back for a while, and we can't do anything until we know what to expect. Right?"

"Yes, that's right, but—"

"But nothing. Sleep, *Aba*. I'll make sure no one bothers you." Teren pointed to a corner, where Rakesh saw a rolled-up blanket.

"You planned this?"

"No. It was Ayani's idea."

"Thank her for me?"

"Of course. Now get some sleep."

Rakesh didn't need to be told twice. He stumbled over to the blanket, wrapped it around himself and lay down on the ground. He was asleep in minute.

———◦———

ARE YOU COMING?

Rakesh grumbled in his sleep and rolled over. *I do need to sleep, Spider.*

But when are you coming?

As soon as we know what to expect! I can't lead anyone into the un-known. Why? Is something wrong?

It comes soon.

What? What does?

The choice. It comes soon. You must be here to choose—

"*Aba* Rakesh?"

Rakesh jerked awake and rolled over to see Teren, standing in the cave mouth.

"Teren? What is it?"

"Tarsis and the children are back. I have some food for you, so you can eat and hear the report."

Rakesh nodded, slowly getting to his feet. "All right. I'm coming." He stumbled out of the cave and accepted a cloth-wrapped bundle from Teren. It proved to be a roll of some kind, bread filled with a mixture of vegetables and some kind of spiced meat. Rakesh wasn't sure what the meat was, and, at the moment, didn't care; he wolfed the roll down, much to the amusement of Teren.

"Ayani says I eat like that," he said. "Two gulps and a swallow, she calls it."

"I haven't eaten since... I don't even know what time it is."

"It's almost dawn up above."

Rakesh stared at him. "Is that it? It feels like it's been days!"

"I know. Come on. Tarsis is this way."

Rakesh followed Teren into the large cavern where everyone had originally gathered and saw Tarsis sitting on the ground. Tarsis rose when he saw Rakesh.

"Spider Priest," he said, bowing slightly. "I did what you asked. The Red Hunters are out in the streets, killing everyone they can. So there are only a few in the ruins. We saw the children. I counted twenty-three."

Rakesh took a deep breath and let it out. "That's all of them. They're all okay?"

"Looked like it. Didn't see the man, though." Tarsis scratched his head. "Heard them talking about him, though. His name's Gavir?"

"No," Rakesh answered, wondering where Tarsis had heard that name. "No, his name is Virin."

"Huh. There's an old Red Hunter. Heard him talking about his prisoner. Called him Gavir."

"That's... bizarre. Gavir was Virin's father," Rakesh said slowly. "All right. You can take us in?"

"Sure. I left Sortag there, to keep watch for a bit, with Asa to run. He's a good shadow. No one's gonna see him. If he sees anything, Asa will come back and let us know. Otherwise, they'll both be back in twenty minutes."

"Good. Thank you, Tarsis." Teren said. "Rakesh, I've had Ayani taking stock of what weapons we have. We have enough to arm everyone."

"Really?"

"Well, some of the packs scavenged on the way in. They weren't happy, but I told them that we'll trade for the weapons. Food, clothes, medical care. Anything they want within reason."

Rakesh nodded. "Good thinking. And yes, I'll make sure that the deal is honored. All right. Let's get everyone ready and armed."

Teren's lips quirked. "They all are. We're just waiting on you, *Aba.* This way."

"You sure you're not taking Sword training, Teren-*na?*" Rakesh asked, following Teren out of the cave, hearing Tarsis behind him. "You're damned good at this."

"I still haven't made up my mind," Teren answered, his voice quiet. "I haven't had time to think. In here." He turned into a cavern that was not quite as large as the one they'd just left. It was full of people. Rakesh looked around and saw that all of them were armed.

"We have a gun for you, *Aba,*" Teren said. "Ayani has it." He paused. "You can shoot, can't you?"

"Virin taught me," Rakesh told him. It was only partly the truth. He'd known the basics since childhood, the same as any child born and raised on a farm, and who had taken a turn on night watch during foaling season. Later, Virin had taken him to the Ishkarin shooting range, honed what he already knew, and taught him to handle an Ishkarin-issue stun blaster. But the gun that Ayani brought to him was something he'd only ever heard of—a pulse gun. They'd been developed for use during the war, and were capable of both narrow and wide-beam shots, and could be locked on for a continuous, high-power beam that would punch through ferro-cement like it was paper. One gunman could mow down an entire assault line, or bring down a small building. For that reason, pulse-guns were highly illegal.

"This is what they're using in the streets?" Rakesh asked, horrified.

"I think this is the only one we got. I wouldn't give it to just anyone. If you don't want it, I'll give you mine, and I'll take this one."

"I'll use it," Rakesh said. He took the gun from Teren, silently hoping that he wouldn't have to use the thing. A quick examination showed that it was in locked into narrow beam, single shot mode. "You've doctored this?"

"Yeah. That's a nasty piece. I didn't want any of ours getting in the way. It's already going to be chaos up there."

Rakesh nodded, then turned to look at the cavern full of people. "How many do we have?"

"One hundred and seventeen," Teren answered. "Ayani is thinking four assault teams. Two from underground to start. Two to attack above ground once we have them distracted."

"I'll defer to Ayani. You both know the area, and you both are better tacticians that I ever will be. I assume you have the teams picked?"

"Yes. She's leading one of topside teams. Hagari has the other. Tarsis is leading the initial underground team, and is going after the Collared. You and I are leading the second wave. We're the ones going after the children and Virin. She figured they'd come to you, but they wouldn't with anyone else."

Rakesh found himself surprised. "You're not leading a team?"

"Ayani ordered me to stay with you." Teren hesitated. "*Aba*, I... Is it like this for you, when someone you love goes off and you don't know if you'll see them again?"

"What? The feeling that you want to scream, but nothing will come out? That you're torn between going with them to keep them safe, and locking them in a deep, dark hole so that they can't go into danger? That feeling?"

Teren's eyes were wide, and he nodded. "Yeah. That one."

"Every single time. You learn to live with it. But you never get used to it, and you never, ever like it."

"I...see," Teren said softly. "Will you excuse me? I want to see her before we send them off."

"Go ahead. If I see you again in anything under twenty minutes, I'm going to make you go back and do it again properly."

Teren looked startled, then blushed furiously. "That wasn't what I meant!"

"It should have been. Go on, off with you. We'll move out in thirty minutes."

Teren vanished into the crowd. Rakesh watched him go, then picked another direction and entered the crowd himself. Best not to intrude on Teren and Ayani's goodbye.

It might be their last.

Chapter Twelve

Virin had always told him that the waiting was the hard part. Rakesh had never believed him before. Now, though, he understood. He and Teren waited side by side in the cavern, waiting for the signal from above that it was time. And it seemed as if they'd been waiting for years.

"How long were we supposed to wait?" he whispered.

"Five minutes, or until the shooting starts," Teren answered, his voice low. "Two minutes left. Have you ever killed anyone, *Aba*?"

"No."

"Neither have I."

Rakesh closed his eyes, starting to recite the Litany. Then he heard it —the sharp whine of gunfire. He looked at Teren, who nodded once, his face a pale study in stone. He'd heard it, too.

"Time to go," Rakesh said. He drew his gun and started forward, hearing Teren at his left, the shuffle and press behind him. With no warning, the passage opened, light flooding the space—Rakesh narrowed his eyes and kept on, moving to hug the wall. More gunfire ahead, and a figure in red moved into view. Rakesh reacted without giving himself a chance to think, raising his gun and firing. The pulse-gun shuddered and coughed, and the Ishamar fell without a sound.

"Good shot," Teren muttered.

Rakesh nodded and kept moving, peering around a corner. There was no one in sight. He glanced back at Teren. "Where's Asa?"

"Here, sir," a girl pushed forward. "The children are this way."

Rakesh fell back and let her lead, watching over her head for red or robes—red uniforms or ragged robes being the two markers Teren had told him to look for. But despite the sounds of gunfire off in the distance, they saw no one else.

"Only one guard?" Teren whispered, his thoughts apparently echoing Rakesh's own.

"There's weren't a lot of people here to start with. They're all off fighting. The children are locked in there," Asa said, nodding towards a nearby part of the palace, one of the few sections that was still standing. "There might be people there."

"Right. Stay alert," Rakesh said. Asa started out. Rakesh followed her, flinching at the sound of gunfire, even closer than before. Hopefully, they'd be able to get in, get the children and Virin, and get back out before anyone noticed they were here. He saw movement ahead of them and stepped back under cover, watching as Asa dove into the shadows and vanished. A figure in red darted up the path and into the structure, too quickly for Rakesh to aim.

"Well, we know there's one person in there," Teren muttered. Rakesh nodded, waiting until Asa came out of the shadows and waved them forward. He followed her, picking his way through the rubble until he entered the shadows and the way into the structure. Ahead, he could see an intact wall, a door that hung half-open and Asa. She was already at the doorway.

The moment that Rakesh passed through the door, he froze, startled by what felt like an electrical charge running up his legs. He looked down, saw nothing but a dirt floor, and moved further into the room. The sensation got stronger, and he heard a gasp as Teren came in.

"What in Darkness' name?" Teren gasped, looking around.

"You feel it, too?" Rakesh asked. He scanned the large room they were in, saw Asa standing not far away. She was looking at him, an odd expression on her face. "She doesn't."

"I didn't, the last time I was here," Teren said. "This... this is weird."

Rakesh nodded, looking around again. "Where are we? What was this, before?"

"This..." Teren paused. "Oh. This is the outer chamber to the temple."

"Are you two coming?" Asa hissed. "There's no one here, but that won't last. Let's go!"

Rakesh nodded and followed her, trying to ignore the feeling, which got stronger the further into the room he went. The rest of the team ranged out behind him, following the directions Ayani had given them before they'd left the caverns. They were to form a chain, each of them staying under cover and waiting until the children were free. And each of them was to form another brick in the wall around the children, surrounding them completely before they left the ruin, the better to protect them on the trip back into the caverns. Rakesh and Teren would follow with Virin. So when Asa stopped at a closed door, Rakesh and Teren were the only ones with her.

"The children are here," she whispered. "Simple locks. Ready?"

"Yes. Let's get out of here," Rakesh whispered back, taking his place on the far side of the door. She did something to the locks, grinned and shot the bolts back, swinging the door open as she stepped back, out of the way. When nothing happened, Rakesh peered around the door, only to see a familiar face looking back at him, her eyes wide and scared, her arms wrapped protectively around the child in her arms.

"Jiren?"

She gaped at him, then whispered, "Rakesh? Darkness, Rakesh?"

"It's all right, Jiren," Rakesh said, moving into the doorway, seeing the children ranged around the room. "Come on, let's get out of here."

"*Aba?*" Rakesh turned at the small voice, went to one knee and opened his arms; Gira rushed to him and hugged him tightly, her small body shivering violently. "*Aba*, I knew you'd find us."

"I wasn't going to let them take you away, Gira-*sa*. Now come on. We need to get you out of here, and I need to find Virin." He squeezed Gira again, then rose, keeping his hand on her shoulder. "Jiren, Asa will take you out of here. There are people waiting all along the way, people who are there to guard you and the children."

"What about you?"

"Teren and I are going after Virin. Don't wait for us, just get out." Rakesh jumped at the sound of a distant explosion, one that was somehow different from the sounds he'd heard earlier. "I... think the reinforcements are here. This is going to be over soon. Get the children out of here now."

Jiren nodded, looking around. She stopped, hesitated, then leaned forward and kissed Rakesh firmly on the lips. Then she looked around again. "Come on, dears. Let's go. Everyone stay together, and not a peep. Understand?"

"Yes, *Ama*!" The children followed Jiren and Asa out and down the passage, and Gira waved as she joined the group. Rakesh smiled as they hurried out of sight, then turned to Teren.

"All right. Where now?" He started forward, then jumped back as the ground in front of him exploded, sending pebbles and dirt everywhere.

"Don't move," a woman's voice warned. Rakesh went cold, recognizing the voice. But it wasn't possible!

"Hands up, the both of you." She walked into view, her gun raised. "Hello, Rakesh. Miss me?"

"Janera?" Rakesh stared at her, at the red synth-leather uniform. He raised his hands without letting go of his gun. "I... what are you doing?"

"Didn't I always tell you I'd look amazing in red?" she asked, laughing. "Oh, come now, darling. Surely you didn't think we wouldn't send some of our own through your silly training? We had to have someone on the inside, after all. Someone close." She came closer, smiling. "You're so very trusting. And so very, very sweet to the little no-caste girl."

"But... you're a Tarken," Rakesh said, his words slurring with the effort to get them out past his shock. "You're one of the best I've trained!"

"All a lie," she said. "Although I did enjoy my time in Virin's bed. He's very good, for a Blunt. So thank you, for that."

"Where is he, Janera?" Rakesh asked. "If you're going to kill me, I want to see him before I die."

She made a face and shook her head. "Oh, sorry. Can't do that. My Commander will have a fit if I disturb his new plaything. Honestly, if I could, I would. And who says you're going to die that quickly?"

Rakesh went cold. "I won't let them do that to me again, Janera."

"You don't have much of a choice." She aimed, her gun pointed not at Rakesh, but at Teren. "You'll behave, or he dies."

There was another distant explosion, and Rakesh closed his eyes and nodded. "That was closer. You know what that is, Janera? Those are the reinforcements that Molari sent. They're going to take this ruin, and they're going to kill everyone they find in red."

"Oh, we won't be here," Janera said. "By the time they reach this point, we'll be gone. I am disappointed that you stole the children back. But not surprised. I told the Commander that there might be some kind of rescue attempt."

"Which is why you were waiting for me here?" Rakesh asked.

She smiled. "Naturally. Now, come along. My Commander is going to enjoy the both of you. And, since I'm bringing you in, he might reward me and let me have some time with your pretty friend here."

Teren was standing close enough that Rakesh felt him shudder. He glanced back over his shoulder, saw Teren looking at him, the question in his eyes. And the fear. Rakesh turned back to Janera and closed his eyes.

You don't have to do that to talk to me.

You're listening?

You're in my temple. Of course I'm listening.

Can you do anything?

That, I cannot. I cannot act outside of you.

Rakesh thought he heard the whisper of the word 'yet' at the end of the Spider's sentence, but he wasn't going to ask. Not now. He opened his eyes, lowered his arms, and walked forward. Janera's eyes widened.

"You... you're walking. You're *walking*! Your canes... where are your canes?"

"You're not going to kill us, Janera," Rakesh said gently. "You and I, we've got too much history together. You won't kill me."

"I told you. I'm taking you to my Commander," Janera said. She leveled her gun at his chest. "Now get back there. And drop your gun!"

"No, little sister," Rakesh said. He kept on walking, using one hand to move Janera's gun off to the side so that he could stand in front of her, looking into her eyes. "You're not. Help me find Virin, and come back with me. Come back to the collar."

"That was a lie!"

"Let this be the lie." He reached out and rested his hand on her shoulder, ran it up to her neck. "Janera, please?"

She looked stricken, then reached out with her free hand to touch Rakesh's bare throat. "I've never seen you without your collar or your canes," she said softly. Then she shook her head. "I can't, Rakesh. This is my life!"

Rakesh closed his eyes and sighed. "I was afraid you'd say that," he said softly. Then he fired.

———●———

TEREN STOOD GUARD OVER Rakesh while he was thoroughly sick, heaving until there was nothing left but bile and his stomach ached.

"All right?" Teren asked.

"No. But I'm done, I think." Rakesh wiped his mouth on the back of his hand and grimaced. "Wish I had some water."

"You surprised me," Teren admitted, handing Rakesh his gun. "I didn't think you'd kill her."

"More important, she didn't think I'd kill her." Rakesh took a deep breath, holding it until the need to vomit once more had passed. "All right. Let's go."

"You're sure? We can wait for the reinforcements," Teren said. He turned, looking out to where they could see smoke billowing. "They're getting closer."

Rakesh shook his head. "No, we don't have time. Ja— she said that they were leaving. There's a transport somewhere in here. If the other team didn't find the Collared, they're on that transport. And probably Virin is, too."

"Right. And by the time the Swords get here—"

"It will be too late. It's the two of us." Rakesh raised his gun and looked at the charge. Still nearly full. "Let's go."

"Where?"

This way.

I thought you said you couldn't see him!

I cannot. But there is pain at the heart of my temple, and terror. I can show you where.

Pain? Terror? Oh, Creator. "This way," Rakesh murmured, feeling a phantom tug leading him forward, deeper into the building.

They passed through another door, and found working lights on the other side, and floors that had been cleared of debris. The walls were covered with elaborate carvings—spiders, intricate webs, and symbols that looked oddly familiar.

"Where are we going?" Teren whispered. "I haven't been this far in."

"The heart of the temple."

"How do you know?"

I am telling him.

Teren froze. "You didn't say that!"

"You can hear Her?" Rakesh asked.

He is of the Blood. In my own place, my children can all hear me.

"Oh."

Rakesh looked back. "You hear the Spider. She's showing me where we're going."

Teren's face was pale, his eyes wide. "Can the weird shit please stop happening now?" he asked softly.

There was a soft chime of laughter. *I like this one. He is a worthy son of mine.*

"Thank you," Teren said. "Can we keep going?"

Of course.

"Not too fast. We're not sure what's ahead of us," Rakesh said, feeling the tug once more. It seemed more urgent now, and from the muttered curse behind him, Rakesh wasn't the only one feeling it.

Another door, and they found themselves in a large, open room dominated by a pair of tall pillars in the center. Linking the pillars was an enormous web made from shimmering, cream-colored fibers, and at the center of the web...

"Darkness!" Teren blurted out. Rakesh darted forward, knowing already that it was too late, that the woman in red hanging in the web was dead. He stood at the base of the web, looking up into sightless eyes.

"Her name was Esha," he said, turning. "We trained togeth—Teren?"

There was no answer—he was alone. Rakesh moved away from the web, his gun raised. "Teren!"

"Thank you, for bringing him back," a voice said. An older man in red stepped out of the darkness, pushing a struggling Teren in front of him. He had one hand clamped over Teren's mouth and nose. "Lay your gun down, or I'll snap his neck."

Rakesh considered taking the shot, then dismissed the idea—Teren was struggling too much, and the Ishamar would kill him the second Rakesh fired. So he nodded. "I'm putting it down," he said, crouching and setting the gun on the ground. He rose and held his hands up. "Let him go."

The Ishamar smiled and shoved Teren forward; Rakesh caught him before he hit the ground.

"You all right?" he asked.

"Yes," Teren answered. "Sorry. I never heard him—"

"Well, now. You're the celebrated Rakesh?" The Ishamar chuckled. "You? You're one of them!"

"Them?"

"An Aakari dog. No better than an animal. Good for prey, for slaking lust, and for nothing else." He laughed again. "I suppose that's the reason that poor, blunted Gavir chose you. He couldn't find a real mate—"

Rakesh interrupted, "If you want Gavir, you're twenty years too late," he called. "Gavir is dead."

The Ishamar looked startled, then smiled. "Yes. Yes, of course. You'll forgive me. I...meander. The price of so many years locked away, you understand. Virin. The son's name is Virin. And he is no better than the father."

Rakesh licked his lips, lost. The man was mad. Of that much he was certain. He needed to defuse the situation, somehow gain the upper hand. "Who are you?" he asked. "Shouldn't we know the name of the leader of the Ishamar?"

"You recognize my rank? Good dog," the man said, his praise dripping with contempt. "Yet you don't know my name?"

"We haven't been introduced," Rakesh said coolly.

"You've never heard of me, then?" The Ishamar's eyes glittered as he stepped forward. "Oh, come now. Does Gavir say nothing of Demarti?"

Rakesh frowned, thinking. Then he shook his head. "I don't know that name. Should I?"

The old man looked shocked. "He has not mentioned me?"

"No. Virin hasn't mentioned you at all. And I never had a chance to meet Gavir." Rakesh looked at Teren. "If you'll take me to him, I'll ask him."

Demarti started to laugh. "You think I'm a fool, do you?" he asked. "An old, mad fool. No, dog. Although...perhaps I will let you see him. Let him see you. Let him watch as I peel the skin from your bloody, broken back." He smiled. "Yes, I think I will enjoy that."

Rakesh swallowed. He couldn't hear the explosions any more, had no idea how far away the Swords were. If they'd get here in time, or if they'd even be able to find their way. He and Teren were alone.

You are not.

Spider, what do I do?

You come to me.

What? Rakesh looked around. *Come where?*

The web. Come to the web, my son, my own.

Rakesh nodded. *All right. Can... can you make Teren hear me?*

He can hear you now.

Teren?

Teren turned to stare, his eyes wide. *Rakesh?*

Listen to me. I'm going to try something. Whatever happens, you get out of here. Find Virin and get out. Understand?

I... yes. But—

*No buts, Teren-*na.

Aba!

Just listen, Teren. And tell Virin I love him. Rakesh stepped back, slowly, hunching his shoulders, averting his eyes. "I... Please... Please don't?" he whispered, not having to fake the fear in his voice. As he hoped, Demarti laughed.

"Oh, the cowering dog. And here I thought you were something special!"

Rakesh stole a look at Teren, who had moved away from him, shuffling slightly off to the side. Demarti's attention was on Rakesh, though, and he didn't seem to notice. He followed Rakesh, moving closer, a thin smile on his face.

"I will enjoy making you scream, dog," he crooned.

"I don't think I'll be screaming for you," Rakesh answered. He reached back and grabbed on to the web with his right hand. There was a sharp pain in his wrist, right where the fidelis bracelet rested against his skin. His ears rang with the sound of the Spider's laughter, and he watched as Demarti's face went pale.

"What... what is that?" he screamed, staring at something over Rakesh's head. Rakesh looked up, and his jaw dropped.

The web was glowing.

Chapter Thirteen

"Make it stop!" Demarti screamed. He raised his gun and aimed it at Rakesh. "You filthy dog, you make it stop!"

What do I do now? Rakesh demanded.

Let me take you. Let me come through you, and into the world. Let me devour the world at long last!

"What?" Rakesh gasped. He tried to let go of the web and found his hand sealed closed around the strands, more strands appearing over his fingers, binding him in place, starting to twine up his arm. "You're supposed to be helping us!"

Who told you that? The Spider laughed. *You stand between the Spider and the world, your father told you. Did he never tell you why? Oh, I see. He never knew. He never knew that he was not meant to be the custodian. He was meant to be the warder. Tragar's madness had finally served its purpose. I am free to walk the world once more.*

"No! No, I won't let you!"

"Rakesh!" Teren shouted. Rakesh turned, saw Teren struggling with Demarti, fighting him for control of the gun. That was the last thing Rakesh saw as a surge of power pulled him into the dark.

He was back in the room with two doors. Only this time, a spider the size of a small air-car was sitting in front of the doors.

"Welcome, my Priest."

"I'm not letting you through me," Rakesh said. "You're as mad as he is."

The spider laughed, a terrifying sound. "Possibly. Probably. But all gods are mad. Did you not know this?"

"I haven't had many dealings with gods," Rakesh answered. "Was this all your doing? The attacks, the revolutionaries? The Ishamar? Did you do this, to get me here?"

"No," the Spider answered. "No, I have been locked away, sealed in my webs since your distant grandmother defeated me and took her place as the sentry between me and my prey. I thought I would never find a passage through, ever since my daughter Sarjana drown in her own blood. Her son was too young to take his place as my Priest, and so I was alone. I had no power. I had no vessel, no bridge. No one I could speak with. No one I could use. Not until you made your ignorant offering, until you entered my webs, not knowing that you should never have trusted me. That I was never a benevolent spirit. I will take back my place in the world, through you and the boy. I shall rule, and I shall feast. And you will be rewarded, my distant son. You will be my Voice, and the boy shall be my Warrior. You shall be my Priest, and he shall rule in my name. He shall give life to my blood once more."

Rakesh grimaced, rubbing his wrist, and thought fast. "He has no siblings. No sisters. I have no children. The bloodline will die in a single generation."

The Spider scoffed. "He has a female. She is acceptable. And there is always your line. The female children and grandchildren of my son Akrashesh."

"Akrashesh?" Rakesh repeated. "Is that my father's name?"

"He did not tell you? He named you for himself, my Priest. Now, it is time."

"No." Rakesh folded his arms over his chest. "I'm not letting you through."

"The son of your heart will die if you do not. Your mate will die if you do not."

Rakesh turned away. "I won't be blackmailed, Spider. I won't be forced. If you think you can hurt me to make me do what you want, all I can say is that others have tried."

"You will be— No! No, you cannot!"

Rakesh turned, startled by the panicked sound of the Spider's voice. Then something hit him, and pain lanced up his arm, worse than anything he'd ever known. He screamed...

And opened his eyes to find himself once more in the ruined temple, curling up on the ground, and staring at a blackened, smoking hand.

His hand.

He clutched his arm to his chest and gasped, trying to deal with the pain, trying to move through it, damp it down. Distantly, he heard Teren's voice, calling his name. Then there were hands on his shoulders, helping him to sit up. It was a few minutes before he could hear the words in Teren's sobbing.

"... sorry! I'm so sorry! I was trying to get the gun away from him and it went off and I didn't mean to shoot you! Darkness, your hand! We need to find a medic, we need to find someone to help you, *Aba*. *Aba*, please forgive me, please, I didn't mean to hurt you I was trying to stop him—"

"Teren," Rakesh croaked. "Teren, stop."

"But your *hand*!"

"My life, Teren. You saved my life." Rakesh blinked, trying to force himself to focus. "Demarti?"

"Over there." Teren nodded. "I... When the gun went off, when you screamed, I got it away from him. My second shot took his head off."

Rakesh felt his lips twitch. "Good thing your aim got better the second time around."

"*Aba*!"

Rakesh looked at Teren, saw the tears running down his face, and pulled the boy close with his good arm, hugging him and kissing the top of his head. "Teren, Teren-*na*, you saved my life. I am not mad at you. I'm not going to turn on you because of this. Once I see a medic, I'll be fine."

"But your hand—"

Rakesh forced himself to look at the charred end of his right arm. The smell of burned meat was turning his already-empty stomach. "I... I'll be fine. The shot cauterized the...the wound. And we have very good prostheses in Tyese, Teren." Rakesh took a deep breath. "Help me up."

"No... No, you need to stay down until we get a medic."

"No, I need to find Virin. And we need to get out of here before the Spider figures out how to reforge the bond."

"What?"

"She's insane, Teren. And She wanted to take over everything, with me as her Priest, and you repopulating her bloodline. She would have had us conquering everything. Worse than Mad Tragar." Rakesh shuddered. "If She takes me again, I don't know if I can fight her."

"Oh. Is there anything we can...do about that?" Teren asked, hooking his hands under Rakesh's left arm and helping him to his feet. "Can... How do we fight that?"

"I don't know."

"The marks are gone, you know. I noticed when you fell."

The marks? Rakesh looked down at his bare chest and his good arm—the pattern that had crossed his skin had vanished. "When you... When you shot me, you destroyed the bracelet I was wearing. The spidersilk bracelet. That must have been the link the Spider was using."

"She needed that?"

"Every time but once. That other time... I don't know. I don't know how she did it. But if She shows up in my dreams again, She can get stuffed." He raised his voice. "Hear me, Spider? You have no priest! I repudiate you!" He looked around, then studied the web for a moment. "Teren, where's my gun?"

"I have it. Why?"

"Can you blow that thing up for me? A lot?"

Teren looked startled, then snickered. "Yes, I can. Come on. I want you out of the way for this."

Rakesh watched from behind another pillar as Teren used the pulse-gun at it's widest setting, strafing back and forth until the web and the pillars that supported it were smoking ash and pebbles on the ground. He stepped out as Teren turned back towards him, dimly surprised at how steady he was.

"Better, *Aba*?"

"Much. Let's go find Virin."

⸻ ◈ ⸻

ONCE OUTSIDE THE TEMPLE, Rakesh stumbled and nearly fell as pain shot up both of his legs. Teren caught him, holding him steady.

"What happened?"

"Whatever She did, it's gone," Rakesh muttered through clenched teeth. "My feet—"

"Let me bring you out of here," Teren urged. "I'll come back and find *Aba* Virin. But you can't do this!"

"I can. I will. He'd come in after me." Rakesh met Teren's eyes. "Let me lean on you, Teren-*na*. We'll find him together."

It wasn't so much leaning as it was Teren carrying Rakesh through the halls. "Where are we going?" Teren asked, panting.

"Someplace close by," Rakesh answered. "In one of the cleared rooms. He can't have been too far. The Spider said there was pain and terror in the heart of the Temple. And Esha had been dead for a long time. So it wasn't her. The Spider meant Virin. And that means...here. Somewhere."

"All right." Teren stopped, helped Rakesh sit down on the ground. "I... You told Ayani you could feel other peoples' emotions."

Rakesh frowned. "Did I? I don't remember. Is it getting colder, Teren?" He looked around, blinking. The pain was starting to grow distant, but so was everything else.

"*Aba*!" Rakesh turned back to see Teren crouched in front of him. "*Aba*, stay with me. Can you feel *Aba* Virin? Can you find him that way? Because this place is huge, and if we just search, we'll never find him."

The words took a moment to sink in, longer to make sense. "Shock," Rakesh murmured. "I... I'm going into shock."

"And...that's bad?" Teren asked.

"Yes." Rakesh blinked, hard. "We need..." He stopped, tilting his head to one side. What was that noise? "I... Do you hear that?"

"Hear what?" Teren asked. He looked up and down the corridor, then back at Rakesh. "Hear what, *Aba*?"

"Sounds...like a heartbeat?" Rakesh closed his eyes and listened. "That way. It's coming from that way."

"I don't hear anything," Teren said softly. "But...all right. Do you want to wait here?"

"No."

"Thought not. Come on." Teren helped Rakesh up, slung his left arm over his shoulder, and started forward. Rakesh stumbled along with him, feeling more and more disjointed. Bad. This was bad. He knew enough about medicine to know that. But he wasn't going to leave Virin behind.

"Door ahead."

"Inside." Rakesh closed his eyes for a moment, struggling to keep a hold on what little coherence he had left. The sound was getting louder. Stronger. Coming from...

"*Aba*, there are two doors."

Rakesh opened his eyes, and his jaw dropped. It was the room from his vision. He shook his head. "Am I seeing what I think I'm seeing?" he asked slowly.

"I don't know?" Teren answered. "What are you seeing?"

"Two doors? And... lots of cobwebs? Looks like they haven't touched this room at all?"

"Yes."

"I... Virin is in here. Behind one of those doors." Rakesh let go of Teren and hobbled forward. "And... if I was that madman, the other door would be a trap."

"That makes sense, I suppose." Teren went to the doors, examined each one. "Which one do I choose?"

Rakesh studied them both for a long moment, cradling his injured arm to his chest with his other arm. "Choose the door. Choose love, or love."

"What?" Teren looked at him, a puzzled look on his face.

"Something the Spider told me. She showed me this room." Rakesh moved forward. "Twice... no, three times. I've been here before. In dreams."

"All right," Teren said slowly, and Rakesh heard the doubt in his voice. "Then...which door?"

Rakesh studied the doors again. Then he shook his head. "You go outside. Into the corridor. And close the door behind you."

"What?" Teren came over to stand in front of Rakesh. "I'm not leaving you."

"And I'm not losing you," Rakesh said softly. "If I choose wrong, you'll have a chance at living. If... If it goes badly, take Ayani and go to Tyese. Take Gira with you. Go to my father and tell him who you are. He'll make sure you're taken care of."

"*Aba*—"

"Teren, please!" Rakesh met his eyes. "Do this for me, son of my heart?"

Teren stared at him for a moment, then nodded. "I'll be right outside the door, though. So if you need me, shout."

Rakesh smiled. "I will do that. Now go."

Teren swallowed, then leaned in and kissed Rakesh's cheek before hurrying out of the room. Once the door was closed, Rakesh turned back to the pair of doors and sighed. One of them was right. Which one?

He staggered forward, reached out and touched the door on his left. The wood was rough, scarred. But the lock was shiny and new. There was an identical lock on the right hand door.

"Virin?" he called out. "Virin, can you hear me? I'm here!"

No answer. He hadn't really been expecting one. But there was a surge in the incessant heartbeat that only he could hear. Rakesh reached out and touched the right hand door, then narrowed his eyes.

"I need to choose," he said softly. "I can't open both doors. How do I choose?" He closed his eyes and rested his head against the door. "Virin, how would you choose?"

The answer came almost at once. Demarti had been as mad as the Spider. This was some kind of revenge against a dead man. Would he be able to keep from gloating over his prisoner? Rakesh didn't think so. He straightened, licked his lips, then leaned forward and examined the lock on the left hand door. The metal was bright, shiny, with a single, smudgy fingerprint. The right hand lock, though, was covered in smudges. Rakesh hesitated for a moment, then reached out, grabbed the lock, pulled the bolt back and swung the door open.

Nothing happened. He opened his eyes, saw the bound figure inside the tiny, dark room, and nearly wept with relief.

"Teren!" he shouted. "Teren, I found him!"

Chapter Fourteen

"He's waking up."

Virin didn't recognize the voice. Who was waking up? Oh, *he* was waking up.

He considered it. Waking up sounded like a good idea. He was hungry. How long had he been asleep? He opened his eyes and blinked. The ceiling was bare. No staring pattern, so he wasn't in his own bed. Where was he?

"Virin?"

The voice was tentative, quiet, and so very welcome. Virin turned towards it, and felt his world wobble.

Rakesh. Looking older, thinner, and so very tired. And sitting in a hover-chair.

"I... I'm still asleep?" Virin asked, hearing how shaky his voice was, and hating it. "I'm dreaming?"

Rakesh smiled sadly. "No, love. You're awake. Finally."

"Finally," Virin repeated. "What do you mean, finally? Where are we? What happened?" He tried to push himself up and ended up panting, exhausted from the effort. "What happened?"

"*Aba*? They said he was awake?" Virin turned towards the door, and was surprised to see Teren standing there. Teren laughed aloud, coming in and taking Virin's hand. "It's good to see you awake, *Aba* Virin."

"Thank you. Why do I have the feeling that I've been asleep longer than I thought?" Virin looked around again. "Where are we? One of you please tell me what happened?"

"What do you remember?" Rakesh asked.

"Ah..." Virin frowned, staring at the ceiling. What did he remember? He closed his eyes. Rakesh, bound and suspended on their bed. Alarms. Explosion. Then...

"Who the fuck was that old bastard?" he demanded, opening his eyes.

Rakesh grinned. "He said his name was Demarti. I talked to Iras, and she knew who he was. Apparently, he had a grudge against your father, back when he served under Gavir's command. And...he shot your father. Twice."

"And Father let him live?" Virin asked dryly.

"Your father was a forgiving man," Rakesh answered. "Demarti was convicted of insubordination and assault, and sent to the camps. Molari is looking into what happened after, but he thinks that the Ishamar movement was born in that camp, and that Demarti was behind it."

Virin nodded, frowning. Remembering the chair. Creator, the *chair*....

"Rin!" Rakesh's hand was tight on his arm. Too tight. Virin opened his eyes and looked, and felt a wave of horror.

"Kesh?" he reached out and grabbed Rakesh's forearm, holding it up to better see the metal hand. "What... Creator, Kesh, what happened?"

Rakesh sighed and pulled his arm back, resting his hands in his lap. "This is why the chair, Rin. Because I can't put too much pressure on the prosthesis yet. It's still healing, and my nerves are still figuring things out. The medics say I should be back on the canes in a month or two."

"But what happened?" Virin repeated.

Rakesh looked down. "It's a long story—"

"Then give me the damned synopsis!"

"Ah... I shot him?" Teren said, sounding embarrassed. "Only it was by accident. I didn't mean to do it."

"You *what?*" Virin shook his head, looking around the bed. "Where's the control? I want to sit up. I want the whole story from the both of you!" Rakesh reached over and picked up the console, passing it to Virin. Once the back of the bed was raised, Virin waved Teren over. "Sit down. Talk to me. Start with where we are. This isn't Tyese."

"Yes, it is. We're in Maryst, at the College of Physicians," Rakesh answered. "This is the only place they felt was qualified to help the both of us."

"And as to what happened, Ayani and I found Rakesh trapped under part of your bed..." Teren began. Rakesh offered occasional explanations, usually having to do with the Spider and Her mad plans, but he let Teren tell the rest of the story.

"He sent me out, so that if he chose the wrong door, we wouldn't all die. Then he called me back in. But by the time I got inside, he had passed out." Teren mock-glared at Rakesh, who laughed. "I went out and started firing into the air until the Swords found me. They got you out of that... monstrosity—Virin, those metal bands were solid! They had to cut you out! Then they brought all of us to Arena City. And then we came here." He grinned. "The craziest three weeks of my life!"

"Three weeks?" Virin repeated.

Rakesh nodded slowly. "Three weeks. From what they told me, when they pulled you out of that chair, you were catatonic. Completely uninjured, and completely unresponsive. Delan says that some Swords react that way to solitary—when they reach a certain point, they...shut down."

"They weren't sure you'd come back, Virin," Teren said quietly.

Virin tipped his head back. "No wonder I feel weak as a baby." He glanced over at Rakesh, reached out and touched the mechanical hand. "Kesh, love, I'm so sorry."

The bed shifted, and Virin turned to see Teren smile, wave, and walk out of the room. The door closed, and he looked back at Rakesh. "Truly. I am."

"I know, love," Rakesh said, his voice quiet. "But it's over now. We'll heal, and we'll be fine. All of us."

"Ayani?"

Rakesh grinned. "Our oldest daughter, you mean? I'm willing to bet that Teren just went to call her. Molari was very impressed by her. She's in training now, and she'll graduate as a Zaan-ti in two years."

"A Zaan-ti? That's unheard of!"

"I know." Rakesh grinned, looking both proud and smug. "The highest cadet rank ever awarded." Then he sobered. "The rest of the children... they're scared. Scarred. *Aba* and *Ama* have taken in the lot of them. It's going to take a lot of time and care to bring some of them out of their fear."

"If anyone can do it, it's Raizi and Akesha." Virin closed his eyes and yawned. "I shouldn't be this tired. Not if I just woke up!"

"You should. You may not have been injured in body, but your mind needs time to heal."

"Janera betrayed us," Virin said.

Rakesh sighed. "I know. And... Rin, I killed her."

"Kesh?"

"Kill her, or lose you? Rin, how is that even a choice?"

Virin nodded. Then, softly, he asked, "How many did we lose?"

"Out of the entire embassy staff, Swords and Collared, there were twenty-two survivors," Rakesh answered. He hesitated, then continued. "By the time Ayani's team found the Collared that were taken captive when they took you, it was too late. All of them were dead." Another hesitation, and he finished in a small voice, "Serris is dead."

Virin shook his head. "Creator, what a waste. And the Ishamar?"

"The ones that were caught in the ruins were either killed out-right or captured and questioned under hypnotics. Molari led the raid on their base himself. Said it was the most fun he'd had in years."

Virin snorted. "He would. And now?"

"Now?"

"What do I do now?" Virin asked. "Retire? If I was....damaged—"

"No one thinks you were damaged, Rin," Rakesh said. "Molari will tell you that himself when he comes. Which he said he would, once you were awake. And...he told me what he was going to ask you when you woke up. So that I could warn you ahead of time."

"Which would be what?" Virin asked.

"Do you want to go back? Molari is going to give us that choice. To go back to Felanore, to rebuild the embassy and finish what we started," Rakesh answered. "He's proud of you, Rin. Of what you accomplished in such a short period of time. He wants you to take over the embassy permanently."

"He said that?" Virin stared at Rakesh, his blood racing in his ears. "He...said that?"

"He did. And, if you decide not to go, then you come back to Arena City with honors."

Virin nodded. He looked up at the ceiling and frowned. "I'll want a new staring pattern. Not having one is bothering me. Makes it hard to think." He looked back at Rakesh. "When they build the new embassy, I mean. Tell them I want a new staring pattern over our bed, will you?"

"We're going back?" Rakesh looked both startled and relieved. "You're sure?"

"We'll take a little time to recover, I think. To make sure the children are settled." Virin smiled, reaching out and taking Rakesh's hand. "Did you think I'd say no?"

"I wasn't sure," Rakesh admitted. "We did so much good—"

"And we'll do more."

"They know who I am now, Rin," Rakesh said. "They know I would have been the Spider Priest."

"Ah..." Virin hummed softly. "And?"

"And the temple was destroyed completely," Rakesh answered the unspoken question. "Teren took on the mantle of heir to the Empire long enough to request that of the Ruling Council."

"He did what?"

"Yes. For about two hours, he was Teren the First of Aakar. He made a long list of requests on behalf of his people, including having the palace ruins and the temple razed to the ground and the debris sunk into the sea. If I remember correctly, the temple grounds will become a park." Rakesh grinned. "And at the end of the Council session, he abdicated in favor of the Tyesean Ruling Council. Aakar is now a protectorate of Tyese. And, I want you to know, that was the only time he's left this hospital since we arrived."

"He calls you Father." Virin noted. "Have we adopted him, too?"

"No. I checked, and legally, he's too old for us to adopt. Which I think made him feel better, since he plans to marry Ayani as soon as she has the rank."

"Good for them!" Virin chuckled. "Grandchildren in our future, hm?"

"Eventually," Teren said from the doorway. "But not soon. She's in training, and I'm coming back to Tyese with you."

"You're not entering training?" Virin asked.

"He turned Molari down," Rakesh said. "Turned down Marga, too."

"I'm entering the diplomatic corps," Teren said. "I'll be working with you and *Aba*. I...discovered a taste for politics."

Virin glanced at Rakesh, saw the look of pride, and knew that there was more. "Why, Teren? It's a thankless job. And dangerous. You saw that."

Teren smiled shyly. "Because I decided I didn't want to leave my family," he said softly. Then he blushed. "Although I think I should leave you alone right now."

Virin arched an eyebrow at him, then looked at Rakesh, only to see his husband making shooing motions. Rakesh grinned at him, but waited until the door closed behind Teren before touching the controls of the hover-chair and raising it. He leaned over the bed, resting on his arms.

"Welcome back, Virin," he said softly. "I missed you."

"Going to show me how much?" Virin asked.

"You know I am. Once you're out of that bed." Rakesh chuckled. "I want you to finish what you started that night in our room."

"Oh, I think I can promise that." Virin leaned over, cupping the back of Rakesh's neck with his hand, rubbing his thumb over the collar that encircled his throat. "I love you, Tarkarin."

"I love you, too, Kian-ti-os," Rakesh answered, and leaned in for his kiss.

About the Author

E lizabeth Schechter has been called one of the top erotica and alternative sexuality writers in the world. Her writing credits include the award-winning steampunk erotic romance *House of Sable Locks* and the Celtic fantasy *Princes of Air*. Her shorter work has appeared in anthologies edited by D.L King (*Carnal Machines*), Laura Antoniou (*No Safewords*), and Cecilia Tan (*Jingle Balls; Like a Prince*). Elizabeth Schechter was born in New York at some point in the past. She is officially old enough to know better, but refuses to grow up. She lives in Central Florida with her husband and son, and a most accepting circle of friends who are both very amused and very proud of the pervy, fetish writer in their midst. Elizabeth can be found online at http://elizabethschechterwrites.com[1] or at https://www.facebook.com/Elizabeth.A.Schechter.

---

1. http://elizabethschechterwrites.com/

More from award-winning author Elizabeth Schechter

Playing for Keeps

A novel in the *Tales from the Arena* series!
Rakesh is one of the most skilled of the Collared.
Virin, a mid-ranking sword, takes Rakesh as his lover and hopes to rise high enough in rank that they may marry. But a storm is brewing. Former Collareds are disappearing, victims of a dark conspiracy of renegade soldiers that conspires to utterly control the nation of Tyrese and destroy all who oppose them. And they have their eyes on Rakesh.

Heart's Master
by Elizabeth Schechter

In one tragic night Steven loses everything: his lover, his dreams, and his sight, but he gains the compassionate, caring dominant he has always longed for. Nick must teach Steven not only how to have a healthy and consensual BDSM relationship, but how to navigate the ways of magic. But as Steven begins to wield his new--and terrifyingly strong--powers, he draws the attention of evil beyond our world.

House of Sable Locks
by Elizabeth Schechter

Winner of the Passionate Plume Award

A steampunk novel of dark passion. Dominant and implacable, the Succubus is all that men crave and fear. However, she has met her match in William, a young aristocrat trained to be the perfect submissive. Their idyll cannot last: there is a killer loose in London, and William's dark past is about to collide with the present.

All Genres ☾ All Genders

☾ Circlet Press: Erotica For Geeks www.circlet.com

If you enjoyed this book, you might also enjoy...

Superlative Speculative Erotica

edited by Cecilia Tan and Bethany Zaiatz
Twenty of the best erotic science fiction and fantasy stories published by Circlet Presson our 25th anniversary. A little cyberpunk, some high fantasy, a touch of horror, some superheroes, a bit of space opera, some paranormal... What unites these stories is their quality. The anthology also features characters who identify as lesbian, gay, genderqueer, bisexual, trans, and heterosexual. What label do you put on a book like that? We call it... superlative speculative erotica.

Fantastic Erotica

edited by Cecilia Tan & Bethany Zaiatz
To celebrate the 20th Anniversary of Circlet Press, Fantastic Erotica presents the very best erotic science fiction and fantasy short stories published by Circlet in the past five years. Chosen by popular vote by the readership from among all the stories published by Circlet from 2008 to the present, these favorites are the cream of the crop.

Best Fantastic Erotica

edited by Cecilia Tan
The best erotic science fiction and fantasy as determined by the annual contest run by Circlet Press. Rewarding originality and positive sensuality, the contest inspires well-known and unknown writers alike to excel in this provocative genre. Erotic sf/f combines erotic and sexual themes with magic, futurism, high fantasy, cyberpunk, space opera, magic realism, and all the many other sub-genres.

All Genres ⊂+ All Genders

⊂+ Circlet Press: Erotica For Geeks www.circlet.com

Circlet
Press

About the Publisher

Circlet Press: Erotica for Geeks. All genres, all genders. Circlet Press has been publishing fine quality erotic science fiction, fantasy, and genre literature since 1992. We love a good sexy story, well told, that sparks the imagination.

www.ingramcontent.com/pod-product-compliance
Lightning Source LLC
Chambersburg PA
CBHW071829020726
47502CB00004B/1288